"Layers of corruption—politics, sex, drugs, and more . . . well-drawn, real moral issues."
—*Philadelphia Inquirer*

"SUSPENSEFUL, INTRICATE, FAST-PACED . . . an impressive work that immediatezine

"FIRST-R. *Globe*

"INTRIGUING, PROVOCATIVE."
—*The Anniston Star*

"A COMPLEX, RICHLY TEXTURED NOVEL by a fine writer who has created some marvelous, unforgettable characters."
—*The Naperville Sun*

"Well-written and sensitive."
—*Virginia Quarterly Review*

"A NEW WRITER TO WATCH!"
—*Ellery Queen Mystery Magazine*

THE LOVE THAT KILLS

Ronald Levitsky

AN ONYX BOOK

ONYX
Published by the Penguin Group
Penguin Books USA Inc., 375 Hudson Street,
New York, New York 10014, U.S.A.
Penguin Books Ltd, 27 Wrights Lane,
London W8 5TZ, England
Penguin Books Australia Ltd, Ringwood,
Victoria, Australia
Penguin Books Canada Ltd, 10 Alcorn Avenue,
Toronto, Ontario, Canada M4V 3B2
Penguin Books (N.Z.) Ltd, 182-190 Wairau Road,
Auckland 10, New Zealand

Penguin Books Ltd, Registered Offices:
Harmondsworth, Middlesex, England

Published by ONYX, an imprint of New American Library, a division
of Penguin Books USA Inc. This is an authorized reprint of a hardcover
edition published by Charles Scribner's Sons.

First ONYX Printing, May, 1993
10 9 8 7 6 5 4 3 2 1

 REGISTERED TRADEMARK—MARCA REGISTRADA

Printed in the United States of America

THE
FIRST WEEK

Chapter 1

MONDAY MORNING

Musket Shoals, Virginia, was a town whose fences Tom Sawyer might have painted and whose residents still blinked twice when they read "murder" in the newspaper. Like the front page lying face up on the passenger seat of Jimmy Wilkes's car, as he turned onto Ocean Drive going into work. He kept glancing from the drumming water on the windshield to the headlines. So, one of the Vietnamese had finally gotten killed.

The rain had ruined his whole weekend—his wife and kids down with colds, the family barbecue canceled—and now Monday morning wet and colorless as if smeared with his younger daughter's gray Crayola. As he drove up the promontory and saw that even the great ocean was obscured in fog, Wilkes thought of his ancestors, smugglers of Revolutionary and Confederate days, slipping through the blockade to shore by sense of touch, while he crept through the rain to avoid slipping into a ditch. Already late for work but, as was his custom on such melancholy days of sun and soul, Wilkes stopped to visit Thomas Jefferson.

Opening the car door he walked to the point of the promontory where the bust of Jefferson, resting on a granite pedestal, jutted from the guardrail. Raindrops dribbled from the bust's head and

collar, tumbling across its shoulders into a stream
racing around Wilkes's feet. Jefferson's face was
barely distinguishable, the bronze having turned
green long ago and the nose worn from tourists
rubbing it for good luck. But Wilkes didn't need
to see the face; just standing there was enough to
send a rush of warmth through his body.

Jefferson had stopped here once, while on vacation during his first administration, and made a
few obligatory comments about Musket Shoals
being a bastion of liberty. It was enough for a
grateful citizenry to erect this monument, so two
hundred years later Wilkes could gaze at his hero
and reflect upon the ideals of justice, equality, and
the essential dignity of man. And one thing more.
Julius Caesar had wept in jealousy before the
statue of Alexander the Great. Looking at Jefferson, Wilkes reminded himself that at forty, after
nine years as a servant of the people, he was still
only an Assistant Commonwealth's Attorney for
the county. Not that he ever felt like crying; he
hadn't the ego of Caesar. But it was worth a slow
shake of the head and, on that gray morning, a
shiver.

He felt the puddle seeping into his shoes. That
and the drivers of passing cars slowing to stare
put him back inside his automobile to continue
down Ocean Drive past the patched-up Vietnamese fishing boats, lights from their lanterns drifting ghostlike in the fog. Like a funeral procession
of spirits for the woman who had been murdered,
Wilkes thought as he glanced once again at the
newspaper. What would her family do—send her
out on a burning boat from America the Promised
Land back to the realm of her ancestors? Murray
Saunders would no doubt be assigned prosecu-

tion of the case; he was the specialist in crimes of violence.

Wilkes turned on the radio. After a few minutes of music and commercials, the news came on with the murder as its lead story:

"A few hours before dawn, in the Vietnamese neighborhood commonly known as the Paddy, police discovered the body of a young Vietnamese woman named Nguyen Thi Nhi. She had been shot through the heart. The woman was found in her apartment behind her parents' tailor shop. Police have already taken a suspect into custody. We have this recorded statement, first run during our seven A.M. broadcast, from Lt. Louis Canary, who is in charge of the investigation:

" 'The murder weapon has been recovered from a trash bin in the alley outside the victim's apartment. Fingerprint identification led to our obtaining a warrant for the arrest of Edison Basehart, who we found in his bait and tackle shop at approximately five o'clock this morning. Although verbally insulting, he didn't give any trouble as my men took him down to county jail. The police department is in the process of conducting a thorough investigation. That's all I can say for now.' "

Canary spoke with a soft sure drawl. Having worked with the detective years before on an insurance fraud, Wilkes remembered him as a large, pear-shaped man who blew smoke rings the size of donuts. Respecting nothing more than himself, Canary was the kind of machine that once set in motion rarely failed.

The rain let up enough so that Wilkes could distinguish the long regular piers of the Tyler Yacht Club. Sails were drawn against their masts like the wings of sleeping birds. The road dipped starboard, almost close enough for him to reach out

and touch the clubhouse flag, then rolled back toward shore and began its gradual descent to the
downtown area. Ten minutes later Wilkes was
passing the last rows of neat little shops and tour-
ist traps, all white with blue or green trim. He
turned the corner to park in his reserved space in
front of the courthouse. All the other spaces were
already filled except for his boss's, but this was
the first day of Simpson's vacation. Still, Wilkes
half-expected to see the space occupied.

The offices of Commonwealth's Attorney were
on the second floor, above the police station and
courtrooms. Wilkes shared a common reception
area with Murray Saunders and their boss, Edgar
Simpson. Walking through the double doors
Wilkes saw that Martha, his secretary, was not at
her desk but heard her inside Saunders's office.
Entering his own office, Wilkes removed his coat
and shook off the rain. His feet felt damp, so he
laid his shoes and socks beside the heat register,
sat behind his desk, and thumbed through the
sheaf of papers spread before him.

It was the Randolph Canning Company file, a
case he had just adjudicated. An environmental
issue—his "specialty"—involving violations of the
state's air and water pollution standards. He had
won, after three years of investigation, research,
interviewing witnesses, and two trials, so that a
multimillion dollar company paid a $5,000 fine and
promised never again to poison its neighbors. He
shook his head, pushing the papers to the edge
of his desk, and tried to think of the case as Jefferson would have—a victory of yeoman farmers
over the sinister smokestacks of industry, but he
had been through enough of these prosecutions
to know they never amounted to much.

People didn't really care about dead fish or a

little soot on their laundry. Not like an armed robbery or, even better, a murder—like that Vietnamese woman who had just been shot to death. That was something people could feel in the pit of their stomachs. That was why they turned on the eleven o'clock news. Murray Saunders knew it, knew how to arch his brow on television when promising to get tough on crime. He talked about his conviction rate the way a stage mother talks about her child, and that was why he was going to the top.

A knock at the door, and Martha walked in. She was old enough to be Wilkes's mother and acted like it. "I was worried when you didn't come in on time, with the rain and all. How are Ellie and the children?"

"Working through a box of Kleenex an hour with their colds. Any messages?"

"The boss wants you to run over to his house right away."

"Edgar? He's on vacation. Can't I just call him?"

She shook her head. "Wants to see you in person."

"What for?"

"I just take the messages. I think Saunders knows. He had me into his office, after I took Mr. Simpson's call, and pumped me like I was a well needing to be primed. Then he kicked me out and reached for the phone. Dollars to donuts he called the boss."

Wilkes blew his nose. He considered calling Simpson, to avoid a twenty-minute drive in the rain; besides, he was as curious as Saunders. But orders were orders and, as his boss was fond of saying, Wilkes was a good soldier. Putting on his socks and shoes and throwing the damp coat over his shoulder, he stepped into the lobby.

"Jimmy!" Saunders called from his office.

Wilkes stopped and leaned in the doorway. "Morning, Murray. How was your weekend?"

"With this lousy weather, about as bad as everyone else's. I came in on Saturday to catch up on some work, so it wasn't a total loss." Saunders had been doing that a lot lately, ever since Simpson had announced he would not seek reelection. "Uh, you heading out already?"

"Uh huh. Early lunch."

They both laughed.

"No, seriously," Saunders persisted.

"Now, Murray, you're not checking up on me, are you?"

"Of course not. It's just . . ."

"Bye, Murray."

The rain had let up; a few drops splattered intermittently against the windshield as Wilkes headed up Jackson Street, the main thoroughfare. Several merchants stood under their canopies to chat with passersby hunched under their umbrellas, and some even were dragging tables of produce and knickknacks onto the sidewalk, as if their actions alone would bring out the sun. Indeed, the sky did appear lighter when Wilkes left the downtown area and passed the Georgian townhomes into the more residential areas with freshly painted clapboard houses and low picket fences. Just before reaching the first emerald rolling hill of horse country, he turned up a private road through clusters of magnolia trees, their white blossoms scattered along the wayside by the rain. Up a winding drive and behind beds of tulips, azaleas, and white bunches of candytuft sprawled Simpson's long, rambling house.

It was a good house, filled with enough stair-cases, spare rooms, and root cellars to make any kid happy. Wilkes had loved visiting there as a boy, his father and Simpson having been school-mates and political allies. Simpson's only child Tad and Wilkes had been best friends, right up until Tad was killed in Vietnam. With their son dead, Simpson and his wife were left alone to sit quietly and remember.

Mrs. Simpson answered the door. Over the years she had grown thin and dry like a pressed flower. "Hello, Jimmy, how nice to see you." She reached up to kiss his cheek and, as she did, he embraced her gently. "How you and Tad used to play—two little Indians." She always said that.

"It's good to see you, Miss Florence. Edgar left a message for me to come over."

"He probably wants to say good-bye. We're go-ing on vacation." She spoke distractedly, perhaps disturbed by the thought of leaving her garden and the house in which her son had lived. "Yes, we're going away."

"Away? I didn't know . . ."

"Nor I. What a surprise this morning. Edgar was already packed. He said he'd had enough of this weather, and that we were going to spend a week in Acapulco."

"Acapulco? That's not like him at all."

"We just received confirmation from the air-lines. We take off in two hours. My goodness, two hours." Her face flushed. "Do you think I can trust Ramsey watering the flowers?"

"Acapulco?"

"Edgar's in his study. You'll have to excuse me, Jimmy. I must finish packing. Yes, we're leaving very soon."

Wilkes paused at the stairwell a few paces from

the study entrance. Under these stairs he and Tad had hidden from Prince John's soldiers, General Grant, and a dozen other adversaries. He had read once that places gave off an aura, a tactile sensation based on what they had experienced, and so he took a step forward to see if the warmth was still there, something left from their boyhood fun. He saw a chip in the wall that a toy spear of Tad's had made. He reached forward to touch it.

"Ji . . . y, you, out th . . . e!" Simpson's muffled voice shouted through the half-open door of his study. "C'mon in!"

Wilkes drew his hand away. He had sensed something, more a chill than warmth, but that was probably only his imagination.

His face hidden by a large handkerchief, Edgar Simpson sat behind the massive desk at the far end of his study. Of all the rooms he'd known, this was Wilkes's favorite—the place where his father and Simpson had talked politics over cigars and whiskey. Rows of law books lined the dark paneled shelves and the portraits of great men looked down over the fireplace—Washington, Madison, and Jefferson. It was that last portrait, first seen over thirty years ago, that Wilkes still carried like a locket in his heart.

Dabbing his face, Simpson drew the handkerchief from his crimson nose. "Ah, Jimmy, glad you came by so fast. Not much time before Florence and me catch our plane. We need to talk about some serious business. Ooph!" He leaned forward, adjusting his ample girth between the desk and chair. "Sit down. I don't have to tell you to make yourself comfortable."

Wilkes walked past a suitcase and drew a chair beside the desk, his knees nearly touching Simpson's. "It's not like you to do something in such a hurry. You're always so methodical, like the plaque in your office, 'Take It One Step at a Time.' "

Simpson blew his nose and grimaced. "That's for young men like you who have the time to take. Damn weather. I'm too old to have my vacation ruined by all this rain. Besides, might as well start practicing for my retirement. Why wait till next year to start enjoying life?"

"And all those case files you brought home last Friday to review over vacation?"

"The hell with them! I've looked at enough paper in my lifetime to cover the Great Wall of China. Time to pass the torch to a younger man."

Just then Simpson's servant Ramsey came in. "The Mrs. say she almost ready. I put your suitcase in the car now."

"Yes, yes." Simpson waved his handkerchief brusquely and fell into a coughing fit.

"Edgar, are you all right?" Wilkes asked, edging closer.

One more great cough, a shudder of the shoulders, and Simpson settled back in his chair. He nodded, and the smile spread on his lips. "Damn weather. I plan to lie out on some beach till I get black as Ramsey."

"Why did you want me to come over? Just to say bon voyage?"

"Would it be so strange for someone who's almost kin?"

Wilkes shook his head.

"Actually, Jimmy, it's about the murder last night."

"In the Paddy?"

Simpson nodded. "That Slant girl getting killed—some whore, I think. I've got the preliminary report from Lt. Canary. Here." He handed

Wilkes a typed page. "Not much at this point, but Canary should wrap things up with a nice red bow in a couple of days."

"I heard him on the radio earlier this morning. He sounded pretty sure of himself, as usual."

"Yeah, that old bird gets the job done. I know you don't think much of him. . . ."

"It's not easy to forget how he let the dogs on those civil rights workers back in the Sixties."

"Jimmy, those men were breaking the law. I had to prosecute them. So would you, if you'd have been a public servant back then."

"Those were bad laws."

"It's not our job to act as the state legislature and . . . !" He began coughing again.

"You're right, Edgar. Calm down. I didn't mean to upset you."

Simpson cleared his throat. "I'm not upset. Besides, you're the one who's right. Times have changed. Take a look at the report."

The single page belied Canary's thoroughness. The victim's name was Nguyen Thi Nhi, twenty-one years old, who had been killed by one bullet through the heart just after one A.M. A neighbor lady heard the noise and woke her husband, who discovered the body and phoned the police. Traces of heroin were found in the victim's apartment, and the woman herself was probably an addict. As the radio had earlier reported, the murder weapon had already been found, a Smith and Wesson .38. From a fingerprint identification, police arrested Edison Basehart, who denied any knowledge of the crime.

"Edison Basehart," Wilkes said aloud.

"That's right. Sound familiar?"

"Isn't he the head of some paramilitary organization?"

"It's called 'Guardians of an Undefiled Nation'—G.U.N. Pretty cute, huh? Saunders had him put away for six months a couple years back for illegal possession of firearms, and it wasn't Basehart's first conviction by a mile. Everything from holding a parade without a permit to several drunk and disorderlies."

"Any violent crimes?"

"Couple of fights. But it's been a whole new ball game with these Slants coming here to live. Hell, even the niggers can't stand them. Coming here and settling with taxpayers' money, taking over part of town, working dirt cheap, driving some of our citizens—black and white—out of business."

"They're hard-working people just trying to get their part of the American dream. I wish everyone else was as law-abiding."

"Don't kid yourself. They got their arms elbow-deep in drugs smuggled from their cousins in the Orient. Don't look at me like that, Jimmy. I know what I'm talking about. You remember, last year I took part in a state-wide investigation of drug trafficking. Canary was on that too. He can tell you better than me. We went down to the Paddy several times, but those people are as close-lipped as the oysters they fish for."

"You sound like a candidate for G.U.N."

"Don't get smart with me, boy. I just want you to see how easy someone like Basehart could get riled up. These Slants have been his new project—I'm having his latest speeches and handouts collated for you. He hates these Vietnamese more than the niggers and Jews put together. It wouldn't have taken much to give him an excuse to put one of them away permanently. Why, one of his followers was arrested a few weeks ago for breaking a Slant's store window just a block away from the scene of this crime.''

''Basehart says he's innocent.''

''That's for a jury to decide but, knowing his kind, I'd bet he's guilty as sin.''

Wilkes looked at his watch. ''Yes, well, you've about convinced me. Saunders should get an easy conviction. I'd better be getting back to the office. I want to finish the canning company file before lunch. You and Florence have a wonderful holiday. You deserve it.'' He began to rise, but Simpson grabbed his arm.

''Do I have to feed you the whole pig before you know what you're eating? Look, boy, I'm assigning this case to you.''

Wilkes sat back in his chair and shook his head. ''This type of crime is Saunders's specialty. I do environmental and insurance cases. You know that.''

''Not this time, Jimmy. It's your baby.''

''I don't understand. Why?''

''A lot of reasons. This is a big case, not just something between a no-account like Basehart and some Slant hooker. You were right before when you said times've changed. This is the new South. No more water hoses turned on elderly black mammies. The world's going to be watching how we handle this—at least the Washington and New York papers will be. We can't let Basehart get acquitted by a bunch of cracker jurymen. The F.B.I.'d come marching in, snooping around, and set up one of their civil rights violation cases against Basehart with us on the bench holding the towels. No sir. Can't have that.''

''All the more reason for you to want an experienced man like Saunders to handle it.''

Simpson shook his head. ''There's going to be

television and press coverage. Saunders comes off like a used-car salesman. Hell, I'm his boss, and I don't even trust him. But you, Jimmy, look as clean-cut and dull as one of them Harvard boys. Why, I can just see your face on the late news all pink and clean. This is going to help you a lot. With me stepping down next year, folks'll be looking for a new Commonwealth's Attorney. Might as well be you."

Wilkes slowly straightened in his chair. "Now I understand. You're doing all this for me. You're setting me up for the next election."

"It's not that. Not entirely, that is. You deserve this opportunity. You've earned it."

"Have I, Edgar? You should see Saunders back in the office. He's salivating over this case like it's a two-inch thick steak. He's more qualified for this type of trial. We both know that."

"Damn it, Jimmy, stop being so damn . . . good! Think of yourself for once. Think of Ellie and the kids. And what about your daddy?"

"He's been dead for six years."

"How do you think he'd feel if he were alive today? Why, you're doing the same damn job you were doing the day we put him into the ground— God rest his soul. Your daddy and I grew up together. We started with nothing but the dirt under our fingernails."

"I know, Edgar."

"Well, you never act like you do. Your daddy was the best fire chief this country ever had, and me . . . I didn't do so bad either. Don't know what all these books here mean, but I know how to get things done."

"Like Saunders."

"It wouldn't hurt for you to be a little like Saunders in some ways. He knows what he wants.

He's got the killer instinct. Yeah, like a fighter. With a case like this, he'd make himself a shoe-in for my job. How'd you like to be working for him?''

Wilkes shook his head. ''Don't misunderstand me. I want to do it, and I see where it could lead. It's just . . . Tell me, Edgar, would you've given me this opportunity if the case had been really difficult?''

Slowly lifting himself like a surfacing hippo, Simpson stuffed his handkerchief into a back pocket. ''Commonwealth's Attorneys don't deal in 'what if' questions. All we're interested in is what's de facto. This Basehart case is de facto, and so is his ass. Walk me out to the car.''

The rain had stopped, but Wilkes felt the gray mist like a cold hand upon his shoulder. Mrs. Simpson was already in the back seat, as the Commonwealth's Attorney eased himself beside her.

Simpson said, ''I already told Lt. Canary that you're in charge of the case. He expects you down at the scene of the crime . . . pronto. How's my Spanish? I'll be back in a week. I know you won't let your daddy down. *Adios*, boy.''

Wilkes watched the car move down the driveway and quickly lose itself among the magnolia trees. He went back to sit on the front steps and looked down to the knot stuck in the middle of the second step. When they were kids, Tad had said the knot was really a fingerprint of a would-be murderer creeping up the stairs and only scared away at the last minute by his father yelling inside the house.

It had gone all wrong. Tad should've been the one following his father's footsteps; he was the one who was tough, who had all the plans. Wilkes wanted to lean against the railing and remember his friend but thought he heard Simpson yelling, from down the highway, for him to get moving and meet Canary. Sighing, he stood and walked slowly to his car. Just as he reached for the door, raindrops big as tears splattered against his hand.

Chapter 2

MONDAY MORNING

The last great bump in the road woke Nate Rosen with a start, tossing the birthday card from his lap. He tried looking out the bus window to see where he was going (being on the road so much, he had forgotten), but his neck had grown stiff, allowing him only to bend down and retrieve the card. It was for his daughter, and as usual he had begun, "Dear Sarah," and stopped, waiting for the right words to come. Sometimes it took days. Words were precious when he saw her so infrequently; as the Talmud stated, words were like bees—they had honey or they could sting. And Sarah had already been stung enough by the divorce.

Pulling the briefcase onto his lap, Rosen put away the card and opened the top folder, remembering that he was on his way to some God-forsaken town called Muskrat . . . no, Musket Shoals. He glanced over the notes from the lecture he had given last night and read the name "Edison Basehart" scribbled on the top sheet. Yawning, he remembered the phone call from his office that woke him before his alarm. "Your vacation's been put on hold. Go to this . . . Musket Shoals and see about an accused murderer, Edison Basehart."

Putting his briefcase on the empty seat beside

him, he looked out the window into a countryside filled with rolling meadows interrupted by an occasional paddock and grazing horses. The sun suddenly broke through the dark clouds, and after three days of rain every color was brilliant, like a Van Gogh, so that his eyes blinked several times before growing accustomed to the light. Horses had always fascinated Rosen—their strength tempered by gentleness, endurance by service, beauty by humility—the very qualities God required of man and so seldom found. For an instant he thought of getting off the bus there and then, leaving his briefcase behind to take that long walk among the horses, but he sighed (so loudly the people across the aisle turned their heads), supposing he had done enough running away in his life. Or maybe he was simply tired from the long ride.

Rubbing his eyes and wondering if it was worth trying to get more sleep, he asked the people across the aisle, an elderly couple, "Is it much longer until we reach"—he had forgotten the name again—"before we reach town?"

The old man shook his head and smiled. "We're here. That sawmill we just passed, that was the beginning of the city limits. Downtown's just up ahead. You're a stranger, huh? Business or pleasure?"

The old man was getting ready for a conversation, but Rosen was in no mood. He preferred getting back to the horses, and so he replied, "Business," and turned to the window.

It was too late. The pastures had given way to a straggling of frame houses which in turn organized themselves into rows of streets with larger homes, stores, and cute little colonial shops—the kind spelled "shoppe" and found on picture postcards. Rosen saw a sign brightly painted with the words "Ye Are Welcome" written in colonial script, and a moment later the bus wheezed to a halt directly in front of the station's doorway. He waited for everyone to exit; in passing the friendly old man smiled a good-bye. After all the other passengers had departed, the bus driver lifted himself from his seat and, seeing Rosen still on board, hesitated like a ship's captain waiting for his last charge to disembark safely.

"Need any help?" the driver asked, looking at his watch.

"You really don't want to know," Rosen replied softly while he pulled down his suitcase from the luggage rack, grabbed his briefcase, and stepped out into Musket Shoals. Once again it was drizzling.

Someone called, "Mr. Rosen?"

He looked carefully at the other man before answering, a habit formed by over a decade of journeying to small towns like this, the stranger in town seeing everyone else as a stranger. The other man smiled good-naturedly and, despite his massive shoulders and arms, seemed harmless enough. "You are Mr. Rosen?"

"Yes. And you must be Basehart's attorney, Mr. . . . ah . . ."

"Collinsby. Yes sir, Lester Collinsby." He came forward with a slight limp and shook hands firmly.

"Of course. Can we start off by me calling you Lester and you calling me Nate? If that's o.k."

"That'll do just fine."

"Unless you've got one of those colorful regional names—like Lester Joe, or Lester Lee, or Lester Sue. . . ."

Collinsby laughed. "You don't want to know

what they call me. Lester'll be just fine, Mr. Rosen . . . Nate. Any more luggage?''

"No, I'm used to traveling light. Thanks for meeting me. I know you weren't given much notice.''

"Telegram came first thing this morning to the Commonwealth's Attorney's Office, and they forwarded it to me.'' He pulled the piece of paper from his pocket as proof. "It's kind of confusing, to tell the truth.''

"Is there a place to eat? I didn't have a chance to get breakfast before leaving Charlottesville.''

"Sure. There's a coffee shop right across the street. Here, let me take your suitcase. I made a reservation next door at the Custis Hotel. It's clean and reasonable.''

As they left the bus station, Rosen saw a squad car parked down the street. The officer behind the wheel was staring at him while talking into his radio. Putting down the speaker, the policeman continued to watch the two men walk into the coffee shop.

It was almost nine thirty; the restaurant was nearly empty. They took a table near the window and, despite Collinsby's suggestion of the "house special''—country ham with red eye gravy and grits, Rosen ordered scrambled eggs and whole wheat toast.

The waitress asked Collinsby, "Can I get you something, Cowpie?''

Blushing, Collinsby looked down at the table. "Just coffee.''

"Cowpie?'' Rosen said.

"I . . . played football in high school and college. One day a bunch of the team got drunk and scrimmaged in a pasture. I took the ball, plowed through the line, and fell square onto a pile of . . .

Well, it's a small town. The name kinda stuck, though if it's all the same to you, I'd rather you called me Lester."

Biting his lip, Rosen nodded. "All right, Lester. Tell me about the Basehart case."

"Wait a minute," Collinsby said. "You've got some explaining to do first."

Rosen shrugged. "O.K."

"Well . . ." He scratched his head. "Maybe it'd be best if you just told me what you're doing here."

"In other words, why I've poked my nose into other people's business. That's all right—I'm used to this kind of reaction. You've heard of my organization, the C.D.C.?"

"Uh . . ."

"The Committee for the Defense of the Constitution. We're based in Washington."

"Sure. Well, sort of."

"I don't blame you. We're not as big as the A.C.L.U., but we get around. Last year in Texas one of our attorneys helped a group of Mexican aliens get the minimum working wage while fighting for naturalization. You might say we're like Basehart's G.U.N., only pointed in the opposite direction. One of our directors heard about this case, and Basehart's political leanings, on the radio early this morning. I was close by—I've been attending a conference on Jefferson and the Bill of Rights at the University of Virginia. So he called and ordered me on a bus to your fair city. C.D.C. is offering your client me as your associate, free of charge. That is, of course, if you and he agree."

Looking down at his plate, Collinsby folded his napkin into a small square then began tearing the edges. "Look, Mr. Rosen, it's not like I don't appreciate the offer and I'm not usually one to look a gift horse in the mouth, but maybe you don't understand about this organization of Basehart's—this G.U.N. It's the kind of thing your group's fighting.''

"Yeah, it does sound crazy. But some people, like my bosses, really believe all this Constitution crap about free speech. Even the slightest hint that Basehart might be tried because he has some unusual political beliefs . . . well, it sends them up the wall. They lose sleep. Their ears get raw from talking to each other about it on the telephone. They'd tear their clothes and heap ashes on their heads for this guy if it'd do any good.''

Collinsby stared at him for a long time. Finally he said, "There's something else you'd better know. I guess you don't understand. I hope you won't be offended, but Rosen—that's a Jewish name.''

Rosen nodded.

"And you're of the Jewish persuasion?"

Laughing, the other man nodded.

"Well, Mr. Rosen, your people are exactly who Basehart gives his speeches about—you and Negroes and Slants . . . Vietnamese. He calls you . . . your people, that is . . .'' He paused to swallow hard. "All sorts of names.''

"I'm sure I've heard them all. I appreciate your concern for my feelings, Lester, but my skin's about as thick as an elephant's. I've dealt for and against a dozen Edison Baseharts.''

"He might not want you representing him. I don't want you expecting too much.''

Just then the policeman who had been watching them outside entered the restaurant. He looked the same as the thousand other small town cops Rosen had seen in his career. The only difference was the policeman's eyes; set so closely together, they continually blinked as if making sure both were seeing the same thing. He stopped at their booth. "Hello, Cowpie. Damn if it ain't raining again."

"Hi, Landon. I heard there could be a break in the weather sometime middle of the week. It'd be nice to see the sun for a change."

"Ain't that the truth. Well, I'm just gonna grab myself a cup of . . ."

"Nice bit of police work," Rosen said, "finding that suspect Basehart so quickly."

The policeman blinked hard, as he looked the attorney up and down.

"The news said you found the murder weapon in a trash bin right outside the victim's apartment. Talk about a lucky break. Then to find the prime suspect sleeping in his house, just waiting for you to pick him up. Yeah, I'd say that was lucky. A little like lightning striking twice in the same place."

"Meaning what?"

Sipping his second cup of coffee, Rosen said, "Meaning I can't wait to find out what else your department has found. Should be quite a lesson in law enforcement procedure."

Again the policeman blinked. He was about to say something but stopped, sauntered down the aisle, and sat in a corner booth, his nervous eyes still staring at Rosen.

"You shouldn't have done that," Collinsby said. "I've got to work with those people."

"Why was he leaning on me?"

"What do you mean?"

"He's been watching me ever since I got off the bus. Why am I so interesting to him?"

Collinsby shook his head. "Landon came in for

a coffee break. So he stops to say hello to me. You're just imagining things, Nate."

"Maybe." Rosen rubbed his eyes. "Didn't get much sleep, and I wasn't expecting another assignment so soon. Been on the road a lot. Too much."

"Sure, I understand. To be honest, I think you've made this trip for nothing. I don't think Edison Basehart'll take you on as co-counsel. Your . . . religion and all."

"Let Basehart stew in jail today. Let him think about facing a murder charge and the electric chair. Tomorrow we'll see how he feels about being represented by a member of the Jewish persuasion. If you're right, fine with me. I can start my vacation like I'd planned. Have you visited the murder scene yet?"

"Uh, no. I hadn't really planned on . . ."

"Let's go."

"You mean now?"

When Rosen nodded, Collinsby pushed back his chair. "All right. Let me call the Commonwealth's Attorney's Office and get the visit cleared." He hesitated. "Nate, excuse me for saying so, but you don't seem so keen on doing this job. Are you?"

Rosen shrugged. When Collinsby stood, however, he said, "Wait a minute, Lester. Since we may be working together, you've got the right to have that question answered, though I don't know if you'll understand." He played with his fork upon the plate. "No matter what my feelings are concerning Basehart, I know how to do my job. It is written that the righteous man doesn't merely read and speak the word of God, he lives it through his actions. He follows the Law. Not the inconsequential law of man, which may deprive Basehart only of his life. I'm talking about the six hundred and thirteen commandments, the disobedience of which threatens your very soul. I'm talking about the Supreme Hanging Judge Who only needs an excuse, Who stands over me, like you are right now, every moment of my life. No, Lester, I know how to do my job. Make the call.'' His fork scraped against the plate, making sounds like claws.

"Sure," Collinsby replied softly. "Sure, Nate."

While the other attorney went to the public phone, Rosen took out a handkerchief and wiped his face. His hand was trembling. He shouldn't have been saying such things to a stranger. Suppose they did wind up working together; would the other man trust him? He took a glass of ice water and downed half of it. Perhaps it wasn't a question of free will. He felt sometimes he had to cry out as Jonah or Job had done, or maybe it was simply releasing the "bad humours" like a medieval bloodletting. Whatever the reason, Rosen felt better. He looked forward to the case, as he did to all those in which he defended people brought before the law. Whether the law or the Law, he knew on which side he really belonged—a victim defending victims.

Collinsby returned, coughing loudly before he reached the table. "All set," he said smiling, "I was patched through to Lt. Canary, the investigating officer, who's at the dead woman's apartment. He said for us to come ahead anytime. I thought we'd stop by the hotel first, give you a chance to freshen up and unwind. Long bus ride," he quickly added.

Rosen paid the check. "I'm fine. Just let me splash some cold water on my face. I'll be right back, then we can head out."

The men's room was located in the rear of the

coffee shop. On his way Rosen passed the policeman, who was sipping coffee over a newspaper
headline screaming the murder.

"Spell your name right?" he asked but stepped
inside before the cop could reply.

Running the water cold as possible, Rosen
washed his hands while remembering, as a boy,
washing them every morning before prayers. He
splashed his face and neck, trying to wake up.
More than that, trying to feel something toward
Basehart, whose life might ultimately depend on
Rosen's skill. And what was skill without compassion, his rabbi had once asked, like a knife that
could be held by either a gangster or a surgeon.
Where was his compassion?

The door opened, and the policeman stood at
the sink beside him. Each looked at the other man
through the mirror, as if watching a movie. Did
the cop realize how much he was blinking?

"You say something to me out there?" the policeman asked.

"Nothing worth repeating."

"You a friend of Cowpie's?"

"No, actually . . ."

"Because he's got a lot more manners than that.
He ought to teach you some of his manners."

"I'll try to remember that, officer. Sorry."

Wadding a paper towel, the policeman threw it
just past Rosen's ear into the garbage can.

"Nice shot," Rosen said. "Do the Washington
Bullets know about you?"

The policeman took a step forward but stopped
suddenly, blinking hard. "Yeah, Cowpie ought to
talk to you about good manners." Brushing past
Rosen, he walked from the room.

Rosen watched the door sweep shut, then
turned to the mirror and faced someone not him-

self, yet not a stranger either. Younger, darker, smaller—struggling to scream while shrinking under the long black gaberdine until no longer there, and Rosen once again stared into his own countenance, eyes wide with fear.

Shaking his head he tried to concentrate on the case. It was just another case, that was all. One more client to defend, despite this stupid mistake. The worst thing someone like him—a stranger, a Jew, an out-of-town lawyer—could do was to make the police angry. Yet not one hour off the bus, and he acted like a smart-mouth kid. He had a job to do. He had chosen freely his own destiny and nothing, including that image in the mirror, would stop him. The anger buzzed in his ears. Words are like bees, Rosen reminded himself again, and closing his eyes to look into that small face deep within his soul, he felt their sting.

Chapter 3

MONDAY

It rained more steadily, as Jimmy Wilkes took the highway leading back to the ocean. Nearing the yacht club he turned left down a road which meandered along the beach. The shore had changed over the centuries, its weaker edges bitten away by the waves like chunks of an apple. Water had already crept over the edges of the embankment, and in low spots the road was beginning to flood. Several times Wilkes slowed to test the brakes.

The area he was heading into, on the edge of the ocean, was the original Musket Shoals. It had been settled in the late sixteen hundreds, before malaria moved most settlers to higher ground several miles inland. A few remained to hunt and fish, that and a little smuggling. Their descendants had stayed on, taking out their fathers' oyster boats before dawn and keeping to themselves. They preferred to call their home simply "Old Town." The inhabitants of the new Musket Shoals, like Wilkes, referred to it as "The Swamp" until ten years ago when the Vietnamese came to settle, first by the dozens; later almost four hundred arrived from camps in Arkansas and Texas. Then it became known as "The Paddy."

The newcomers kept to themselves, building their own houses and setting up businesses—tailor shops, arts and crafts, and restaurants.

Wilkes once had taken his family to dinner there. His younger daughter spit the spiced fish all over the table, but the owner smiled, cleaned the mess without saying a word, and returned five minutes later with a hamburger. That was the way they were. They worked hard and studied, gave more than their share to charities, contributed to both political parties but never mixed in politics, and at night—when everyone else in the world was asleep—they were still working. That was why there was so much prejudice and hate. Not the slant of their eyes or the smell of their food. Like ants they never stopped working.

The Paddy grew from the ocean's edge, and as Wilkes entered the area he smelled the salt spray almost as strongly as the pervasive odor of fermented fish sauce. The street was narrow, barely two lanes, while the cross streets were mere alleys; he glimpsed dark twisting passages filled with deep puddles and signs he couldn't understand. Everywhere walkways were crowded with as many vendors as passersby, vendors with little pushcarts selling everything from delicate multi-colored paper fans to thin rice cakes and bowls of steaming soup smelling richly of beef and onion. Wilkes glanced at the report Simpson had given him and tried to read the address, which was almost as incomprehensible as the signs.

He pulled over, rolled down the passenger window, and motioned to an old man who was holding a newspaper over his head to keep off the rain. Huddled beside him was a girl, probably his granddaughter, dressed in a bright green slicker.

"Excuse me, sir. Can you tell me how to get to Kim Van Kieu Street, number six?"

The old man smiled sheepishly and shrugged his shoulders, but the girl answered in perfect English, "Oh, you're here about the murder. Are you a policeman? A reporter?" She rattled some Vietnamese to the old man who nodded silently, drawing the girl closer. "Police cars have been coming in and out all morning," she continued. "They had those big red lights that whirl around, just like on TV."

"Sorry to disappoint you," Wilkes replied. "Can you tell me where I can find the address?"

"Sure. Keep going straight for two blocks, then turn right toward the ocean. Nguyen Thi Nhi's place is almost at the end of the block, behind her father's shop."

"Thanks." Wilkes was about to roll up the window, when he asked, "Did you know her—the victim?"

"Oh sure. Around here everybody knows everybody."

"Thanks."

As he pulled away, the girl shouted, "Bye-bye, copper!"

He smiled, almost laughing aloud, because she sounded so much like his daughters. Turning right at the second corner, Wilkes nosed the car down an even narrower side street, edging close to the curb to let a racing motor scooter pass. The buildings were frame, mostly two stories with shops on the first floor, and crowded so closely together he couldn't tell which door led to what building. Darker than he would have expected, even with the rain and closeness of the street, perhaps due to the numbers of people upon the sidewalk, everyone hurrying from one place to another, yet no one distinguishable from another. He resisted the analogy of ants and accelerated toward the flashing red lights. He rolled up the passenger window, but not before the car was filled with the pungent odor of fish sauce.

Wilkes parked behind one of the two police cars and hurried over to a patrolman directing traffic around the vehicles.

"I'm from the Commonwealth's Attorney's Office. Where can I find Lt. Canary? He's expecting me."

Without taking his eyes from the road, the officer replied, "Go down that little alley beside the tailor shop over there on your right. You can't miss it. With us, the forensic team, and the neighbors, it's been a regular party since early this morning."

Trying to avoid the puddles, Wilkes stepped gingerly into the alley and followed a slender path between garbage cans and broken produce crates. He could barely see a step ahead, while along the way yellow eyes of cats blinked slowly like rows of Christmas lights. Above him through open apartment windows, smells of lunch lay thick upon the alley. Occasionally a pot clanged or a chair scraped, but no voices; not even the cats meowed. Ahead light filtered through an open doorway. Wilkes hurried there, water splattering his pants.

Lt. Canary stood inside the doorway, leaning against the wall and smoking a cigarette. A notebook flapped lazily in his large hand. Without looking at Wilkes he said, "Expected you about an hour ago."

"Sorry. I was tied up with the Commonwealth's Attorney."

"Old Edgar. Going off to get a tan while you and me catch our death of cold. Guess being the boss has its privileges. Been a while since we worked together. Glad you're on the case instead of Saunders. He's a smart-ass boy, like those hot-shot Congressmen we catch speeding from the capital—think they got all the answers.''

Canary shifted his weight, and a sigh emerged from the depths of his great body. He had grown larger than Wilkes remembered but was still solid, the weight evenly distributed so that his belt had not yet slid under his stomach. His sandy hair, streaked with silver, was cropped short. Closely set gray eyes, bulbous nose, veins reddened from drink, and thin lips curling like a snake around the cigarette which he inhaled deeply, releasing a series of small dark smoke rings, the only indication that he was peeved at being kept waiting.

"Body's down at the morgue," Canary continued.

"May I look around?"

The policeman shrugged.

Had it been more fashionable, people would have called the place a studio apartment. It was a small room, not much bigger than the bed and night table, the latter containing a lighted makeup mirror and pile of assorted lipsticks and rouges. The bed was unmade, its orange silken sheet stained with blood, several brownish-red droplets leading to one great dark oval. Above the headboard hung a large poster of John Lennon and Yoko Ono. On the other side of the bed was a straight-back chair on which rested a vase of freshly cut flowers and a half-burned incense stick smelling slightly of sandalwood. Beside it was another chair containing the telephone, a book, and three travel brochures. Another brochure was on the floor at the foot of the bed.

"O.K. to touch them?" Wilkes asked.

Canary nodded. "Everything's been dusted for prints.''

The book was one of those romance novels; on the cover a woman in a crinoline dress was being embraced by a buccaneer. The brochures were the kind found in any travel agency and dealt with the Caribbean and the Yucatan Peninsula. Next to the chair was a wastebasket filled with soiled Kleenex, a few wadded tissues having fallen over the side onto the floor.

"O.K. to touch them too," Canary deadpanned.

"That's all right."

"Not curious?" He clicked his tongue. "We found traces of cocaine on some of the tissues buried about halfway down. Sometimes if you want to find something bad enough, got to get your hands a little dirty."

"I'll try to remember that. So the victim was involved in drugs."

"Up to her little slanty eyes. C'mere, let me show you something."

He led Wilkes into the bathroom. The sink was dirty and filled with rust stains. Caught between faucet and plunger was a spoon, the bottom of which was blackened by heat.

"See here, near the drain. Those white granules." The detective pointed with his stubby finger. "Heroin. This little lady was into about everything. Sex, drugs—not a very pretty picture."

"Did you find anything else? An address book of her customers?"

"Can't find any so far. Gonna talk some more to her daddy and sister. Maybe they'll talk to you. You got nice manners."

Wilkes ignored the last comment. "You think Edison Basehart did this? The report said it was his gun you found."

Canary dropped the cigarette stub onto the floor and crushed it. Immediately he lit another. "Yeah. Found it in a trash can in the alley just outside. A Smith and Wesson .38. Basehart must've wiped the handle clean, but if he'd of been a little smarter, he'd of cleaned the barrel too. We found a partial print there—his. No, Jimmy, ain't much chance of Basehart seeing the light of day. They may even throw the switch on him for this piece of work. So don't worry; you can start printing up your campaign posters."

Wilkes glared at the policeman, who merely smiled as he brought the cigarette to his lips.

"Is that all, Lieutenant?"

"There is one minor little piece of evidence you overlooked. See here, right by the doorway. On the doorframe and down here on the floor—a few drops of blood. Probably went out into the alley, but the rain washed it away."

"It can't be the victim's, can it? I mean—so far away from the bed?"

Canary shook his head. "We had them analyzed—different blood types. Anyways, she died instantly. The neighbor, who heard the noise and woke her husband, said there might've been two shots. She was a little confused, being woke up suddenly. But we know there was more than one shot. Two bullets were fired from the gun. What do you make of it?"

Wilkes moved closer to examine the bloodstains. There wasn't much blood and, searching the floor between the doorway and bed, he found nothing else. "When you arrested Edison Basehart, was he examined for wounds?"

"He was clean. That means someone else was there. Either someone helping Basehart commit the murder . . . maybe this accomplice and the woman struggled over the gun, and it went off and shot him first. Or . . ." Canary grinned around a cigarette.

"Yes?"

"Or there's a witness bleeding out there somewhere. We're checking all the area hospitals. We'll find whoever it is."

Wilkes said, "Or maybe it means Basehart is innocent. He says he didn't do it."

"We gave him a paraffin test and found traces of gunpowder on his hand. He said he'd been target shooting earlier. Well, what do you expect him to say? Confess to first-degree murder? Basehart did it all right. We got no problem with this one."

Wilkes said, "You're very concerned about making everything easy for you."

The detective folded his great arms. "Don't get your hackles up. It's what you and Simpson want—right? Else why wasn't Saunders assigned this case?"

Wilkes shook his head and looked at the ground.

"C'mon," Canary grumbled. "This way . . . well, hello, Cowpie."

Lester Collinsby limped into the room followed by a tall thin man wearing a corduroy jacket. "Morning, Lieutenant. Kind of a surprise to see you here, Jimmy. I was expecting Murray Saunders."

They shook hands. Wilkes said, "Edgar assigned me to the case."

"That's fine. Good to work with an old friend. This here's Mr. Nate Rosen. He's with the . . . uh . . ."

"Committee to Defend the Constitution," Rosen said. "Nice to meet you both."

"Nate Rosen?" Wilkes repeated. "Weren't you on the U. Va. Jefferson program this past weekend? I wanted to make it but just couldn't get away."

"That's right. My organization was asked to provide a speaker on the Bill of Rights. You might say that's why I'm here now in Musket Shoals."

"I don't follow you."

"As you know, the purpose of my organization is to guarantee that the constitutional rights of all individuals are protected."

Wilkes said, "I can assure you that the State of Virginia will do everything in its power to secure justice for the Nguyen family."

"It's not the Nguyens we're concerned with. It's the accused, Edison Basehart."

"Basehart? But he's a . . . I don't understand."

Canary leaned against the wall. "What the hell you here for?"

"I may be representing Mr. Basehart as Lester's co-counsel."

"Basehart want you?"

"We haven't yet discussed . . ."

"So you're a goddamn ambulance chaser. What the hell you doing in my town? You already gave my man Landon some smart-ass talk earlier this morning. We don't need you around here."

"You know what happened in the coffee shop. . . . He radio in to tell you all about it?"

Canary pushed off the wall and walked toward Rosen.

Wilkes stepped between the two men. "Lieutenant, what's gotten into you? You've never met Mr. Rosen, and yet . . ."

"I knew his kind back in the Sixties, when we was having all that trouble, just trying to do our job, just trying to keep the peace. They come down from the North, them bleeding-heart white boys quoting the Constitution like it was Scripture. Crying to the TV cameras about police dogs and water hoses, making me and the rest of the police look like we was the criminals. Now those same white boys wear a suit and tie, but ain't nothing changed. I bet you was one of them, Rosen. Where was you in the Sixties?''

Their eyes locked, and Rosen said, ''I was in a synagogue.'' The room fell into silence for nearly a minute, then he turned to Wilkes. ''Tell me about the gun the police found.'' He began looking around the room.

Eyeing Canary, who sat heavily on the bed and looked away, Wilkes answered, ''Ballistics has established it was the murder weapon. The serial number had been filed off, but Basehart's fingerprint is on the barrel.''

Rosen stepped into the bathroom, returned a minute later and continued to inspect the bedroom. ''Traces of heroin in the sink. The woman was an addict?''

''The autopsy will determine that.''

''If she was a junkie and a prostitute, she was probably involved with other addicts. Then there's her pimp. . . .''

''I can assure you that the police are checking all possible leads.''

Rosen knelt by the doorway. ''Blood. If the Nguyen woman was shot in the heart by the bed, then . . . was Basehart wounded?''

Wilkes shook his head. He couldn't believe how quickly the other attorney found and interpreted the evidence. Even Canary adjusted his bulk and turned toward the lawyer.

Rosen continued, ''Then there's someone else

who saw what happened. Either the witness, or maybe the real murderer."

Canary lit a cigarette. "We found the murderer. He's locked up in jail right now."

"I assume you dusted for prints."

"Yes," Wilkes said.

"Checked the stain's blood type."

Canary blew a smoke ring and nodded.

"Brushed the bedspread."

"What?"

"Checked the bed to see if there were any fibers, hair, semen which might've come from someone who slept with her, who might be the murderer." Rosen said more loudly, "If Basehart is innocent, this evidence could've cleared him."

Canary shrugged. "Didn't do that. Guess it's too late now—half a day since the murder and who knows how many people been sitting on the bed. Hell, now my fibers are all mixed up with the rest of them others. Brush the bed now, might think *I* slept with the woman and killed her."

Rosen barely controlled his anger. "No, Lieutenant, she was shot, not crushed to death."

"Son-of-a-bitch!" Canary struggled to his feet, Wilkes again stepping between the two men. "Get the hell outta here before I break you in two. You hear! Get the hell outta my town!" Wilkes could barely hold him back.

Collinsby grabbed Rosen. "Come on, Nate, we'd better go."

By the time Canary had pushed Wilkes out of the way, the other two attorneys had left.

"Asshole!" Canary shouted, crushing his cigarette on the floor until there was nothing left. "The next time I see him . . ."

"Forget it," Wilkes said. "There's not much chance that someone like Basehart will accept Mr.

Rosen as counsel. Now, you were about to take me to the Nguyens.''

The policeman lit another cigarette and inhaled deeply several times. "All right. Let's go. Let's get this damn circus over with.''

Next to the bathroom was a door, which Canary opened and led Wilkes into a large workroom. A half-dozen tables were filled with sewing machines, rulers, and rolls of fabric. The stools were inverted on the tabletops while the workers, little men with stooped shoulders, huddled in one of the corners, talking quietly while bringing cups of tea to their lips like a collection of windup toys. Past the tables ran a long counter parallel to the wall. On one side stood two uniformed policemen, while on the other—nearer the wall—were an elderly Vietnamese man and a woman in her mid-twenties, both silent.

Canary righted a stool and sat down heavily, flipping ash onto the floor, then signaled for the two Vietnamese to join him.

"Now where were we? Oh, yeah . . . Mr. Nguyen, sorry to bother you again. We'll be clearing out of here in a few minutes, but I wanted to introduce Mr. Wilkes from the Commonwealth's Attorney's office. I'm sure he has a few questions for you. This is Mr. Nguyen's daughter—his other daughter, I mean, Miss''—he referred to his notebook—"now don't let me get this wrong, Miss Nguyen Thi Trac. Damn if it don't all sound like something you'd order in a Chinese restaurant. Go ahead, Jimmy, ask your questions. Miss Nguyen can help you with any translation problems, though the old gentleman knows a hellava lot more English than he lets on—ain't that right? Getting any answers, well, that might be another problem.''

The old man bowed slightly to Wilkes and avoided his eyes. The workers suddenly stopped their chatter, so that in the entire room the only sound heard was Canary once again flicking ash from his cigarette. Mr. Nguyen wore a clean white shirt outside his trousers; its brightness emphasized his dull pallor and the deep sadness in his eyes. They were pools—those eyes—and Wilkes forced himself to look away before sinking under his own desperation.

"I . . ." Wilkes began. His throat felt so dry, he coughed and began again. "I'm sorry all this has to be done during your time of grief. I just want you to know that we all want the same thing— justice, to find your daughter's murderer. As you know, Lt. Canary has arrested a man the police believe is responsible for this terrible crime, but we would certainly welcome any help you might give us. Do you understand all this, sir?"

The old man nodded. Nothing more.

"Good. Well . . . do you have in mind any person or persons who might wish to harm your daughter?"

Mr. Nguyen shook his head.

"Did you see anyone last night? Hear anything suspicious?"

A shake of the head. Not far away stood the workmen, one of whom pursed his lips as if the old man's response had a greater meaning. The other employees also seemed to understand, like the silent communication that is intelligible only to members of the same species. Like ants.

Wilkes grew impatient. "Mr. Nguyen, if you expect us to be of any help to you. . . ."

"My father does not expect anything from you."

Mr. Nguyen said a few quiet words to his

daughter in their native language, and she replied in kind, only with a sharpness that made one of the workers raise his eyebrows. Wilkes hadn't paid any attention to her before; she was like the other women he had passed earlier in the street— thin with straight black hair framing her narrow eyes. Only now she wasn't quite like the others. She was taller, reaching his shoulders, and her eyes blazed. It was those eyes, as much as her mouth, that spoke to him.

"What has happened has happened, and there is nothing you or anyone else can do to change that." She spoke perfect English with only a trace of an accent.

"Miss Nguyen, I don't think you understand. There's a murderer or murderers whom we're trying to bring to justice."

"No, it is you who do not understand. My father's only concern is to prepare my sister for her burial and to make certain that her spirit will remain alive. If you would only leave us alone to do that, we would be grateful."

Wilkes heard Canary snicker followed by a smoke ring drifting between him and the woman.

The detective cleared his throat. After another moment's pause he said to the daughter, "I'm kind of surprised to find you and your daddy so unsociable. After getting to know your brother Van, and he being such a real jaybird when it comes to talking."

Mr. Nguyen smiled politely at the mention of his son, but his daughter bristled. "What has he to do with this!"

"Yeah, Jimmy, you should meet her brother Van, a real credit to the community. Junkie, pusher, why I wouldn't be surprised if he was pimping for his dead sister. A real go-getter, that boy. Simpson and I met him when we did that big drug investigation. Old Van gave us a name or two and saved his neck that time. I wonder why Van ain't here. What do you think, Miss Nguyen?''

She leveled her gaze at the policeman but said nothing. Again the workroom was filled with a silence rigid as glass. Wilkes not only was afraid to speak but even to move, for it was all so unreal, so distant from the early morning and the bust of Jefferson. The oil smell from the sewing machines mixed in his nostrils with incense from the dead girl's room and stuck in the back of his throat, so that finally he did cough, cracking the silence into jagged edges.

The woman winced. ''My brother is out with the fishing boats. He lives a few blocks away He always goes out before dawn and doesn't know yet about my sister.''

Rocking as if he were a stuck car, Canary pushed off his stool to stand beside Wilkes. ''He ain't in his dump—we checked it. Out fishing, you say? Now why didn't I think of that? You sure . . . I mean, you saw him leave? Got up in the middle of the night and packed him a nice peanut butter and rice sandwich for lunch?''

Her jaw trembled in anger, but she waited a moment to reply. ''He always goes fishing early each weekday. That's his job.''

Canary dropped his cigarette butt, rubbing his foot back and forth until the butt was welded into the floor. ''Yeah, his job. Well, Jimmy, think I've had enough of this ring-around-the-rosy. Unless you got any more questions?''

Without waiting for a reply, Canary signaled the other policemen who followed him back into the dead girl's room. A minute later Wilkes heard

the two police cars drive off, sirens blaring to em-
phasize their departure.

For all his contemptible behavior, Canary had
been the ballast holding Wilkes to a world of some
familiarity—the voice, the uniforms, even the casual cruelty, but now that was gone and he was
alone among these strangers who might as well
have been Martians with their secret smiles, their
way of reaching one another without saying a
word, and their infinite patience that left him feeling that he was the real subject under scrutiny.
Yet as difficult as it was to remain, it was harder
mustering the courage to leave. What should he
do—abruptly walk out of the room like Canary?
What to say—an apology for disturbing their grief
or a stern warning, as they said on television, not
to leave town? The old man still smiled politely
with his eyes averted, while the workers stood as
statues, no one complaining, no one tired of his
posture. Wilkes sensed his limbs growing heavy,
the sweat forming ice-cold on his forehead, and
the silence buzzing in his ears until he felt they
would burst.

"The men can return to work?"

Wilkes blinked, forcing a hand to rub his eyes.

"Is it all right for them to return to work?" the
old man's daughter asked again.

He nodded, and as if the mechanism of some
great toy had been activated, the old man turned
and shuffled back to the counter as his workmen
each took a spot at a table to measure or cut or
sew; even the bell above the entranceway tinkled
to announce a customer's arrival. For a moment
the activity let Wilkes believe that all along he had
been merely an observer and not a player, until
he saw the old man's daughter staring at him.

Pretending not to notice, Wilkes turned to leave and, in doing so, glimpsed the woman begin to cry. So, he thought—not daring to look a second time—they are, after all, just like everyone else.

Chapter 4

TUESDAY MORNING

Walking from the coffee shop, Rosen paused to pull his shirt collar tight around the back of his neck. Yesterday's gray mist still clung to the town like an old drunk afraid to go home. Rosen felt a little afraid too. He always did in a new place on a new job, wondering what the people there were really like. An old man walked by and smiled hello; wasn't he the same person who had been so friendly on the bus?

It was better than most, Rosen supposed—this Musket Shoals with its magnolia trees, antiques shops, and street names well over a hundred years old. He could respect a place with a sense of history, like a tree with deep roots. It took a creeping vine like himself to respect such a place. Yes, he liked it despite Landon the blinking cop, Lt. Canary, and the prospect of having to defend a racist bigot. And so he smiled back at the old man, wanting to believe with all his heart what God had told him as a boy—that man was by nature good. Despite the fact that nearly every day, his work told him the opposite.

Lester Collinsby pulled up across the street in front of the hotel, just as the clock on the corner bank struck ten. He was right on time.

"Morning," Collinsby said. "Jimmy Wilkes is meeting us at the jail. He's going to introduce you to Basehart. Just don't get your hopes up about Edison accepting you as co-counsel. C'mon, hop in.''

"Wait a minute, Lester. Let me take in this work of art.''

Collinsby was driving a two-year-old Jaguar, fire-engine red, that shone as if it had just come from the showroom. After strolling around the car, Rosen slid into the passenger seat and inhaled the smell of real leather as one would a fine cigar. Chuckling, Collinsby shifted gears, and the Jag glided into traffic, quickly distancing itself from the hotel.

Seeing Lester behind the wheel was like seeing him for the first time. There was a gold watch, a gold ring, and probably a gold chain around his neck, all looking like they belonged on a golden boy like Collinsby. Only the limp didn't.

"Looks like you're doing O.K.,'' Rosen said.

Collinsby smiled. "Yeah, guess so. Heck, I'm not the greatest lawyer in the world or even in the county for that matter, but people around here have been good to me.''

"You said yesterday that you played football.''

"Guess it's kind of hard to hide when you're as big and clumsy as I am. Yeah, I was pretty good in my day—no John Riggins, but I had a shot at the pros. Busted my knee in college.''

"Must've been tough.''

"When the doctors told me, I felt like blowing out my brains. But I didn't, and it passed. Like I said before, people in this town didn't desert me. They helped me back on my feet. I've gone through two wives and three houses, everything I guess America is about. You can make it through just about anything if you have somebody to count on. Know what I mean?''

Rosen looked away. After a moment he said, "What can you tell me about the case? I've read both local papers, but that's it."

"There's not a whole lot more I can tell you. The police report's on the back seat . . . here."

Rosen scanned the file. "The murder weapon's a problem?"

"His fingerprint's on the gun, all right. As for the weapon itself—a throwaway, one of those Saturday night specials. The police have confiscated a ton of guns like the murder weapon from Basehart's organization, the Klan, and even some Nazi group over in the next town. It's that fingerprint, the paraffin test, plus all the hate literature. His group's even been suspected of a couple fire-bombings of Vietnamese stores during the past few weeks."

Rosen shook his head. "What about the dead woman?"

"What about her?"

"The police report lists her occupation as a prostitute. We know that drugs were found in her apartment. Maybe the shooting was by somebody else—a dissatisfied customer, a pusher, or a junkie. What about her brother?"

"Still missing. He didn't go fishing—the police checked. I hate to say it, but Basehart doesn't stand much of a chance. Bet I can work out a pretty good deal with Jimmy Wilkes, the fella you met yesterday with Canary—Jimmy's the Assistant Commonwealth's Attorney handling the case. We went to school together. He doesn't have too much experience in criminal trial and won't be especially anxious to take this one to court. Anyways, I never met a prosecutor who wasn't interested in saving himself time and the state some money."

"Don't be offended, Lester, but do you think any pressure might be put on this Jimmy Wilkes by some of these cockroaches in white sheets crawling out of the woodwork? I mean, how sympathetic are the people around here to Basehart and his group?"

"I'm not offended, Nate. Maybe a little tired of hearing that kind of talk, that's all. I'll just chalk it up to you being a Northern boy. This isn't the Sixties; people don't go gunning down civil rights workers anymore. Sure we've got our share of Baseharts. Times are bad for some, and people are always looking for someone else to blame; that's just human nature. From what I've read, you've got the same trouble up North, maybe worse. Folks around here are good people—I already told you that. Wait'll you get to know Jimmy. You'll think you're talking to Thomas Jefferson himself. Here's the courthouse."

The two attorneys checked in with the desk sergeant, then walked down the long gray corridor, where afternoon suddenly gave way to the dim glow of lamplight. Rosen looked around and said, "Nice place, early Kafka," then the men continued in silence. In the gray loneliness just before they reached the door, Sarah flashed before Rosen's eyes, the image of his daughter as he had last seen her, a pink ribbon in her jet black hair and below the newly cut bangs her dark eyes looking softly up at him. Two months ago he had gone home to Chicago for vacation. On his last day they went to a Cubs game, and she had been as giggly as he supposed any twelve year old was, until he brought her home and she sat at the piano. It was her big surprise, to have spent two months learning to play "Lulu's Back in Town" choppy, the way Thelonius Monk played the tune, because he loved it so. It had driven her mother and her piano teacher crazy, she said. How Sarah played it, and how she looked at him after finishing, melting his heart and almost bringing him to make peace with God. When the door opened to the interrogation room, Rosen followed Collinsby inside with the same gentle steps he had, as a boy, followed his father into shul.

The room was small with steel-gray walls and, below a fixture caked with dust, Jimmy Wilkes sat in one of the four wooden chairs surrounding a small square table. The fixture lighted a tight circle barely reaching the walls, so that the edges of the room remained in shadow, and at first Rosen didn't notice a stenographer adjusting her machine in the corner.

Wilkes and Collinsby shook hands. "Hi, Jimmy. You remember Nate Rosen of the . . . what's that group, Nate?"

Wilkes said, "The Committee to Defend the Constitution. Of course I remember. Nice to see you again, Mr. Rosen. I was hoping we'd get a chance to talk about Mr. Jefferson and the Bill of Rights. I am sorry about yesterday. Lt. Canary's a good police officer. He's lived and worked through some pretty rough times. Hard for some people to forget those days."

"Sure. Did Lester make it clear to you why I'm here?"

Before Wilkes had a chance to reply, a low moan sounded deep within one of the far walls. Rosen leaned forward, cocking his ear toward the sound, which grew in intensity, a harsh grating merging into a rumble. A loud shudder, then silence followed by a crack of light breaking the dark, the crack growing larger until he saw it was an elevator.

A policeman stepped out followed by a tall gangling man dressed in faded jeans, a torn checkered shirt, and a vest filled with punctures where fishing lures had hung. They walked to the table, the tall man staring down at the lawyers and grinning, so that the gaps in his brown teeth showed clearly.

"All right, Edison," the policeman said, "just sit down and behave yourself. The nice men want to ask you some questions."

Basehart sat across from Rosen, between Wilkes and Collinsby. He said, "Well, who brought the cards?" His voice was dry and gravelly, as if he needed a drink of water.

Collinsby said, "You remember me, Edison, I defended you two years ago on a drunk and disorderly. I'll be representing you again, if that's all right."

"Sure, throw in any warm body. Hey, Cowpie, still slipping in manure piles during football practice?"

Collinsby blushed. "Now, Edison, that was a long time ago. Some things are best forgotten." Nodding toward Rosen, "This gentleman is . . . an associate of mine. You know Mr. Wilkes, the Assistant Commonwealth's Attorney? He has some questions for you."

"Sure. Nothin' I like better'n shootin' the shit."

Wilkes cleared his throat and looked down at an open file. "Good. Now, Mr. Basehart, I notice here that . . ."

"Wait a minute," Rosen said, "aren't you going to warn him that a stenographer is recording everything being said and that he doesn't have to answer any questions?"

"Yeah!" Basehart shouted. "I got my rights!"

"Of course," Wilkes replied. "I'm sorry. Uh,

as I was saying, you've had several run-ins with
the law—seven, counting this one.''

''Harassment, that's all.''

''The last one involved assault on a Vietnamese
man and damage to his store.''

''I don't mind sayin' I can't stand the sight a'
those Slants. We was just fine, us fishin' folk, till
they come here. What right do they have fishin'
our waters and sellin' for less 'cause all they eat
is rice? Rice mixed with that stinkin' fish sauce.
Hell, it stinks up the whole river. Sure I hate 'em.
Any real American would.''

''This 'real American' business. Let's talk about
your organization—G.U.N.''

''Guardians of an Undefiled Nation,'' Basehart
said proudly.

''I understand you're a general, the group's
leader.''

''Commander in chief. I give the orders.''

''Can you tell me an order you gave recently?''

Basehart shifted slightly. ''Well . . . 'bout three
weeks ago we went over to Cherryville where
some niggers were causin' some problems.''

Once again Wilkes looked at the sheaf of papers. ''I see you're referring to a Negro voter registration drive which you and your friends—''

''My soldiers.''

''—disrupted. You served three days in jail for
disorderly conduct.''

''Harassment. Just like this.''

''You think I'm harassing you?''

''You work for the government. Everybody
knows the Hebes control the government. Hebes
'n niggers 'n now Slants. Ain't but a few real
Americans left.''

Glancing at Rosen, Collinsby said, ''Now, Edison, you've got no call to use that kind of language."

Wilkes's face had reddened. "You killed the Nguyen woman, didn't you? Killed her for no other reason than your blind hate."

"You're crazy," Basehart said.

"Your gun was found outside the victim's apartment—your fingerprints. We can prove you fired a weapon."

"I was nowhere near the Paddy last night! I was asleep in my store *all* last night."

"No witnesses."

Basehart leaned forward and showed his teeth. "That's where I gotcha. My ol' buddy was with me till five in the mornin'. Ask him—Billy Lee Pelham."

"You told the police there were no witnesses."

"Didn't want to get Billy Lee involved. Besides, ain't none a' their business what I do and who I do it with."

"This Mr. Pelham, is he a member of your organization?"

"A colonel."

"I see. How do you explain your fingerprints found on the murder weapon?"

"Can't. Don't know."

"That's not a very good answer."

"You're so damn smart. Whaddya you think?"

"I think . . . !" Wilkes caught himself. "I think you're in serious trouble, and if you don't come up with a satisfactory explanation, I'm going to move for an indictment of first-degree murder. That carries the death penalty."

The room grew quiet. Basehart looked into his lap while muttering something under his breath. His head sank slowly onto his chest, and Rosen noticed the prisoner smelled of liquor—more than that, it was the smell of decay. He was decaying, from the crusted bald spot on the top of his skull to the emaciated shoulder blades spreading like the wings of a vulture.

Collinsby cleared his throat while fumbling with the papers in his briefcase. He stretched his massive arms, nearly touching Basehart and Rosen. "Jimmy, I think it'd be best if my client doesn't say anything further, until we have a talk. Then I'm sure we'll all be able to work something out."

Basehart jerked up his head. "Whaddya mean by that?"

"We have to talk, Edison. No need to get upset about anything."

"Not get upset! You don't believe me either. You're all the same, you lawyers. You're either kikes or bought off by kikes. I didn't do it, I tell ya! Ask Billy Lee, he'll tell ya!"

"Let me talk to him," Collinsby said to Wilkes. "I'll call you later."

Wilkes nodded and walked out the door, followed by the stenographer.

After the door was shut, Rosen said, "You're in serious trouble, Edison."

"Who the hell're you?"

"Just one of the mourners."

"Huh?"

Collinsby leaned forward. "This is Mr. Rosen." As if hypnotized, Basehart kept his eyes on the stranger. "He's an attorney sent by the C.D.C.—the Committee for the Defense of the Constitution—to offer you his services free of charge. We'd be co-counsels on your behalf."

Basehart's limbs moved snakelike up and down the chair, while his eyes remained transfixed by the other man.

"Well, Edison, what do you think?" the lawyer persisted.

"He's a Jew, ain't he?"

"That has no bearing one way or the other. Mr. Rosen is a professional, who would never let any personal feelings interfere . . ."

"What's a Jew doin' here? Get him outta here."

"Now, Edison, be reasonable."

"Get him outta here I said! Do I havta call a cop? Get him outta here!"

Basehart suddenly grew silent under Rosen's gaze, as his last outcry receded into the dark edges of the room.

Rosen said, "Lester, why don't you let Mr. Basehart and me clarify a few things between us. You wouldn't mind stepping out of the room for a few minutes."

Basehart cut in, his voice trembling, "I t-t-told you . . ."

"You don't have anything to worry about. Remember, we Jews only eat babies, never full-grown men."

Collinsby looked from one man to the other. "You sure . . . ?"

"Of course. It'll be all right. Go ahead."

As Collinsby rose, Basehart's eyes darted to him, but the prisoner said nothing. Only when the door closed behind his lawyer did his gaze, like some insect, crawl from the floor up the chair and back to Rosen. It was then Rosen noticed how red Basehart's eyes were, with circles so deep they might have been etched into the skin.

"Have they been treating you all right? They're feeding you properly, letting you exercise, not interrupting your sleep?"

Basehart looked down at his hands where his

middle finger picked at a hangnail on his thumb. For a minute neither man spoke.

"From what I hear, Edison, it's not like you to be so quiet." Rosen leaned forward in his chair. "Bet you could tell me a few good jokes."

Shrugging, Basehart said quietly, "You wouldn't like 'em."

"No?"

The prisoner stretched his legs and said, "Well, maybe so. Maybe you'd learn somethin' 'bout stickin' your long nose where it don't belong. Y'know, you Hebes sure got a lotta nerve. You think that all you had to do was walk in here, like this was Florida or somethin', 'n I'm gonna crawl over 'n kiss your goddamn feet. Well, it'll be a cold day in hell when I need a kike's help. What I could use is a man like Hitler. He'd know what to do with your kind. Why I bet . . ."

Rosen's fist lashed out, catching Basehart flush on the jaw and knocking him off his chair. "G . . . damn it, I . . . bleedin'!" came a muffled cry from the floor, as Rosen walked around and perched on the table directly above Basehart, who screwed one eye up while holding his jaw with both hands. A little blood trickled between his fingers.

Flexing his hand Rosen said, "I guess you've been saying crap like that for so long, you think it doesn't bother people. Maybe now you'll remember."

"H-Hebe," Basehart chattered, his hands balled into fists held tightly over his face.

"That's good, Edison, that's real good. Let your hate work itself out. Then maybe we can talk."

Basehart mumbled something incomprehensible then, moving his hands from his mouth, said, "Talk? Talk with you . . . I'll kill you first."

"Oh, you'll talk with me, Edison, or you'll fry just like a fly hitting that light bulb up there. And don't worry about me getting so upset I'll walk out on you. When I was a kid I used to wear ear-locks and a skullcap. There's nothing you can think of that someone in my neighborhood didn't call me. And I got hit by a lot tougher guys than you'll ever know. So anytime you really hurt my feelings, I'll just beat the hell out of you."

"You're crazy!"

"No, Edison, you're the one who's crazy, because sure as shooting you're on your way to the electric chair, and there isn't anyone between you and the switch but me."

"Shit. No one in this town gives a damn about a dead Slant whore."

"That's where you're wrong. This isn't the good old days when you and the boys could play kickball with some Negro's head. This is the new South, or so I've been told by none other than your lawyer. You're going to be famous, Edison. I can see your face on the covers of *Time* and *Newsweek.* Little children across the country are going to wear T-shirts with your picture and the caption, 'Pull the Switch on the Son-of-a-Bitch.' See, you're going to show the world that the South has a conscience after all."

"My lawyer . . . he'll take care a' everything." Basehart raised himself on one elbow.

"Collinsby? Sure, he'll take care of everything. You know what he wants to do—plea bargain you into prison so that they throw away the key. Guess he and the prosecutor are real cozy—high-school pals."

"That's right," Basehart said. "They was awful friendly. That son-of-a-bitch."

"But then, maybe he's right."

"Whaddya mean?"

Yawning, Rosen rubbed his eyes. "Well, if you murdered the woman, Collinsby's doing the right thing. In fact, you'd be getting off easy."

"Shit."

"Gee, Edison, you're so eloquent, maybe you should conduct your own defense. Anyway, I'm wasting my time. You did it."

"Says who?"

"Did you?" When Basehart pressed his lips together, Rosen said wearily, "Idiot. You might as well choose which white sheet and hood you want to be buried in. Good-bye."

As Rosen turned to walk away, Basehart blurted, "I ain't no part a' the Klan! Don't truck with the idea a' sneakin' 'round with your face all covered up. A man who doesn't have the guts to say his mind clean out in the open is weak as piss." He glared at the other man, his face twitching. "Just don't call me one a' them."

Turning to meet the prisoner's gaze, Rosen looked at him curiously. "All right. Did you kill the woman, Edison?"

One quick shake of the head.

"Do you want me to represent you, along with Collinsby?"

Basehart bit his lip but said nothing.

Rosen shifted his weight. "Let me put it this way. Do you have any objections to my tagging along with your lawyer, as sort of an advisory counsel?"

Basehart's lower lip slowly pulled away from his teeth, his mouth opening only enough for him to mutter something.

"What's that, Edison?"

"Shit. You can do whatever the hell you want.

I got better things to do than keep tabs on the likes a' you.''

"O.K. Maybe I'll stick around. And since you're in such a festive mood, maybe you could fill me in on something important.''

"Yeah—like what?''

"About the gun and your fingerprints?''

"I told you, I told everyone, I don't know. My organization owns a lot a' guns. Anyone coulda' taken one, 'n I don't mean my boys. Some nigger, some ki . . .'' He stopped suddenly, touching his chin. "Even the cops confiscated a pile. Who the hell knows?''

"You wouldn't have any idea who did kill the woman?''

"Hell, no! I told you I was home target shootin' in back or drinkin' beer in front of the TV. Why don't you ask Billy Lee—he was with me. Besides, he's the one always goin' down . . .'' He stopped abruptly then slowly ran a hand through his hair. He spoke distractedly, "Ask Billy Lee. You just ask him.''

Chapter 5

WEDNESDAY MORNING

Collinsby's Jaguar hummed impatiently through downtown Musket Shoals. Gaining speed as it passed the residential area, the automobile reached the outskirts of town where it made a sound, as if clearing its throat, and with a shudder leaped onto the highway. Rosen tightened his seat belt and closed his eyes for a moment, wondering how much of his body would remain intact for identification. His lips began the kaddish, the prayer for the dead, and somewhere very close he heard God's laughter. No, it was Collinsby chuckling, his leather gloves gripping the steering wheel.

"Not used to this kind of speed, Nate!" he shouted over the engine's throbbing. His grin opened like a laceration across his face.

Rosen's ears had become two seashells. He heard eternity in the sound of rushing wind, and his lips moved faster in silent prayer.

"It's my only vice!" Collinsby added, shifting the gear yet again and blurring the fields ahead into a kaleidoscope of yellows and greens. "Only time I feel really free! Besides, you're the one who wanted to get right on the case!"

"Isn't one dead body enough for this town?"

Collinsby ignored him, and Rosen resigned himself to the speed. He unclenched his hands, settled into the seat, and closing his eyes once again turned inward to his daughter—the serenity of her face before the piano. He remembered her birthday card, barely begun, in his briefcase; if the car crashed it would be his last words to her. "Dear Sarah" and that was all, a great void following the two words. If he could but finish the card . . . what would he write . . . he was sorry for having sinned against her? Hadn't God decreed that a man's home was sacred as the Great Temple; therefore, hadn't the divorce sent Rosen's home tumbling down as surely as the Romans had destroyed the Lord's Holy Place? And left Sarah his Wailing Wall.

No, that was going too far, making him some sort of tragic figure—a Job shrinking from the Voice in the wind—when he was no more than one of a million stories acted out each day and just as inconsequential. Like the one to which they were speeding, the home of the dead woman with her family grieving the loss of a daughter and perhaps their dreams as well. But, after all, that was justice in this world, everyone having an equal chance to suffer.

Rosen felt the car gradually slow and, opening his eyes, saw the Paddy's narrow streets and Oriental signs. A moment later he smelled the salt air of the ocean mingling with a dozen other odors of fish, oil, and decay. It reminded him of Chicago's Maxwell Street years ago—of the hundreds of dirty peddlars calling him down into their dimly lit stores, of pushcarts filled with hot dogs and flies, trays of cheap watches and pinwheels, of life smelling strong as the sweat of a frightened man.

"Got you here safe and sound, after all," Collinsby said. "Bet you thought we weren't going to make it."

Rosen continued looking out the window without replying.

The other lawyer clicked his tongue. "Sure is something. Wasn't that long ago when I was a boy, we used to play hookey. Come down here with our fishing poles, drinking Dr Peppers, and cast our lines off the piece of land right down there. There weren't but a couple of shacks and lean-to's for the fishermen. Caught some nice-sized ones, but the biggest fellers always got away. Always got spanked when I came home, but it was worth it. Now . . . heck, everything's changed. I don't know this place anymore—it's like you're not even in America. Guess you can't totally blame Basehart for the way he feels."

A sudden chill rushed through Rosen's body, and he repeated the kaddish silently, this time for the dead woman.

"Here we are," Collinsby said as they turned the corner. "There's Nguyen's shop, where all those people are. What a crowd!"

He drove past the tailor shop, searching for a place to park. Rosen stared at the Vietnamese congregating at the entrance, but they carefully avoided looking back. There were about two dozen men, women, and children. Many were draped in a flimsy white material thin as gauze, a few wearing turbans of the same material and holding crudely fashioned walking sticks.

Collinsby pulled into a parking spot where the street ended and the pier began. They stepped from the car and, for a moment, both men gazed into the ocean. Sunlight danced upon a horizon interrupted by an occasional fishing boat, its sail a speck of shimmering white.

"Sure can be pretty out here," Collinsby said. He stretched broadly, lifting his face toward the sun. "Yeah, makes you remember the way you were as a kid. I could stand here all day."

Rosen tried not to think of his childhood, as he looked out onto the water. The ocean was beautiful yet vast and immutable in its power, so that even the whale of Jonah was but a minnow in its midst. And the ocean, in turn, was the size of a raindrop to the Creator. A raindrop that could flood the world upon a whim, killing everything but a floating zoo. How could Man be expected to find justice in such a world? "Let's get this over with," Rosen said, but he too found it difficult to turn away. The ocean was so beautiful.

As the two men walked toward the tailor shop, Rosen noticed another Jaguar parked across the street. It was the same model as Collinsby's, even the same color, but brand-new, glowing like fire among the street's brown and greenish hues. From habit he made a mental note of the license plate.

He nodded toward the automobile. "I can barely tell it apart from yours. Pretty flashy for this neighborhood, wouldn't you say?"

Collinsby laughed nervously. "Yeah, two peas in a pod. Look, Nate, I bet those people are gathered for some kind of service for the dead woman. Could even be the funeral. I don't feel very good about disturbing the family just now. Know what I'm saying?"

Rosen turned to his companion. "Do you have any children?"

"A boy and a girl."

"You must know how the parents feel. We should see them at least to pay our respects. If not for ourselves then as emissaries for our client, to give Basehart this one mitzvah—good deed—so that when he dies he won't face God empty-handed.''

As soon as he spoke, Rosen looked away ashamed. Those were his father's words, yet he said them with such conviction. And said, they could not be unsaid, so the two men continued up the street into the crowd which parted like leaves stirring in the wind. At the doorway stood a woman wearing a white garment; past her, other mourners mingled quietly inside the shop.

"Yes?" she asked, looking at Rosen.

She was slightly taller than the other women, with the fine delicate features common to Vietnamese; only her eyes were large and piercing. The white garment nearly touched her sandals but was open at the shoulders, revealing her arms. They were beautiful, very slender, as were her hands, though her fingernails were clipped short, and Rosen imagined her legs to be as shapely.

"We're sorry to come at this time but, if possible, we'd like a few words with Mr. Nguyen.''

"Who are you?" Her directness surprised him.

"My name is Nathan Rosen, and this is Lester Collinsby. We're representing Edison Basehart.''

She didn't blink. "This is my sister's wake.'' The sentence was said as a statement not an accusation, and she waited for him to make the decision.

"If possible, we would like to see your father just for a few minutes. We'll make it brief, I promise . . . Miss Nguyen.'' He noticed she wasn't wearing a wedding ring.

"I would rather you go away. This has been very difficult for my parents.''

"I know. We wouldn't intrude if time wasn't pressing. Right now an innocent man might be unfairly imprisoned while a guilty man, your sister's murderer, is free. We'll take just a few minutes of your father's time. I promise."

"Very well, then, just a few minutes. I will speak to my father. My mother will not speak to strangers—that is just her custom. This way."

The two men followed her in a convoluted path past the mourners, until they reached the open casket. It had been placed on two work tables drawn together, and before it was an altar containing three bowls of rice, three cups of tea, and three smoking joss sticks emitting the heavy aroma of sandalwood. The entire area around the body was heavily scented with spices. The corpse was dressed beautifully in traditional Vietnamese attire—a white overdress form-fitting to the waist, with long tight sleeves and a high collar, and black satin pants. A white handkerchief covered the dead woman's face, and resting on her stomach was a knife.

Collinsby leaned over and whispered to Rosen, "This gives me the creeps. I told you we shouldn't have come. Let's get this over with and get the heck out of here."

Miss Nguyen said something in Vietnamese to an old couple standing near the coffin. The man nodded, approached the two visitors and smiled politely, not looking into their eyes.

"My father will speak with you," the young woman said.

"Thank you," Rosen replied. "Mr. Nguyen, we're sorry for this intrusion, but there are some important questions we need to ask. I have the police report, so I won't bother you with the same questions you answered for them. What I'd like to know . . . is there any reason why Edison Basehart in particular, or any of his friends should want to hurt your daughter?"

The man replied in his native language, and the young woman translated, "She was Vietnamese. For some that is enough."

"Yes, but why your daughter? You and your wife also live in the building but weren't disturbed, and there was no attempt to break into the shop itself. This seems to indicate that your daughter might have known her assailant. Do you have any idea whom this person might be?"

Mr. Nguyen shook his head.

"It's important that we speak with your son, Van. Is he here?"

The old man, still smiling politely, fell into a deep silence. Finally his daughter said, "My brother is not here. He has not been home since the day before my sister was murdered, nor have we heard from him."

"Isn't that odd? He was supposed to have gone fishing early that morning, yet it seems he didn't."

"Apparently not, after all. Van was not always consistent in his actions. My brother often went away for several days at a time. As for his present whereabouts, perhaps he is grieving by himself. My sister and he were very close. Is that all?"

"Yes." Rosen was about to turn, when he added, "Mr. Nguyen, I deeply regret what happened to your daughter. One of my holy books compares a man's child to a precious jewel entrusted to him by a king. All the while in his possession, the man worries until the king repossesses what is rightfully his. Your daughter was a precious gift from God, and He has only reclaimed what is His."

The old man looked up momentarily, nodded and returned his gaze to the floor.

"I'll show you out," the woman said. Rosen

walked beside her, while Collinsby followed
closely behind. There seemed to be an even
greater crowd of mourners and, as they passed
the counter, Rosen glimpsed a young white man
wearing a crimson polo shirt. His hair was slicked
back, which accentuated his fleshy lips and eyes
green as emeralds. The man caught Rosen in his
gaze then quickly ducked behind the crowd.

"Who's he?" Rosen asked.

"No one. A friend of my father's perhaps. I
don't know."

"Lester, who was that man?"

"Who?"

"The Caucasian."

"Didn't see him. Come on, let's go."

Rosen looked back toward the counter, but the
face in the crowd had disappeared. After they
walked through the doorway, he said to Collinsby, "You go ahead to the car. I have to pick
up something across the street."

The other man hesitated then, shrugging,
limped down the street in long strides, quickly
distancing himself from the house of death.

Rosen asked the woman, "If I may impose one
more time on your kindness. There's a gift shop
over there, and I'd like to buy my daughter something special for her birthday. Would you help me
pick it out?"

"I really should . . ."

"Please."

She pressed her lips together and looked up at
Rosen. "Very well." As they crossed the street
she added, "That was a nice thing you said to my
father. You're the only outsider who seemed the
least bit sincere. You sounded like a priest."

He laughed. "Did I? I guess old habits die hard.
I don't know your name—your first name."

"It's Trac, Nguyen Thi Trac. Not very pretty-sounding in English, but very special to my people. My sister and I were named after two great sisters who fought the Chinese centuries ago. I'm the *chi-mot*, first daughter, and my sister's the second, *chi-hai*. That is to say, she was."

They entered the shop, which was crowded with aisles of dolls, incense, candles, cups, and rows of blouses, shirts, and slacks of the same type in which the dead woman was dressed. The proprietress, a wizened old woman smoking a long thin pipe, smiled a toothless grin and chatted loudly in Vietnamese, her voice sounding like an out-of-tune guitar. Trac replied—it was the first time Rosen had seen her smile—and led him to the counter, upon which were many rings and bracelets from brass to what appeared to be gold.

"Old Li says she has some special jewelry for your daughter. With Li it's special if the gold doesn't rub off in your hand. Many of us feel she missed her true calling as a used-car salesman. Don't let her take advantage of you."

Meanwhile the old woman had taken out a tray of gold-braided necklaces and draped one on Trac's shoulder, clapping her hands with a squeal of delight.

"It's very beautiful," Rosen said, "but I think a little too grown-up for Sarah. She's just twelve. What about the outfits over there?" He walked to the clothes rack. Removing the necklace Trac followed him, the old woman trailing behind.

"What do you call these?"

"That is the *ao-dai*, the 'custom dress' which is our traditional outfit. Three pieces, the blouse covered by these panels front and back over the pants. They are all handmade, see—each embroidery is slightly different. Do you know your daughter's size? These run small, as you've probably guessed.''

"I think this one, yes, with the white pants. It may be a little big, but she can always grow into it.''

"It is lovely. What's her coloring?''

"She has dark eyes and long black hair, like yours." For a moment their eyes locked.

"Yes, I think you've made a wise choice.''

Again the old woman clapped her hands gleefully, took the outfit to the counter and wrapped it carefully. Rosen paid for the gift, thanked her, then followed Trac from the store.

A large hearse, one entire side covered by a dragon, was parked across the street in front of the tailor shop. Some of the mourners were decorating the sides of the vehicle with flowers, slips of rolled paper, a portrait of the dead woman, and attaching an altar with more flowers, incense, and a flickering oil lamp.

"My parents still believe in the old ways," she said. "Putting the knife on my sister's stomach, and now the dragon—to keep away evil spirits. The pieces of paper are prayers for my sister to carry to our ancestors.''

"And the three bowls of rice and tea I saw inside?''

"They will be placed before the altar of my parents' house three times daily for the next three years. For some of the old people, a hundred days of mourning is enough, but not my father. He believes we must offer prayers to our ancestors of the past five generations. It is a contract; you lawyers can understand that. We help assure them a place in heaven, and they in turn will protect us from evil." She paused. "Some help they provided my sister. Well, we're in America. Something must have been lost in the translation.''

"It's a beautiful ceremony. Your parents must've loved your sister very much.''

Trac bit her lip. Only a momentary weakness, for she quickly cleared her throat and shook her head. "Nhi was a woman and therefore not of great consequence. Had it been my brother, their only son, it would have meant that the family line was broken and our souls and those of our ancestors would wander aimlessly in the spirit world forever. Yes, let Nhi and me go to hell, but let the gods protect Van by all means.'' She was struggling not to cry.

"You're worried about your brother, aren't you?''

She broke into nervous laughter. "Do you worry about your cat when you let him out for the night? Van knows how to take care of himself. That is the first lesson all of us younger ones learned in the United States and something the old ones, like my parents, never understood. My father keeps praying to the dead as if they could hear and, if so, as if they would care. Van knows better; there is no one who will help you but yourself. He taught Nhi well, didn't he?''

Rosen watched her angrily brush away the silent tears. Her parents' ritual he could understand—the mourning clothes, the altar with candles, and most importantly the sense of community, of present mingling with the past as if old friends. It was the way of his people too—ripped clothes and ashes, the swaying of the congregation as they recited the kaddish, the yahrzeit candle flickering as fragile as life. But this grief of hers was different because it was so alone, a stranger wandering aimlessly in a world of strangers, and there was nothing he could say to assuage it. So he looked down at the gift under his arm, until she gained control of herself.

"Thanks again for helping me choose the present."

She nodded.

"Well, good-bye." Neither moved, and he said, "I'll probably be in town for a few weeks. Could I see you again?"

"Haven't you asked enough questions?"

"It's not that."

A long pause.

"I don't think . . ." she began.

"I'm divorced, if that's the problem."

She gave a short laugh. "Morality is something I left behind in Vietnam, like the pagoda. Seems so old-fashioned in this town. It's just, I don't know how long I'll be here. I took a leave of absence from the Smithsonian to help my parents with the funeral arrangements and share their mourning."

"Really? What kind of work do you do at the Smithsonian?"

"I'm a musicologist. I restore instruments for the museum."

"That's why you have short nails, so as not to scratch the wood."

She smiled. "You'd make a good detective."

They stood looking at each other for a moment, then Rosen said, "Musicologist. You wouldn't happen to like jazz?"

"I like all music."

"Good. I'll call you, and perhaps we can get together. Let me walk you back to . . ."

A "bang" came from across the street, like someone striking a kettledrum. Trac fell against him and, inhaling her perfume, Rosen let a hand reach up to touch her shoulder. As she turned slightly, he saw that his hand was bleeding; a small glass shard was sticking where his thumb and forefinger met. The street had suddenly grown silent, but while cleaning and wrapping the wound in a handkerchief, he heard someone crying softly. Then, as if the street had a volume control, the cries grew louder into screams and shouts ringing against his ears.

Looking across the street next to the Nguyens' tailor shop, Rosen saw that the display window of a grocery store had been blown apart. Torn heads of cabbages and other produce lay strewn across the sidewalk among pieces of shattered glass. Several of the mourners wandered into the street holding their faces or arms, too dazed to cry. Trac hurried alongside an old man with a deep cut on the side of his face and spoke to him in Vietnamese. He muttered something as she helped him back to the sidewalk, where a young couple took him.

Following Trac to the storefront, Rosen asked, "What happened? What did the old man say?"

She shook her head. "All he said was 'Viet Cong attack.' He was in shock, remembering how it was in Vietnam." She looked around. "This was how it happened during the war. All the time. You would be walking and then . . ." Her eyes fixed on the broken window, and Rosen sensed her slipping away. He shook her, and she blinked, bringing a hand to her forehead. "I . . . I must see if my parents are all right." She ran into the tailor shop.

He bent to examine the shattered window more carefully. There had been little damage to the store itself. The bomb must have been small and planted somewhere in the display, blowing the glass outward. It seemed that whoever placed it there wanted the explosions to scare not kill; in that he had been successful.

Rosen stepped inside to the counter, where a man and boy sat. "Are you the owner?"

The man stared straight ahead, not moving, but the boy answered, "My father is. He doesn't speak English."

"Is he hurt?"

The boy shook his head. "He is afraid . . . the explosion."

"Ask him if he knows who did this."

The boy exchanged a few words with his father. "He says they are bad."

"Who?"

The man blinked and stared at Rosen, as if seeing him for the first time. He shook his head and muttered to his son who said, "My father wants to be left alone."

"Sure, I guess it probably was the V.C."

Father and son stared at one another but remained silent.

Back on the sidewalk, Rosen watched the Vietnamese busily cleaning the street; vegetables and broken glass were being swept into neat little piles, placed into garbage bags, and carried away. The injured people had disappeared into the buildings. He signaled to Trac, who walked from the tailor shop.

"How are your parents?"

"They were not hurt. The funeral will begin as soon as everything is cleaned."

He looked at the hearse. There were a few scratches on the hood, which a boy was buffing carefully, and the photograph of Trac's sister had been torn.

"The police should be here soon," he said. "Maybe then we'll find out what happened."

"The police will not come. No one has called them. No one will call them."

"But the bombing . . ."

"What bombing? Look around. Nothing has happened."

Glancing up and down the street, Rosen saw that everything had been cleaned. From where he stood, he couldn't even tell if the window was missing from the grocery store. Only the slight throbbing in his hand and the murdered woman's torn picture proved something had happened.

"Why won't anybody call the police?"

"They don't want trouble. Whenever the police come, there is more trouble. You've seen for yourself. My sister died, someone called the police, and look what has happened. Now . . ."

"So the two events are connected."

"I didn't say that."

"Didn't you?"

She stood close to him, her arm brushing against his sleeve. "Please, you are here at my sister's wake. I ask you to honor the feelings of my people. Forget this has happened."

Her face was close enough for Rosen to feel her breath against his cheek. He need only pull her close and . . .

He took a step back. "The Caucasian I saw earlier in your father's shop—who is he?"

"I . . . I told you I don't know. Forget it. You must excuse me—my parents are waiting." She forced a smile. "So much sadness. We should think of more pleasant things. You did say you would call me. I would like that." She turned and walked into the tailor shop, and everything seemed as it had been when Rosen and Collinsby had first crossed the street. He looked at his injured hand. Had there really been a bombing?

Walking down the street to the car, Rosen still smelled her perfume and felt his face grow warm. Even after three years of divorce, he wasn't comfortable with other women. He wanted to see Nguyen Thi Trac again, not because of the case (what did he really care about Basehart), but because they were both alone, both wandering spirits. That was reason enough.

Reaching the car, he slid inside next to Collinsby and asked, "Did you hear anything?"

"No. Like what?"

Rosen stared at the other man, who looked back innocently. "Nothing. Let's go."

Collinsby drove slowly up a street that had covered its wounds. Nguyen Thi Nhi's funeral procession appeared ready to begin; the coffin was being carried from the shop. Rosen looked at the opposite curb and noticed the other red Jaguar had gone, doubtless the white face with it. Concentrating, he saw the face clearly and the license plate number, so that the first thing he did after Collinsby dropped him off at the hotel was to call his home office and check on the car registration. While waiting for the return call, he bandaged his hand, lay back in bed with Sarah's birthday card on his stomach, and fell asleep.

Chapter 6

That same morning Lt. Canary left Jimmy Wilkes
a message to meet him for lunch at Lois's Cafe.
No one in Wilkes's office had heard of the diner
except for a custodian, who sometimes helped his
brother-in-law haul freight on the weekends and
was able to give directions. On the highway near
the ocean and not far from the Paddy, it was quite
a distance to travel for lunch—Canary had left no
further message, but Wilkes looked forward to
getting away from the office. Although only a day
had passed since his assignment to the case, everything was going better than expected. The
murder weapon had been found, a suspect arrested, and even the defense counsel Lester Collinsby seemed ready to make a deal. Yet, Edison
Basehart not only refused to confess but vehe-
mently maintained his innocence. And Murray
Saunders, the other Assistant Commonwealth's
Attorney, hovered like a vulture around Wilkes,
waiting for a mistake.

Sunlight had finally broken through the clouds,
and rolling down his car window, Wilkes hoped
the warm dry air would be good for his cold. He
even drove the long way to take in more coastline
and watch the fishing boats move lazily through
glittering water, their reflections delicate as
sketches on a china plate.

Lois's Cafe stood just inside the highway where it bent like an elbow to move away from the ocean. A long driveway led into a spacious parking lot half-filled with trucks, pickups, and Canary's brown Ford. Parking beside it, Wilkes leaned against his own hood, lifting his face toward the sun until he could feel it seeping into his skin. Maybe the weather would hold, and his family could go on a picnic next weekend. He dabbed his nose with a handkerchief then walked up the drive and into the restaurant.

Canary sat alone at a booth next to the window; in front of him was a bowl scraped clean of chili surrounded by a graveyard of cracker wrappers.

"Sit down," he said, wiping a napkin across his face. "I was just having an appetizer until you got here." He called to the waitress, "Two more bowls of chili over here, Inez! More coffee and crackers too!" To Wilkes, "This place is a dump, but they make the best chili in town. Got a real Mexican working in the kitchen."

Wilkes sat across from the policeman and took a cup of coffee the waitress poured.

"Yeah," Canary continued, "this place is famous for its chili and the scenery." He patted the waitress's bottom and laughed. "Ain't that right, Inez?"

"Now, Lou, behave yourself. Remember, you're on duty. Chili's coming right up. Here's some more saltines to keep you quiet."

After she left, Wilkes demanded, "Why did you bring me all the way out here?"

Tearing open a package of crackers, Canary said, "Business, and you're paying for lunch. After all, you big shots in the Commonwealth's Attorney's Office have those expense accounts for taking your secretaries to dinners and motels. I'm only a poor honest cop trying to make it with Inez now and then. Wanted to see you, because I got some news about the Basehart case.'' The waitress set down the bowls of chili. ''Easy on the Tabasco sauce, Jimmy. I told you, they got a real Mexican in there.''

Wilkes pushed his bowl aside. ''I don't have time for your games. What is it?''

''There're two things. Did you know Basehart got himself that Northern lawyer?''

''I saw Mr. Rosen with Lester Collinsby yesterday at the courthouse. He was awfully quiet during Basehart's interrogation. In fact, I got the impression that Lester was planning to plea bargain his client. Are you sure Rosen's come on as co-counsel?''

The policeman nodded.

''How'd you find out about him so quickly?''

Canary paused to build a mound of chili on a cracker then, cranking open his mouth, swallowed it. ''A good cop knows his town. That ambulance chaser and Cowpie went over to the Paddy this morning. I wouldn't worry about it. What the hell they gonna find that we didn't see first? Have to admit I'm disappointed in Basehart, hiring some out a' town slick. That's just not his style.''

''He has a right to retain anyone he wants for a proper defense.''

''Yes, your majesty, I appreciate you reminding me.'' He blew his nose into a napkin. ''Can't shake this damn cold.''

''Is that why you had me drive all the way out here? You could've told me this over the phone.''

''Oh no, that was just a little piece of small town gossip which I figured you'd be far above. No, I asked you here to go shopping. That's right. Take a look across the street." He leaned back to light a cigarette.

Looking out the window and across the highway, Wilkes saw the large wooden sign, "Edison's Bait and Tackle Shop," and below that in smaller letters, "National Headquarters of the Guardians of an Undefiled Nation." Set back a few yards from the road was the shop itself. It was not what Wilkes would have guessed from Basehart's personal appearance, but a neat little house of green shingles and shuttered windows with flower boxes. In the driveway a brand new pickup gleamed in the sun, while on the front porch a hammock swung gently back and forth. Two men sat on the steps; the taller one was whittling while his companion sipped a beer. The whole scene looked like a Currier and Ives print.

"That's Basehart's shop?"

Canary blew his first smoke ring of the afternoon. "Bet you didn't know our Edison was such a country gentleman."

"To look at him, he's just a . . . How can he live so well?"

"Probably sells a helluva lot of worms. You know about his worm farm? Last time we ran him in, he told me about it—the only experimental worm farm in the world. For years he'd been trying to crossbreed different kinds of night crawlers for better bait. That's the kind of man we're dealing with, but that's not why you're here. The man swinging in the hammock is Billy Lee Pelham, our wandering boy come home. My men have been sitting here since the murder, waiting for Billy Lee. He finally turned up a few hours ago."

"Basehart's alibi."

Canary snickered. "Billy Lee's so used to lying, he probably couldn't tell you who his real mother is. He's been in and out of jail as much as his fishing buddy. No, I wouldn't worry too much about Billy Lee, counselor, but just the same, let's take a walk over and find out where he's been since the murder. Right after you finish that bowl of chili. Inez, how about bringing me more coffee and a nice slice of pecan pie!''

Ten minutes later Wilkes followed a belching Canary out the door. Crossing the highway they approached the front porch. The two men sitting on the stairs looked up nonchalantly, and the whittler said, ''We got company, Billy Lee.''

''Customers?'' asked the voice inside the hammock.

''Not likely. Besides, don't think we have enough worms to feed this canary.''

The policeman smiled. ''Hello, Billy Lee.'' The hammock slowly came to a halt. ''What you whittling, Rupert?'' He took the piece of wood—a half-formed whistle—from the man's hand, examined it carefully then, grabbing Rupert by the neck, stuffed it into his mouth. ''You were saying something?''

Spitting out splinters and blood, Rupert dropped his knife and crawled away, the other man on the porch hurrying after. Canary took the knife and wood, walked up the steps, leaned against a post, and began whittling. Wilkes stayed below, resting a foot on the first step while watching the hammock grow still as a stone.

Finally a pudgy leg emerged over the side, followed by the other, feet yellow with dirt, then the rest of the body slunk from the hammock. Billy Lee Pelham was short and stocky, as if his limbs had been pushed together like pieces of clay. His face was unshaven, stubbled with several days' growth. The flaps of Pelham's overalls were unclasped so that they hung over his lap, revealing a hairy chest streaked with sweat. He blinked hard in the sunlight and smiled, his teeth as brown and mangled as Basehart's.

"Well, well, well. If it ain't my old friend, Lt. Canary." His voice was high-pitched and sing-song. "Been awhile, ain't it. And how're you to-day?"

"Just fine, Billy Lee."

"Come lookin' for some worms, have ya?"

"Let's just say a snake."

Pelham scowled for a moment, but the smile soon crept back upon his lips. "Who's he?"

"Well, I'm shocked, Billy Lee, that a man as active in public affairs as yourself doesn't know one of Musket Shoals' leading citizens. This is Mr. Wilkes, Assistant Commonwealth's Attorney in charge of electrocuting your fishing buddy."

"Yeah?" Pelham looked Wilkes up and down. "What's he doin' here? What's this all about?"

Canary resumed whittling the whistle. "Do I need to spell it out for you? Edison Basehart's been yelling for the past day and a half that he was with you the night the Slant woman was murdered. You're his alibi, Billy Lee. How about it?"

Scratching his head, Pelham did not answer.

"Well, boy?"

He pursed his lips and tossed up his hands. "Sure he was with me. I mean, guess he was."

"What do you mean, you guess?"

"We was playin' some cards the night you're talkin' 'bout, then I got tired 'n fell asleep. I woke up real early in the mornin' to go fishin'."

"How early?"

"It was still dark out. Maybe 'bout five A.M."

"That's why you weren't there when we arrested Basehart at seven. Too bad for your friend." Canary took a step closer. "What time did you fall asleep? That's real important, Billy Lee, because if it was after midnight, Basehart can use you as an alibi—for all the good it'd do him. But if it was before twelve, and you were dead to the world until five in the morning, how're you supposed to know what he did? See what I mean?"

"I know what you're sayin', 'n I been thinkin' on it long 'n hard, Lieutenant. Lord knows it's a heavy burden havin' a man's life hangin' on exactly when your head touched the pillow." He looked at the sky, contemplating a flock of passing seagulls.

Canary had almost finished the whistle and pointed the knife at Pelham. "I just had a big lunch. That always tires me out and makes me cranky if I'm put under any undue stress, which is what you're putting me under right now. It's a heads or tails question, either yes or no. Are you alibi-ing for Basehart or ain't you?"

"Well, Lieutenant," he said rubbing his jaw, "if you put it that way—so clear 'n all—guess I'd have to say no. I had a few beers—musta fell asleep 'bout eleven. I'll be on the witness stand 'n have to put my hand on the Bible, swearin' before the Lord. Not to mention perjury 'n goin' to jail for lyin'. Look, Edison's one a' my dearest friends. We're both officers in this fine organization to keep America pure. But, hell, my ass is on the line."

"So that's it."

"The truth will be told. Anything else I can do for you all?"

Puffing on a cigarette, Canary blew a large smoke ring. "Yeah. Take off your clothes."

"What?"

"You heard me, boy."

"Shit . . . you're jokin' . . . ain'tcha?"

Canary shook his head. "When the Nguyen woman was killed, someone else was shot in the same room. Wasn't Basehart."

Pelham stared at the policeman for a long time, then his face brightened. "Oh, I get it." Pulling down the flaps, he wiggled off his overalls and, wearing no underwear, stood naked as a bloated tick. Walking in a small circle to show his backside, he said, "See, no scars, no marks, not a damn thing—pure as the day I was born. All right to get dressed?"

"Yeah, before I lose my lunch."

As Pelham pulled up his overalls and grinned, Wilkes remembered Basehart's bravado and smile quickly melting into a desperate fear, so alone. "Ask Billy Lee!" the accused had cried. Something was wrong. Wilkes would have been the last person in the world to condone perjury, but any human being, even a creature such as Basehart, deserved some loyalty, if it was only a hesitation before throwing him to the wolves. Yet, Pelham couldn't wait to betray his friend. "Ask Billy Lee!" Now they had.

Wilkes took a step up the stairs. "Where have you been the past two days?"

"This is a free country," Pelham said, sitting back in the hammock. "Ain't nobody's business where I been."

Canary flicked the whittling knife so that it stuck in the floor a shade below Pelham's left foot. "The man asked you a simple question. How about a simple answer?"

Pelham shifted his feet. "Sure. Ain't nobody got more respect for the law than me." He paused momentarily, half-closing his eyes deep in thought. "Like I said . . . from Sunday night to Monday about five in the mornin', I was with Edison. Then I went fishin'. Didn't have me no luck, so I left off fishin' couple hours later, got in my pickup 'n drove out to Morgan's Creek to do a little squirrel shootin'. Camped out there last night—slept in the back of the pickup. This mornin' I got up early to shoot ducks 'n caught a chill. I crawled back in the truck 'n slept it off. Just got back a little while ago. I feel a whole lot better, in case you're interested." He had spoken slowly and carefully, as if trying to repeat something from memory. Having finished he relaxed, even started the hammock rocking again.

"Anybody see you?"

"Don't think so. You know how bad Morgan's Creek can get, especially after a big rain. Not too many folks get out there this time a' year."

Wilkes asked, "Why didn't you come forward after Basehart was arrested?"

"Radio's broke in the pickup. Just heard about Edison's misfortune from Rupert not but an hour ago. Anyways, what the hell can I do? Ain't really none a' my affair."

Furrowing his brow Canary stared at Pelham, who looked down at the floor and stopped rocking. The detective blew his nose, stepped down from the porch and walked to the pickup in the driveway, Pelham hurrying after. Canary carefully inspected the vehicle, bending to examine each of the wheels, the mud-flaps, and bumpers. Opening the car door and leaning inside, he brought out a rifle.

"This what you went hunting with?"

Pelham nodded.

"Looks mighty clean."

"I cleaned it," Pelham answered almost before Canary finished.

"The truck too? I do know what Morgan's Creek is like. With all the rain we've been having, that road going in there must be full of mud, let alone all those side trails. Your tires should've been swimming in mud up to the axle. This truck is mighty clean, Billy Lee."

"Like you said, Lieutenant, I cleaned it. Cleaned it real good at one a' them new quickie car washes. After all, it's my prize possession. Just ask any a' the boys."

Returning the rifle to the truck, Canary walked back to the porch. This time Pelham followed like a whipped dog, knowing he had to come but not wanting to get too close.

"Well, that's something, that sure is something," the policeman said to Wilkes while lighting another cigarette. "Here's poor Billy Lee, so sick he has to crawl into his truck to get some rest. Crawl, mind you. Then he feels so much better, first thing he does when he gets back home is to clean his gun and wash his truck. My, he's a tidy one. Look at him, Jimmy, don't he strike you as a tidy one?"

Running a hand through his greasy hair, Pelham said, "T-Told you, I'm feelin' better now. What's all the fuss 'bout anyway with me bein' up at Morgan's Creek? I told you what you wanted to know—that I can't be sure Edison was with me. That's the truth and ain't no one can make me say any different." He looked anxiously from Canary to Wilkes.

"Leaving all that be for now," the policeman said, "you got any idea why Basehart's gun was found outside the dead woman's apartment?"

Pelham shook his head.

"You got a gun."

"Just my huntin' rifle."

"We found gunpowder traces on Basehart. Said he was target shooting with you on Sunday. There was a squirrel rifle in the shop that'd been fired recently, and some bullet holes in the trees out back. You remember shooting with him?"

"When?"

"Sunday."

Pelham crossed his arms. "Don't rightly remember, Lieutenant."

"Did your buddy ever threaten any Vietnamese?"

"You know as well as me, Edison has no use for them Slants—just talkin' 'bout them would get him real worked up. But neither do any a' us."

"You think he killed that woman?"

"Oh, no," Pelham said, taking a step backward to avoid Canary's smoke rings. "You don't trick me into talkin' down my friend. I ain't helpin' you anymore."

Wilkes and Canary looked at each other. Shrugging, the policeman said, "All right, Billy Lee, that's all for now. Just don't go and get lost again. I may be wanting to talk to you real soon. In fact"—he pulled out the wooden whistle—"when you hear this, you better come running quick. You do understand."

Pelham nodded, trying to smile.

"Good. C'mon, counselor."

As Canary passed him, Wilkes suddenly had a thought. He asked Pelham, "Do you know where Nguyen Van Van is?"

"Who?"

"Nguyen Van Van—the dead woman's brother."

"Some S-Slant? You're askin' me 'bout some

Slant? How the hell should I know? H-How the hell should I know anything 'bout any of 'em?''

"I understand that he got around quite a bit." Wilkes took a step closer. "This is a small town. You sure you haven't . . ."

"I told you, I don't know no Slant . . . no Slant! Can't you leave a man in peace! I know my rights, I know all about police harassment! It's against some part a' the Constitution, some . . ." He quieted under Canary's gaze.

"You're mighty touchy, Billy Lee," the lieutenant said, "but I guess we can just chalk that up to your recent illness. Don't mind saying, I didn't believe you before, but now . . . well, you do look mighty pale. Maybe we should drive you over to the doctor."

Pelham took out a dirty blue bandana and wiped the sweat from his face and neck. He tried to laugh, but it sounded more like a croak. "No. No, thank you. Guess I just got worked up a little, my best friend bein' in jail 'n all."

"Yeah, I see how you'd worry. Got some good news for you though." He waited.

Pelham narrowed his eyes. "Yeah?"

"Your friend's got himself another lawyer. He come in from no less than Washington, D.C."

"How's that?"

"Yeah, some big city sharpie to help Collinsby. So you see, if he's innocent, Basehart's got nothing to worry about. Ain't that good news?"

"Say, Lieutenant, about this here lawyer . . ."

"Bye, Billy Lee."

Pelham said something which was drowned out by the traffic, as Canary and Wilkes crossed the highway and walked up the driveway into the parking lot.

Opening his car door Canary said, "This case

is getting a lot more interesting than I first thought."

"So you think Pelham is lying?"

"Through his teeth. I told you, with Billy Lee lying's a religion. We just got to figure out how much and why. See, it would've been the easiest thing in the world for him to alibi Basehart, say he didn't fall asleep till one and Basehart was still there. Even if you and me didn't believe him, he might've given the defense some help in court."

"And besides, if he's Basehart's friend . . ."

"Right. Those boys stick together like horse shit. In the old days one of them might go kill a nigger, while the rest would swear he was leading a prayer meeting. No, something's wrong. And when you mentioned that Slant girl's brother—like you hit him in the gut. What made you think of that?"

Wilkes shrugged. "Nobody else seems to know where Van is. I thought it was worth a try."

"Yeah, sure was. I'm gonna put a few more men on that missing Slant's tail." Both men took out handkerchiefs and blew their noses. Canary laughed. "Damn cold, can't seem to shake it. Well, be seeing you, counselor."

"You know," Wilkes said as Canary got into his car, "it might be worth checking the owner-ship papers and financing on the bait and tackle shop. Maybe Pelham has something to gain with Basehart in prison, though I doubt anyone would betray a friend for a few cans of worms."

"You don't know Billy Lee. I'll look into it. I still think Basehart is guilty as hell, but he didn't do it alone. Sure would like to fry Billy Lee along-side him and maybe a few others of his white trash friends. We'll get them, get them all, and there ain't nothing Lester Collinsby and that bleeding-heart Hebe lawyer can do about it." Canary paused to blow a smoke ring. "Jimmy, you didn't do too bad today."

Driving back to the office, Wilkes found it hard to stay within the speed limit, exhilarated as hunters were after the hunt. He couldn't wait for Murray Saunders to ask, "How did it go?"

Chapter 7

THURSDAY MORNING

A telegram was waiting for Rosen, as he passed the front desk after breakfasting in the hotel coffee shop. Having contacted Virginia's Bureau of Motor Vehicles, his Washington office identified a Richard M. Dickerson as owner of the red Jaguar that had been parked near the Nguyens' tailor shop. Stepping into a phone booth, Rosen thumbed through the directory and found in bold letters, "Richard 'Dick' Dickerson, State Senator." He dialed the number.

"Senator Dick Dickerson's office, Miss Reynolds speaking." Her voice could have belonged to Scarlett O'Hara.

"Hello, this is Nathan Rosen representing the Committee to Defend the Constitution. You've no doubt heard of my organization."

There was a pause. "Well, I'm sure it does a great deal of good. What may I do for you, Mr. Rosen?"

"I'd like to speak with Senator Dickerson, please. It's very important."

"I'm sorry, but the Senator will not be in today."

"Could I reach him at home?"

"Sorry again, but I cannot give out the Senator's private number. You understand."

"Of course." Rosen did his best to sound heartbroken. "It's just that our organization is holding its annual banquet this weekend, and our keynote speaker has suddenly taken ill. Senator Dickerson's name came up as a replacement, because of his fine record on civil liberties, but we really do need an immediate confirmation. This would be quite a feather in the Senator's cap."

"Oh dear, that is a problem. Well . . . I really can't give out any numbers, but I suppose it wouldn't hurt to tell you the Senator's spending the day on his yacht. At the Tyler Yacht club. Not that he usually takes time off during the middle of the week, but with the state senate in recess . . ."

"I understand perfectly, and I want you to know my organization appreciates your trust. This will be quite a surprise for the Senator. Thanks very much."

He sat in the lobby to wait for Lester Collinsby, who had promised to drop by. On the inside of his left wrist Rosen scratched the scar made by a switchblade meant for a client, an atheist trying to ban a nativity scene from a town square. He looked from the scar to his bandaged right hand where glass from yesterday's explosion had cut him; it would form a new scar to join the others on his body. He thought of the ancient ascetics who whipped themselves as a kind of penance. Was he so very different?

Closing his eyes he tried to remain very still, as the stone sunk to the bottom of the ocean is oblivious to all the waves it has caused. His mind was clearing itself of everything, when he heard a sound like the rushing of wind—God's voice speaking to Job? No, the click of metal upon metal as the hotel door shut.

"Hey, there you are. Sleep well?" Collinsby's voice, and Rosen could feel the big man's shadow fall across him.

He opened his eyes slowly. "Yes, thank you."

Collinsby sat on the couch adjacent to him. "I heard from Jimmy Wilkes that Billy Lee Pelham finally showed up—right at Basehart's bait and tackle shop. Guess he lives there too. Jimmy says Pelham won't swear to Basehart being with him the whole night, only until about eleven when Pelham fell asleep. That doesn't sound good, especially with them being friends and in that organization together."

"That is interesting."

"Thought we could take a ride out to the bait and tackle shop. If Pelham really isn't going to alibi Basehart, we'd better think about cutting a deal with Jimmy."

"Lester, this case sure hasn't caused you any undue stress."

Collinsby laughed. "Ever hear of the football term 'forward progress'? Means you run with the ball, until the other team throws you back. The referee marks the ball as far as you got. That's the way I feel about this case. From all the evidence, there's not a heck of a lot we can do. Fourth down and long yardage, Nate."

"Time to punt. Not much choice, huh?"

"Not from where I stand. Besides, we can probably work out a good deal—at least keep Basehart out of the electric chair. Like I said before, Jimmy doesn't have too much experience in cases like this, so he shouldn't be anxious to take this one to court. What do you say—let's check out Pelham's story and then call Jimmy."

Rosen shook his head. "Maybe later. Right now I feel like an ocean breeze. Looks pretty warm outside."

"We still got the sun, though it's supposed to rain tonight. I'd be happy to oblige, Nate, but don't you think first things first? Maybe after lunch we can take a drive.''

"Something pertaining to the case we need to check. Could be important. I'll tell you on the way.''

Rosen walked from the lobby without waiting for Collinsby and was sitting in the car when the other man emerged from the hotel.

"Anywhere in particular?'' Collinsby asked, accelerating quickly from the curb.

"Tyler Yacht Club. I checked out that red Jaguar we saw yesterday at the funeral. It belongs to State Senator Richard Dickerson.''

"Dick Dickerson? No, there's some mistake. What would his car be doing in the Paddy? You must've mixed up the numbers on the license plate. I think we're on a wild goose chase.'' As Collinsby spoke, the car slowed to ten miles below the speed limit, as if he were a child dragging his feet before some unpleasant task. "I really think it's a waste of time.''

"Drop me at a car rental. You can interview Pelham, while I visit Dickerson.'' He looked out the window but from the corner of his eye saw Collinsby's jaw tighten.

"No, that's all right.''

The tremor in Collinsby's voice was obliterated by the automobile's acceleration. Streets thinned into pastures, and Rosen sniffed traces of salt spray in the wind. As the highway gradually veered to the left, the land turned brown and rocky, piling into a ridge that grew larger in the distance until curving back the other way like some primordial snake basking in the sun. At the promontory where the land curved, Rosen noticed a widening of the road—a small rest area and some sort of monument.

"What's that up ahead?" he asked.

"An old statue of Jefferson. He spoke here once on his way to Washington. I used to stop to see it in high school with Jimmy Wilkes. The way he'd stand in front of the thing, you'd think it was some sort of idol. Here's our turn."

Collinsby slowed to make a quick left onto an asphalt road that dipped between the ridge and wound its way toward the ocean. Soon they came upon the sign, "Private Lane," and then another, "Tyler Yacht Club, Founded 1843, Members and Guests Only." The road straightened; a half mile ahead the ocean stretched so calm that one could barely distinguish it from the sky. Nearing the dock Collinsby drove into a parking lot, where he pulled between a Cadillac and a Mercedes.

Rosen said, "Looks like car thief heaven."

Collinsby laughed. "You should see this place on a weekend."

Rosen wandered through the lot, finally signaling Collinsby to join him. "This is the car I saw across the street from the Nguyen tailor shop. A newer model of yours—same color. You've never seen it before?"

Collinsby scratched his head. "Can't say as I have."

"Why would Dickerson have gone there?"

"Maybe . . . maybe it wasn't Dickerson. Maybe somebody else was driving his car."

"His wife?"

"He's a widower. I don't know who it could've been. It was just a thought. Look, are we going in or not?"

The two men walked back toward the clubhouse, a large building modeled after a colonial tavern, white planks ribbed with cedar beams. The entrance, a double door of polished oak, was opened gingerly by a doorman in a traditional sailor suit—tasseled cap, striped shirt, and baggy pants.

Pausing at the door Rosen asked, "Senator Dickerson inside?"

"No, sir," the doorman replied. "He's over on his boat, second one down. The *Richard III*."

The two attorneys walked down to the dock. Rosen didn't know a thing about boats. Growing up in Chicago, he had never paid much attention to the ones on Lake Michigan. Seeing them up close, however, was something else. They were machines of wonder—from the colorful pennants lilting in the breeze, to the long smooth curves of the cabin and deck, and the broad sleek hull. The *Richard III* was one of the larger yachts—big enough to accommodate a half-dozen people—and it was cleaner, white trimmed with crimson stripes vibrant as flowing blood. A small boarding ramp was in place but unattended. Nobody was on deck.

Rosen was about to call out, when he heard a loud noise and something breaking inside the cabin. A woman screamed, "No! Help! Help!"

He took a step onto the ramp, when Collinsby's powerful hand stopped him.

"Wait a bit," the other man almost whispered.

Another scream, which subsided into a series of giggles followed by an irritated, "Now you just stop that," and more giggles. Suddenly a young woman in a bikini stumbled up the stairs, hitching the top back over her breasts. "Oops!" She blushed seeing the two men, but before she could say another word, a hand reached up from the cabin stairway and pulled her ankle so that she collapsed upon the deck. The hand was so scrawny that its veins stood out, deeply tanned skin devoid of hair, with a large gold band weighing down the ring finger. "Oww, that hurts!" the woman squealed, and the hand finally released its grip.

Up the stairs bounded Senator Dickerson, wearing an outlandish Hawaiian shirt. Grinning wickedly he leaned over, as a swimmer does, to pounce upon the woman, who nodded toward the dock.

"Eh?" he asked until noticing the two visitors. The leer quickly changed to a broad grin, while he put on a pair of sunglasses to mask his emerald eyes. Rosen had seen those eyes somewhere before. Dickerson's bermuda shorts were as ridiculous as his shirt, billowing around his bony knees. He walked to the railing and leaned forward, brushing back his coppery hair to show off his remarkable tan. Everything about Dickerson's appearance was perfect—hair bronze as his skin, teeth whiter-than-white—as if all colors had been painted then covered with several layers of lacquer, making it impossible to tell his true age.

"Hello, Lester. Long time no see." His tone was even, betraying nothing. Because of the dark glasses, Rosen didn't know at which of the two men Dickerson was staring.

"Sure has been awhile," Collinsby replied. "Think I last saw you at that charity dinner the Mayor gave a few months back. How have you been?"

"Fine, just fine. Trying to keep fit. And you?"

"Fine."

They spoke too formally. Rosen remembered being in the company of a recently divorced couple who conversed in a similar manner; whole histories floated ghostlike around the few words spoken. Collinsby wasn't looking up at Dickerson; maybe the sun was in his eyes. The woman sauntered beside the Senator and, looking at Collinsby, purred, "Who's your friend, Dick?"

Ignoring her Dickerson asked, "You here visiting someone?"

"No. I mean . . ." Collinsby took out a handkerchief and wiped his hands.

"We're here on an errand, Senator," Rosen said. "My name's Nathan Rosen. I'm an attorney, who, along with Lester, is representing Edison Basehart. I'm sure you've read about the case. Mr. Basehart is accused of killing a Vietnamese woman, Nguyen Thi Nhi."

For a long time Dickerson stared through his dark glasses at the two men. His next words burst like machine-gun fire. "Representing Basehart!" More quietly to Collinsby, "I read you were defending him. I had no idea you had an associate."

"Not exactly. Mr. Rosen just kind of showed up. He's from the . . . what's that group, Nate?"

"Committee to Defend the Constitution. You've heard of my organization?"

"Uh . . . of course. Great job you all are doing, I'm sure. But . . . why are you involved in this case?"

"I've been sent to help Lester protect Basehart's constitutional rights."

"And Basehart agreed?"

"He was most cordial. A delightful fellow, one of the great raconteurs of our generation. You've met him, Senator?"

"No. No, of course not. It's just . . . I've heard of his reputation, and you are a . . . never mind. You said you're on an errand. One that involves me in some way?"

Rosen ran his gaze across the length of the vessel. "I've never been on a yacht before. Could we

see you for a few minutes? What are you supposed to say—permission to come aboard, sir?"

Dickerson paused, as if his mind were a computer referring to earlier data, cross-checking and
analyzing various options before finally spitting
out a response. "Very well."

The two attorneys joined Dickerson and his girlfriend in four lounge chairs behind a buffet table,
Rosen counting four glasses and four half-filled
plates of food. He looked at the cabin door which
was slightly ajar.

"A drink, gentlemen?" Dickerson asked. Rosen
nodded. "And you, Lester?"

Collinsby sat on the edge of his chair. "No,
thank you. I feel bad about coming here unan-
nounced. At least I should've called to . . . make
an appointment."

"Nonsense. Bonnie, pour Mr. Rosen a glass of
champagne while he tells me about his little errand." He was smiling, and, lifting a silver case
from the table, offered the men a cigar. Collinsby
shook his head.

"No thanks," Rosen said. "This may be nothing at all, but in the interest of our client, we need
to be as thorough as possible. I'm sure you understand. Thank you." He took the champagne.

"You're welcome, I'm sure," the woman said
and wiggled over to Dickerson, leaning against
his shoulder while he stroked one of her knees.

"Yes?" the Senator asked, his hand coming to
a stop.

"We were wondering what you were doing in
the Paddy yesterday morning."

"Wha . . . what?" Dickerson and the woman
burst out laughing. "I can assure you, gentlemen,
I wasn't there yesterday morning. I was otherwise
engaged." Bonnie laughed even harder. "Why I

haven't stepped foot in that place since the last election. I'm afraid you've been misinformed. Sorry you've come all this way for nothing." He lit a cigar and puffed contentedly.

Rosen said, "Your car was there."

"My car? You're certain?"

Rosen nodded.

"Which one?"

"That bright red lunar module in the parking lot. I saw it parked across from the tailor shop belonging to the murdered woman's parents. It was there yesterday morning just before the funeral procession."

Dickerson stroked his jaw and remained silent, but Bonnie said, "Why, it's simple, honey. Your boy Junior must've taken the car. He uses it more 'n you do."

"Hmm."

"All we gotta do is ask him. Junior!" she shouted toward the cabin door. "Junior, company!" No response. "He may be busy with Lu Ann. Junior, put your pants on 'n get up here right this minute—oww! That hurts!" She rubbed her knee where Dickerson's hand had left its mark.

"You needn't be so loud," the Senator snapped. Lowering his voice he said, "Dickie, would you please come up here for a moment."

He must have been standing behind the door, for instantly a young man stepped onto the deck, and just as quickly Rosen recognized him as the white face at the wake. Junior was shirtless, his chest almost smooth as a woman's, and his cutoffs exposed the same skinny legs as his father. His face also closely resembled Dickerson, especially those emerald eyes.

The young man went directly to the buffet ta-

ble, placed a stack of cold cuts between two slices
of white bread liberally spread with mayonnaise
and ate heartily, making loud chomping noises.
Only then did he lean against the table and look
at the two attorneys.

Bonnie clapped her hands. "What you been
doin' to make you so hungry! Lu Ann, you got
any mileage left in you!"

"Shut up," Junior said between bites. "Hi,
Lester."

Collinsby nodded.

"What're you doing out here?"

Dickerson said, "This is Mr. Rosen from the . . ."

"Committee to Defend the Constitution."

"Yes, of course. He and Lester represent the
man accused of killing that Vietnamese woman.
You read about it, I'm sure."

Finishing the sandwich he made another, stopping only to burp.

"Dickie."

"Yeah? What's all this got to do with me?"

"Mr. Rosen claims to have seen our car parked
yesterday near the shop of the dead woman's parents. That's in the Paddy. Were you out there?"

Junior shrugged. "I was at lots of places yesterday."

Rosen said, "Perhaps there's a better way of
expressing this. I saw you inside the tailor shop
at the wake itself. What were you doing there?"

Junior looked at him and burped.

Dickerson cleared his throat. "Now, son, the
man asked a simple question. Let's get this settled
before we waste the whole day."

Another young woman walked through the
cabin doorway. Like Bonnie she wore a skimpy
bikini. She slunk along the railing, dabbing a wet

compress against a puffy cheek, and looked down at the deck.

Bonnie hurried to her. "What's the matter, honey, Junior up to his old tricks?" She glared at the young man. "You know she don't like to be treated rough. We ain't animals."

Dickerson held up his hand. "That's quite enough from everyone." To Rosen, "You'll have to forgive them, but you know how it is—kids will be kids."

"Senator, I don't care what games your son and his playmates have been involved in, as long as they haven't been with Nguyen Thi Nhi, the dead woman. You haven't been playing any games with her, have you, Junior?"

Junior shook his head. "What in the world would I be doing with some Slant?"

"So you deny being at the wake yesterday?"

"That's right. So that makes you either mistaken or a liar."

"Dickie . . ." his father began.

"All right! I never met this Slant you're talking about, or any Slant for that matter. Now get off our boat."

"Sure, I will," Rosen said. "I must've been mistaken. Sorry to have bothered all of you."

"Why, that's quite all right," Dickerson replied. "Mistakes do happen."

"You see . . . guess I can tell you in the strictest confidence . . . Lester and I are worried about more than just the murder. The police autopsy revealed that the Nguyen woman suffered from some sort of venereal disease. I think they're calling it yellow syphilis. It's Asian in origin, takes longer to develop than other social diseases, is more resistant to medication like penicillin, and can be fatal. Seems it creeps up on the brain, paralyzing then destroying the nerve endings. I can see that Junior has all his wits about him—forgive me for being suspicious of a liaison between him and this woman. But after all, she was a known prostitute and, like you said, kids will be kids, and anyone having intimate contact with her within the past few months could've contracted the disease and unknowingly become a carrier, passing it on to innocent young women—well, like Lu Ann. There's a possibility of a real epidemic right here in Musket Shoals. You appreciate the reason why I asked you to keep this information confidential. We don't want to start a panic. I'm sure the proper medical authorities will think of something. I only hope they do in time for those poor souls who've already contracted the disease. I'm glad Junior's not one of them.''

Rosen had rambled on purpose while watching, from the corner of his eye, Junior growing paler by the second. Lu Ann had also blanched, moving toward him and saying, "J . . . Junior?'' Ignoring her, he looked deeply where he had bitten the sandwich, as if his eyes could examine the bacteria in his saliva. "J . . . Junior!'' she demanded, grabbing his arm. He pushed her away and ran downstairs, Lu Ann sobbing and hurrying after.

"Anything wrong?'' Rosen asked.

Through his dark glasses Dickerson stared into the cabin.

"Senator?''

"Nothing. Nothing's the matter.''

"It seems I've upset Junior.''

"He doesn't like being associated with those people, that's all.''

"Those people—you mean the Vietnamese in the Paddy?''

Dickerson nodded curtly.

"Why?"

"You don't understand, Mr. Rosen, but since these people arrived, there've been certain problems. I'm surprised Lester hasn't told you. Yes, I'm very surprised."

Collinsby moved in his seat as if pricked by a needle.

"What about you, Senator?" Rosen asked.

"Me?"

"What do you think about the Vietnamese? After all, they are in your district. I imagine many of them have the vote. Who knows—some day this could be a black and yellow district. In some parts of California already . . ."

"I don't mind telling you that I believe Americans should take care of Americans first. We don't have enough jobs as it is. Why go cutting the pie into even smaller pieces, so that a real American can't even get a taste in his mouth?"

"A lot of people around here seem to agree with you."

"That's the point. I'm merely the representative of the people's will, merely a reflection of their thoughts and feelings. Someone's got to stand up for America. For God's sake, Miami speaks more Spanish than English, and New York—that's a foreign country. But Musket Shoals . . . families here go back to before the Revolution. We've been at the forefront of true Americanism ever since the first boatloads of foul smelling, bearded . . ." He stopped suddenly and looked away from Rosen. "I . . . I sometimes get a bit carried away. You know how we politicians love a soapbox."

Rosen sipped the last of his champagne.

"Gentlemen," Dickerson said rising, "if you've finished your business here . . ."

"Of course, Senator," Rosen replied, as he and Collinsby stood. "You've been most kind to receive us without an appointment."

"Quite all right. Sorry I couldn't have been more help. Nor my son."

They shook hands. Rosen said, "Well, you know what they say, 'sometimes from the mouths of babes.' Good-bye."

He turned and walked down the ramp onto the dock. Looking over his shoulder he saw Collinsby shrug then hobble down the walkway, taking long limping strides until he disappeared beyond the clubhouse into the parking lot. Rosen kept his own pace slow, enjoying the sun and the long shadows cast across his path by the series of boats; he flickered through them like a silent movie. He had not uncovered the truth yet, but that would come. Besides, as the great rabbis had said about the Torah, one does not study to know but to learn.

Collinsby already had the motor running, hands gripping the wheel so tightly that his knuckles were white.

"Turn off the engine," Rosen said, folding his arms and leaning back in the seat.

Collinsby let the motor idle. "Why? Haven't we embarrassed ourselves enough with the Senator? You don't know what an important man he is. I have to live in this town."

"Dickerson's a liar, and I'd guess that Junior's a lot worse. I think they know something. Shut off the engine for a couple of minutes."

Reluctantly Collinsby did as requested. "Now what?"

"Just a couple minutes. Indulge me, please."

"I don't understand a thing you're doing. I don't know what kind of game . . ."

"Well, what do you know. I was wrong. It didn't take a couple minutes after all. Look."

He nodded toward the other end of the parking lot where Junior was hurrying. The young man now wore a pullover and a pair of clip-clopping sandals almost sliding off as he ran. He started his car before closing the door, laying a track of rubber through the lot and onto the road, forcing an oncoming Continental to one side.

"Let's go!" Rosen shouted, buckling his seat belt.

"Huh?"

"As they say in the movies, follow that car. C'mon, Lester, this is your chance to lay your foot on the pedal."

Collinsby accelerated quickly, weaving smartly through the parked cars, until he too forced the Continental back to the shoulder of the road and, fishtailing for a moment, straightened and sped after the quarry. He was driving fast but seemed to be holding back.

"C'mon, Lester, you're sleepwalking."

Collinsby swallowed hard. "I . . . thought you didn't like me going so fast." He shook his head and, holding the wheel steady with one hand, used his other to take out a handkerchief and mop his face.

Rosen said, "I've seen those *Smoky and the Bandit* movies. I know how you Southerners can drive. Of course, if Junior's too much for you."

Putting his hand on the gearshift, Collinsby gave a nervous laugh. "Junior . . . heck." His hand went down on the shift, and the car lunged forward, screaming as it flew like a kamikaze and almost splattered Rosen's brain against the headrest. "This fast enough?" Collinsby asked, but Rosen couldn't peel his lips from his teeth to reply.

In less than a minute they reached the highway, Collinsby slowing just enough to execute a perfect hairpin turn, and in another two minutes they saw Junior's car about a half mile ahead. It was all Rosen could do to get his colleague to maintain a discreet distance. Junior drove impatiently, leaning on the horn and passing other vehicles every chance he could. Collinsby kept up with no problem, gliding around cars and trucks, while spinning the wheel with one hand.

"Lester, I've got to hand it to you. You're a real ace."

He laughed. "Heck, you should see me Sundays on the dirt track."

Junior had to slow down as he reached town, and Collinsby altered his speed accordingly. The two attorneys passed the courthouse, drove another two blocks and stopped, seeing Junior ahead of them waiting for someone to pull out of a parking space. Rosen looked across the street and grinned.

"I'll get out here. Be back in a few minutes."

"Where you going?"

He nodded across the street.

"The Gregson Medical Building? Why?"

"Just calling on a sick friend!" Rosen shouted, running across the street and into the building.

There was a pharmacy to his left, the kind displaying eighteenth-century apothecary equipment and charging twenty-first-century prices. The lobby's carpet was plush burgundy, neatly brushed, and led past groups of Georgian chairs to the silver doors of an elevator, above which hung the symbol of medicine, a snake curled around a staff. It was there Rosen waited, just to the right of the elevator button. He did not have long to wait.

Junior clip-clopped his way into the lobby, pushing an old man aside. He was looking down at the carpet and didn't see Rosen until three quarters of the way to the elevator. Stopping suddenly he edged toward the stairs. The lawyer followed him, both men walking through the doorway almost simultaneously.

"Wait a minute," Rosen said, taking the other man by the arm.

"Leave me alone!" Junior twisted away and fell across the stairs.

Rosen sat on top of the other man. "Hi, Junior. Long time no see."

Junior tried to pull away but only succeeded in scooting down two stairs and scraping his back. He flayed at Rosen, who pinned Dickerson's fists against the steps.

"You're a real pushover, kid," Rosen said, "but I guess that's because of the yellow syphilis working on your system, slowly rotting it away."

Junior strained against the lawyer's grip. "Leave me alone, you son-of-a-bitch!"

"Sapping your strength, digging into all those little capillaries, filling them with poison. Having trouble seeing—I understand that goes first."

"Damn you!" Junior screamed, tears rolling down his eyes.

"Then it starts loosening your teeth and hair, until they all fall out. But that doesn't matter, because your brain'll be too far gone for you to notice anything. You just sort of dribble between splitting headaches, until your whole body oozes into a puddle of slime."

Junior shook uncontrollably, his reddening face

soaked with sweat and tears, but his cries were silent, reverberating somewhere deep inside.

Loosening his grip Rosen sat beside the other man. "What's the matter—was it something I said? You were with Nguyen Thi Nhi. Hey!"

Junior gradually blinked, looked around, and finally sat up. He drew an arm across his eyes, wiping away the sweat, and let his breath shudder hollowly. "I . . ." His voice cracked, but he swallowed and asked, "I'm gonna die, ain't I?"

"Let's talk about more pleasant things, like your relationship with the Vietnamese woman."

"Whore."

"So you slept with her. Did the two of you do drugs together?"

Junior looked away.

"What about some of your other hobbies. Know anything about rigging bombs—little ones that blow up store windows and scare people?"

Crinkling his eyebrows, Junior said, "Leave me alone and let me . . ." He began to shake again but dragged himself to his feet. "Just leave me alone!" Clutching the railing, Junior began pulling himself up the stairs. "Just leave me alone," he kept mumbling under his breath.

Rosen allowed him to climb a few steps before saying, "I made it all up." The other man continued up the stairs. "Didn't you hear me? It was all a gag. There's no such thing as the yellow syphilis—at least I don't think there is. You're O.K."

Junior slowed to a halt, like an old man who must predetermine every move, turned, and brought a hand through his hair. "Huh?"

"You're O.K. I just wanted to find out if you really knew the Nguyen woman. You should've told me in the first place, but then maybe you enjoyed this. Look how rough you like to play with your girlfriend. You like getting the other end of it for a change?''

Rosen didn't wait for a reply but walked back down the stairs, his footsteps clicking loudly in the silence. It wasn't until he reentered the lobby that he heard Junior's savage obscenities, cut short by the closing exit door, hum around the door edges like the buzzing of an angry mosquito.

Chapter 8

THURSDAY EVENING

The Paddy was a different world at night. Rosen's eyes widened as he drove down the main street leading to the tailor shop. Lights looped between buildings like endless strings of pearls, rouge-colored neon signs winked at passersby, and the street pulsated to the beat of a dozen rock tunes. Passing alleyways, Rosen glimpsed women in short skirts lounging on porch steps while beckoning men; some called to him. Small family restaurants alternated with pizza and hamburger joints, making the neighborhood neither American nor Vietnamese but a parody of both.

Reaching the Nguyens' intersection he turned, the automobile gasping fitfully, and parked close to the tailor shop. Before he could shut off the motor, Trac stepped through the doorway and glided into the car. She was as changed as the neighborhood, no longer in her mourning garb or even the traditional ao-dai, but in a gray knit dress. She wore a touch of lipstick and blush, which made her appear older and even more serious. He had been right about one thing; she did have beautiful legs.

"Thanks for accepting my invitation on such short notice," he said, wondering if he should compliment her. He didn't.

"I'm glad you called. Besides, you mentioned

having some important new information. Have you learned anything about my brother Van?''

"I thought you'd be more interested in news about your sister's case."

"What's happened to Nhi is finished, and nothing you or the police do will change it. My brother is still missing, and my parents are very worried. As I told you before, he's the only male, the last of the line."

Rosen made a U-turn—the car sputtered—drove back up the block, and continued through the main street which slowly grew less congested. "Like the car? It was all the rental agency had. Don't sneeze too loudly, or we'll have to call a tow truck."

She smiled weakly. "You were about to tell me something."

"No news about your brother, as far as I know. However, I did have an interesting afternoon. Lester Collinsby and I visited Senator Richard Dickerson and his son on their yacht at the Tyler Yacht Club. Do you know the Senator—Dick, as his intimate friends call him?"

"No," Trac replied. She was staring out the window.

"How about his son, Junior?"

"No."

"Strange, because he knew your sister." Rosen waited for a response, but Trac continued to gaze out the window. "Did you know that Junior Dickerson attended your sister's funeral?"

She turned swiftly. "No, I didn't know!"

"I saw him there. He was the only Caucasian. Sure you didn't notice him? Besides being white, he's incredibly ugly."

She stared at him but said nothing.

"What about the bombing? Could there be any connection between it and your sister's . . . ?"

"Why did you call me? To take me out for a drink or an interrogation? Are my parents and I on trial now? Haven't we been through enough? You people . . . !"

"I'm sorry," Rosen said. "You're right of course. We should forget all about the case for one evening and try to have a good time. Besides, I need your help with directions." He unfolded a sheet of paper and handed it to her. "Ever hear of this nightclub?"

"Top o' the Evenin's?" The paper trembled in her hand, until finally she grew calm. "Yes, it's quite the spot. I used to go there once in a while to hear jazz, before I moved to D.C."

"Good music?"

"Very good. At least it was, and I think Lu still sings there. She's terrific."

"Collinsby recommended it. Says his cousin works there. Do I keep going straight?"

They had left the last lights of the Paddy flickering far behind and were now in open country. Occasionally the eyes of a cow or horse were reflected in the headlights.

"There's a turnoff about a mile ahead," Trac said, "and Top's place is a half mile down that road, just before you get to the Black Bottom, the Negro section of town." She gave a short laugh. "Our wonderful Musket Shoals with its rich section, poor section, white, black, and yellow sections. So much for America, the great melting pot."

"Your family's first generation. It takes time to adjust. If not the parents, then the children and grandchildren."

"Like my dead sister and the children she'll

never have? Or my brother, who doesn't seem to
be anywhere?''

Rosen grew quiet.

"I'm sorry," Trac said. "We weren't going to
talk about Nhi's death. Tell me, how did *your*
family adjust to this new world? Did they live the
typical American dream?''

He laughed. "You can't go by me. Let's just
skip it. Is that the turnoff?''

''Yes.''

Slowing the car which sputtered and shook, Rosen turned left and drove the next half mile in
silence, Trac relaxing in her seat and looking
ahead for the nightclub. "There it is," she said,
but her words were unnecessary. It was the only
building in sight.

Rosen pulled into a parking space near the door.
Leaving the rental he noticed Collinsby's Jaguar
among a half-dozen cars scattered in nearby
spaces. The nightclub was a one-story, box-like
structure resembling a small warehouse. A string
of naked light bulbs dangled just below the roof,
and above the doorway a hand-painted sign read,
''Top o' the Evenin' '' with a hand holding a top
hat. Very faintly Rosen heard piano music coming
from inside. The door opened, and out stepped a
well-dressed black couple. Rosen caught the closing door.

''I think I'm going to like this place,'' he said,
turning to Trac, but her eyes were transfixed by
the red sports car. "Trac?''

She didn't seem to hear him but took a step
backward, her hand reaching out toward Rosen's
car door. She seemed about to fall, so he grabbed
her.

''Trac?''

Blinking a few times, she barely looked at him,

eyes averted as her father's had been during her sister's wake.

He said, "I didn't think it would make any difference if Lester Collinsby was here. No business, I promise. We're all just going to listen to the music."

"What?"

"We're just going to listen to the music."

She gazed at the Jaguar. "Who did you say this belongs to?"

"Lester Collinsby, my associate. You met him yesterday. Are you all right?"

She put a hand to her forehead then rubbed her eyes. "Yes. I'm sorry. It's just that I can't get used to . . . I can't believe that Nhi is really dead."

"Would you rather I take you home?"

"No. It'll be good for me to relax. Besides, I've got to prove to you that the music here is good."

Rosen followed her into the blue haze of flickering bar lights and cigarette smoke. The room was surprisingly large, with a bar running the length of the wall to their right and about a dozen tables arranged in a semicircle around the opposite wall. There the piano stood on a raised platform, where a tall black woman was playing the old standard "Mean to Me" and singing with a sweet sadness that reminded him of Billie Holliday. The nightclub was nearly empty, so Rosen led Trac to a table near the piano. While waiting for the cocktail waitress, he looked around for Collinsby. Five or six men sat along the bar; they were black, as was everyone else in the room.

"Do you see Lester?" he asked.

"No. Didn't you say he had a cousin working here? Maybe he's with him in back."

"I suppose so."

The waitress came over and shouted their orders to the bartender, a tall muscular man wearing a tight-fitting T-shirt.

"This is like I remember," Trac said, nodding up at the piano player. "Even Lu sounds as good. Isn't she marvelous?"

Rosen leaned back and listened. Lu was a handsome woman in her early forties with skin the color of cafe au lait and raven hair that fell in large curls playing peek-a-boo, as she tossed her head, with two gold-looped earrings. Her dress was low-cut, and the moisture on her skin made her round shoulders and heavy breasts shimmer, causing Rosen to loosen his collar. She was singing Peggy Lee's "Fever," teasing him with her cat-and-mouse voice, the tilt of her head and the way her hands played the keyboard.

"She's great," he said.

Lu must have heard him, for she winked in his direction.

"You're speaking about her musical ability, of course," Trac teased.

Rosen's face grew warm. For all his city living and marriage, he still felt awkward in the presence of women. A dozen proscriptions from the Talmud came to mind—"Do not speak too much to women, even your wife." Revealing one's passion, that was worse. Again a dozen warnings, each one old and bearded and shaking a finger at him.

The waitress returned with their order. Rosen took a quick drink then nervously drummed the rim of his glass in time to the music.

"I'm glad you like the place," Trac said. "I thought you would."

"Yes. This lady's terrific. I wonder why she's stuck in a town like Musket Shoals. She's a lot

better than singers I've heard in Chicago and
D.C.''

"That's puzzled me too. I think it has something to do with the owner, Top o' the Evenin'.''

"That's his name?''

She shrugged. "It's the only name I've ever
heard him called. He's quite a character. Maybe
you'll meet him tonight. I'm pretty sure there's
something between him and Lu. I don't know if
they're married, but they've been together for
years.''

She sipped her drink, and they listened to the
music, Rosen gradually relaxing as Lu glided from
one song to another. Jazz was both his rebellion
and therapy, the concept of improvisation so foreign to his ancestors with their 613 commands to
obey. To "waste" time listening to music when
there was so much to study was a sin, yet the
music was beautiful. It was played and sung, as
Lu was doing that moment, from the very soul
and therefore, Rosen was certain, inspired by the
Lord. Songs of longing like the Psalms of David,
of bitter sweetness to which any man would re-
spond if he were only honest. If he were only . . .

"There's your friend, Lester Collinsby," Trac
said. "Oh good, he's with Top.''

The two men approached Rosen's table, the
owner shouting to the bartender, "Drinks all
'round here, Big Ben!'' Top o' the Evenin' was a
small dark man with a head disproportionately
large for his body. His arms swung in rhythm to
Lu's music, and he strutted like a rooster.

The two men sat down, and Collinsby said, "Glad
you could make it. Hello, Miss Nguyen. This is Top
o' the Evenin'. He owns this place. Great, isn't it?''

"Absolutely,'' Rosen said. "Trac's been here
before and told me all about it.''

"Thank you," Top o' the Evenin' replied. "Cowpie said you was a jazz aficionado, and you just proved you got helluva good taste." He laughed merrily, causing the others to join in.

Rosen nodded up toward Lu. "She's wonderful. I don't know which is better, her singing or her playing."

"You see," Collinsby said, "our local culture's as good as any you've got up North."

"Don't pay him no mind," Top said. "He's just prejudiced on account of Lu being his blood."

Rosen crinkled his eyebrows. "Excuse me."

"They cousins. Yeah, had the same granddaddy. Ain't that right, Cowpie?"

Collinsby grinned sheepishly. "I've never tried to hide it. Why, I'm proud to have such a great talent as a relation."

Rosen asked, "Has she ever sung outside of Musket Shoals?"

"Yeah," Top replied, "we been around some. Always wanted to take her to the big city lights and show her off, but she say, 'What for? We doing fine right here.' Besides, she don't wanna leave the kids. We got two kids, and she say first things first. Speaking of the lady, sit down here, honey."

Lu had finished her set and came over to the table, pulling a chair between Top and Collinsby. Rosen noticed a marked resemblance between the two cousins—each was big-boned and good-looking, with a generous mouth that dimpled when it smiled.

Top said, "This here's Mr. Rosen and Miss Nguyen. He was just saying how you was wasting yourself in a dump like this."

"I didn't mean . . ." Rosen began as Top laughed.

"Don't pay him no mind, Mr. Rosen," Lu said. "He's always riling up folks. Thank you for the compliment." She finished Top's drink. "Oh, I'm thirsty. How about some lemonade, honey."

Top called over the cocktail waitress, ordered another round then whispered in her ear. She nodded and walked to the bar.

"You in Musket Shoals on business, Mr. Rosen?" Lu asked.

"Yes. I'm working with Lester on behalf of Edison Basehart, the man accused of murdering . . ." he nodded toward Trac, "Miss Nguyen's sister."

"I read about it in the paper. I'm sorry, Miss Nguyen. It's a terrible thing, losing somebody you love like that. I can see why you've got such sad eyes."

"It's your music," Trac replied. "Although the melodies are very different, your music and that of my country are very alike. So beautiful, so sad."

Balancing a tray of drinks with one hand, the waitress returned and as she handed Top his drink, Rosen saw him nod slightly. The woman moved clockwise, serving Lu, Collinsby, and Rosen, and as she bent forward, the tray suddenly slid from her hand, the glass splashing across Trac's lap. Trac jumped up and shook her dress, while the waitress dabbed at it with a cloth.

"Awful sorry," the waitress said.

Lu took Trac by the hand. "C'mon, honey, let me take you into the back room and put some cold water on it. If we hurry, it won't stain."

"All right, thank you." Both women walked through a doorway next to the bar.

"Sorry 'bout that," Top said. "I'm gonna talk to that waitress."

"Haven't you already?" Rosen asked.

Top and Collinsby exchanged glances.

Rosen leaned back in his chair. "Let's stop the play-acting. The waitress dumped the drink on purpose. You wanted to talk to me without Trac being here, so let's get on with it."

"Yeah," Collinsby said quietly. "Look, Nate, I've been thinking about what you said, about me being too quick to make a deal with the Commonwealth's Attorney's Office. Honestly I think Basehart's guilty, but to cover all the bases, I'm willing to look into the possibility of the murder being drug-related. You suggested it yesterday, when you said the shooting might've been done by some pusher or junkie. I thought it'd be worthwhile talking to Top, seeing as he . . ."

"Seeing that I'm a nigger and so I gotta be hopped up all the time. Right, Cowpie?"

"C'mon, Top. Everyone knows 'if someone wants to get high, Top's is the place where you can buy.' I've represented you a time or two for possession and . . ."

"All right, let's not be getting into that. Just between us men of the world, sure I do a little and sometimes have a transaction. After all, I'm just a businessman. Hell, white folks do it all the time. You think the Mafia's from Africa? And all those big-shot politicians' kids getting slapped on the wrist for snortin' cocaine. Shit."

Rosen drummed his fingers on the table. "Can we get on with this? You have some information that will help us?"

Top shrugged. "Maybe. It's about Van, your girlfriend's brother."

"You know where he is?"

"No, but I'd sure like to. For a crook, Van ain't a very honest man. I'm telling you because Cowpie and Lu are cousins, but I expect you to keep this between the three of us. Among his many business ventures, Van is a supplier of the pleasures of the world."

"Drugs?"

"Yeah, that and women. He was pimping for a bunch a' Slant girls down in the Paddy."

"His sister, the dead woman?"

"If it'd made him a buck, hell yes."

Collinsby said, "Tell him about the drug deal, Top."

"Keep it down. All right. No need to go into details, but Van and me made a transaction. I gave him a lot of money, and he was gonna get something for me. That was over two weeks ago, and I ain't seen the stuff, the money, or Van since. Knowing Van, bet I ain't the only one he skipped out on."

"A lot of money?" Rosen asked.

"Yeah, a lot."

"What did his sister Nhi have to do with all this?"

"He used to stash the shit at her place. I know, cause one time I had one a' my boys follow him. I should a' been as careful this time."

"Maybe you were," Rosen said, leaning closer.

"What?"

"Maybe one of your boys broke into the woman's room to get the drugs and killed her."

"Shit."

"It makes as much sense as some political crazy like Basehart blowing her away. Even more, when you consider that Van's been hiding out since the murder. Why would he be running from Basehart? Now if he was cheating someone on a drug deal, and that someone murdered his sister. . . ."

"That's what I'm saying, man," Top whispered hoarsely, "someone might of. But not me."

"Why not?"

"Ease up, Nate," Collinsby said. "Top here's doing us a favor."

"That's cool," Top said, the grin returning to his face. "In the first place, Mr. Rosen, I told you I didn't do it. In the second place, you might as well pick out of a hat for all the people who'd like to do Van some dirt. Then there's the whole thing 'bout the gun. The paper say Basehart's fingerprints were on the gun that killed the Slant. That means one a' two things—he did it or else someone framed him. With this color skin how was I supposed to get close enough to that white trash to have him put his fingerprints on his gun 'n then obligingly hand it over to me instead a' blowing my brains out? You're supposed to be a real smart lawyer. You figger that one out"—he stuck out both hands—"you can put the cuffs on right now. I'll go with you real quiet."

Looking into his half-empty glass, Rosen also smiled. "I like the way you put it, in the form of a puzzle. It reminds me of my days as a student when the rabbis would argue over a question and, when there was no resolution, say, 'It is for the prophet Elijah to decide.' That's for whom we leave the extra cup of wine at Passover, in case Elijah decides to come." Rosen nudged his glass to the middle of the table. "Let's leave this for Elijah. If it be his will to discover who's the murderer, so be it. I'll just be around to help him. One thing though. I imagine the police are pretty set on convicting Basehart. That makes everyone happy, except for Edison, of course. But if Elijah, Lester, and I do get him off, the cops aren't going to be happy, and they might start believing in this drug connection with Van. When they start look-

ing for new suspects, on whose door do you think
they're going to knock first?''

"I got nothin' to hide."

"At least you have a lawyer in the family."

Top leaned back in his chair, crossed his arms,
and glared at Rosen. "I'll ask around 'bout what
happened and 'bout Van. But if I was you, I'd
catch the next bus back to the big city. You stir up
hot soup, you make splashes and get burned. You
dig?''

"Yeah, sure. One more thing . . ."

Collinsby grabbed his arm. "The ladies are
coming back."

Rosen persisted, "Do you know if there's any
connection between Van and Senator Dickerson's
son?''

"What? Why the hell would Van be messing
with some big-shot politician's kid?"

"You said it yourself a little while ago. Drugs."

Top shifted uncomfortably in his chair, one
hand balled into a fist and pressed against his lips.

The two women sat down, Lu declaring,
"Looks good as new. Well, time for me to get
back to work. Hope you all enjoy the rest of the
evening."

Trac said, "I didn't mean for you to take your
entire break cleaning my dress."

"Never you mind. This way you have to stay a
little longer and put up with me. Not much of an
audience tonight. Got to keep what I can get."

Flashing a smile Lu walked regally onto the
platform and sat behind the piano. Her fingers
meandered over the keyboard, coming together
for a languid rendition of "Stormy Weather." For
a long time she moaned softly like a clarinet, as if
alone in her room thinking about a lost love. Im-
perceptibly the words formed, growing from a

whisper to a plaintive call and sending shivers down Rosen's back. Trac's hand was on the table, and he moved his close to cover hers but stopped. It was the natural thing to do—the music made it perfect—but he could not bring himself to do it, not in public. After all these years, he was still his father's son.

When the song ended and Rosen moved his hands together in applause, he noticed that Top had left the table; looking around he couldn't find the nightclub owner anywhere. Nothing to worry about, Rosen thought as he settled into Lu's next song; if Top went away angry, he would only work harder to find Van. Something would have to break sooner or later, unless of course Basehart was guilty. Rosen didn't really care about the case at that moment, only Lu's song and how good Trac looked backlit by the blue-gray cloud that settled around her like twilight. He pressed two fingers against his eyes, for he felt drunk, senses unraveling as quickly as the notes in Lu's song, words about to fall from his tongue he would be mortified to say to Trac any other time. Mercifully the song ended; Lu paused to wipe her neck and take a long drink of lemonade.

Taking a deep breath he asked Trac, ''Are you hungry?''

''A little, but they don't serve food here.''

''Why don't we go back to the Paddy, and you can introduce me to some very ethnic restaurant.''

She smiled, and they rose to leave, Lu nodding good-bye.

''Anything we need to do tomorrow?'' Collinsby asked. ''I may be tied up in court all morning.''

''I'd like to see this Pelham who's so reluctant

to give Basehart an alibi. I'll call your office tomorrow around lunchtime.''

Leaving the table Rosen followed Trac along the length of the bar. He opened the door for her, clearing his throat to breathe the cool clean evening breeze and, stepping outside, inhaled even more deeply while watching some constellation track slowly across the crystal blue night.

He was about to comment on the beauty of the night, but she spoke first. At least he thought she started to say something. Turning in her direction Rosen felt a fist crack against his jaw while two arms pinned his hands behind his back. As he straightened, trying to shake his head clear, another fist grazed his cheek, and he tasted the first trickling of blood. He wanted to fall down, but the man behind him was too strong, and so Rosen hung there while someone pummeled his face and body. In the soft fog that was his mind everything had slowed, and he was a boy again pretending to be Floyd Patterson, slapping at his big fluffy pillow with goose feathers puffing out of the pillowcase. Whiteness floating in little crescents before his eyes. He had to be quiet, or else his father would come into the bedroom demanding to know, ''What is this nonsense!''

Bits of white fell more quickly before his face, as if the pillow had burst releasing thousands of feathers, while at the same time he felt himself sinking into bed. Although he was certain his eyes were closed, the whiteness kept falling, trickling into his mouth like melting snow and covering him warm as a blanket.

Chapter 9

FRIDAY MORNING

Just when the pain was beginning to subside, someone flicked a switch on the machine that was the world and set it into motion, cranking him up an inch at a time until he balanced precariously on his feet. That same someone pulled him past dark tight faces, until he collapsed into a seat. The world moved again, and he drifted to the steady hum of what must have been an automobile.

What he saw he knew he couldn't have seen but saw nevertheless. Moses climbed down from Mt. Sinai with the Ten Commandments, as the children of Israel lifted their voices in prayer to Baal, the false god. Moses's brow knit angrily and his eyes flashed, eyes that became those of Rosen's father. Eyes, those terrible eyes, glowering at the worshipper closest to Baal; the worshipper was Rosen.

"Nate, Nate?" a voice was drumming.

He looked in its direction, saw only a blur, yet moved toward it and away from the heat of his father's eyes. The air clung cold to his face like wet taffy, but finally he felt himself being lowered until lying in something soft and moss warm. Layers of darkness folded him into a cocoon. Only the distant sound of angry voices and persistent flashes of light, specks that burned through his eyelids and stayed with him through the night, not fading until he opened his eyes to the morning.

Rosen found himself in bed—not his, for the ceiling was painted a different color and the heavy aroma of incense permeated his pillow. When he tried rising to his elbows, the pain rolled over him in waves, so that he was forced to lie back very still. In the previous instant, however, Rosen had seen enough to realize he must have slept in the murdered woman's room.

He pushed his shoulders back against the silken pillow and found he was alone. Three joss sticks were smoking from the floor near the bed, and a blanket lay draped carelessly across the chair as if someone had slept there. Rosen waited for the aching to subside—he found that as long as he lay still and breathed shallowly, there was no pain—then began to reconstruct what had happened. He had gone to the nightclub with Trac, talked to Collinsby and Top o' the Evenin', listened to Lu's music. Then . . . in the parking lot . . . someone kept hitting him, again and again. After that everything grew murky, no matter how hard he tried to remember.

Only the murmur of angry voices and hot bright sparks still flashed somewhere inside his memory. His eyelids fluttered closed; for a long time Rosen listened to his own breathing and traced the sparks shooting out through the blackness, one after another arcing only to fall gracefully away beyond his vision.

The door clicked open. He turned his head slightly and saw Trac enter with a white paper bag. She hadn't changed clothes from the previous night.

"Good, you're awake," she said. "I have some breakfast for you. Coffee and an English muffin.

I thought you'd better eat light after what happened." She drew the chair close to the bed and sat, putting his food on the night table beside him. Deep lines were etched under her eyes. "How do you feel?"

Opening his mouth to reply, he felt as if his lips had been sewn together with chicken wire. He reached over for the coffee, took a few sips, and tried again. "Did you . . . catch the number of the train that used me for its track?"

"Glad you still have your sense of humor. I was very worried last night. Guess it's really only bumps and bruises, but still . . ." She reached down and came up with a damp cloth, with which she dabbed his face.

He asked, "This your room?"

"My sister's. We used to share it when we were children, even slept in the same bed. This is where she was . . . where she died. I'm staying here while I'm in town. My father's shop is part of the building, but you know that. That's where I first saw you." She tried to smile.

He touched his face; it felt unfamiliar. "Let me have your compact mirror."

Trac hesitated but, seeing Rosen extend a hand, reached into her purse and gave him the compact.

He looked at himself a long time, then returned the mirror. "Trick or treat."

"It's not as bad as it looks."

"Can't be. I'm not dead."

"No, really, once the swelling goes down. The cut on your lip—I put a cold compress on it last night, and the bleeding stopped right away. As for the bruises on your body, nothing seems to be broken. I mean . . . you'd feel it, wouldn't you?"

"All I can do is feel it." He shifted and risked a deep breath, which grabbed at his ribs but grad-

ually loosened. The next few breaths came a bit
easier. "Guess you're right. You . . . you didn't
have a doctor come by last night? You didn't call
the police?"

Trac wet the cloth and returned it to his forehead, soothing the aching around his eyes. Her
face was close enough so that Rosen could feel her
breath warm and moist against his neck, the fine
curve of her mouth almost touching his cheek,
and despite all the pain he felt a deeper stirring. His
left hand, hanging over the side of the bed, brushed
against her leg, which moved slightly as Trac placed
the compress on his swollen cheek. Her skin was
silken as the sheets and made Rosen almost forget
the pain. Almost, but not quite.

"You didn't call the police?"

Returning the cloth to the bowl, Trac shifted back
in the chair. "No. Top o' the Evenin' didn't think
it was a good idea. He said calling the police would
be bad for business—that you'd understand. He and
Mr. Collinsby checked you over and said nothing
was broken, that they'd both seen a lot worse. Besides . . . if the police had come, it would've meant
more trouble for my parents. More questions, more
innuendos about my sister, my brother. I'm sorry,
Nate, I couldn't put them through any more of
that."

Narrowing his eyes Rosen sipped his coffee.
"Why?"

"I just told you. My parents . . ."

"No, I mean why would this involve your family?
It was just a simple mugging, wasn't it?"

She swallowed hard but didn't reply.

"They were after my wallet—no, it's still in my
back pocket. They were just some muggers, weren't
they?"

"Yes," she said quietly.

"Did they bother you?"

"No, my screams must've scared them. That and people starting to come out from the nightclub. They ran, then I heard a car drive away."

"You got a good look at them?" He took the English muffin from the bag, bit into it gingerly, and took a few more sips of coffee. "You were saying?"

"I . . . it was dark."

"How many were there?"

"Three, I think."

"You think?"

"I told you, it was dark."

"Sure. After all, I was there too." Rosen finished one half of the muffin. "You didn't recognize them?"

Trac glared at him.

"Were they black or white?"

"Why are you doing this?"

"Hmm?"

"Don't!" she snapped. "Another cross-examination, counselor? Don't you ever take a break from your precious case? Some people beat you half to death—you're lucky Top and Collinsby heard me screaming—and instead of counting your blessings, you're snapping at the first person who comes along."

Rosen drank the rest of his coffee then shook his head slowly. "I wasn't snapping at you, just asking some questions. Isn't it natural for a guy to be curious about the goons who tried to bash his brains in?"

She rubbed her eyes. "I'm sorry. I didn't get much sleep last night. Guess I'm a little on edge. I . . . let me try to remember." She paused, knitting her eyebrows. "There were . . . three men. They took turns, two holding you while the other did the hitting. It was horrible." She shuddered, knuckles turning white as her hands tightened into fists.

"Were they black or white?" Rosen asked.

"They were black. In fact one of them—he was short and very stocky—looked familiar, but I don't know where I would've seen him before."

"Maybe Top o' the Evenin's club. You said you used to go there."

"That's it. He used to clean the place and help the bartender, Big Ben. I remember because he's short and heavy, while the bartender's so tall and muscular. At least I think so. How did you know?"

Rosen shook his head slowly. "I didn't. It's just one of the many possible answers that fits the questions. If Top o' the Evenin' is responsible for your sister's death, it's only natural he'd want Basehart to take the fall. That means knocking me out of commission, which they almost did. What did Collinsby do, after finding me unconscious?"

"He looked you over with Top then helped you get into the car. He wanted to take you to the hospital, but Top persuaded him not to. Now I understand why."

"Would you be willing to go to the police?"

"I don't think that's a good idea. I'm not positive the man I saw was the same one who worked for Top. I mean, I couldn't swear to it under oath. And the publicity—my family."

"Sure. Your family." He settled back in bed, moving around the pain as best he could. "What time is it?"

She checked her watch. "Only a few minutes after nine. Mr. Collinsby promised he'd stop by later this morning to check on you. He was very worried last night."

"Look, I'm a little tired. Maybe I should try to get some more rest. You wouldn't mind if I . . ."

"No, of course not. You're certain you're all right?"

He nodded.

"Good. I have some errands to run this morning. I'll just be gone a few hours. I'll bring back something for lunch. Is there anything else I can do to make you more comfortable?"

He shook his head.

"Well, then, I'll see you in a few hours."

They exchanged glances, and he wondered if she would touch him—squeeze his arm perhaps, but she merely shut the door very quietly. He closed his eyes, feeling the silken pillowcase caress his cheek, and imagined her walking through the alley into the busy street, watched her long legs swishing the skirt whose material was soft as the silk he lay against. His nostrils filled with the incense of the room, and his forehead began to grow moist.

Angrily he shifted to his side, away from the joss sticks, when the stabbing pain from his rib cage hurled him back. He breathed shallowly for a few minutes until the aching subsided. "Not too bad," he thought. He had been beaten up worse, just needed to take it easy. A few days, that was all, and he'd be himself again.

Sleep was what he needed, but sleep did not come. It wasn't his injuries; he lay perfectly still so that he felt nothing. That damn incense, that was it, coloring the image behind his eyelids flaming red, the color of a lover's bouquet. The color, he suddenly realized, of Trac's lips. He opened his eyes to the morning sun, hoping to wash away the brilliant color, but it remained.

Pushing back the pillow, Rosen carefully sat up to survey the room. For the first time he noticed the poster of John Lennon and Yoko Ono above the bed. Why would Trac's sister have put that picture on her wall; was it a symbol of her own life, East meets West? The whole thing—the poster, the drugs she took, the smoldering incense—was straight from the Sixties, as was the Paddy, something seen on the evening news with Walter Cronkite. A time when all Americans wanted to "help" the Vietnamese. Now twenty years later, Nguyen Thi Nhi was murdered in a town where everyone called her a "Slant whore."

The phone rang. He lifted the receiver and settled back against his pillow. "Yes?"

"Hello, Nate?" It was Collinsby.

"Morning."

"Glad to hear that you're still among the living! How you feeling?"

"Like I was dropped from an airplane and forgot the parachute."

Collinsby laughed. "Now you know what it's like being hit by a couple of linebackers. You just have to shake it off. You'll be O.K."

"I was kind of out of it at the time, so I don't remember, but did you call the police?"

A long pause before he answered. "I was going to, but Top said no—it'd be an excuse for the police to close him down. Anyway, it was a simple mugging, and we scared them off before they got your wallet. No real harm done."

"No, they just turned my face into hamburger meat."

"Top's kind of kinfolk. I'm sorry, Nate."

"Sure. Did you see who did it?"

"No. It was dark, and they had a car waiting. Sorry."

"Trac thought she recognized one of the men who beat me up. Thinks he might have been working for Top around the club."

Another pause. "She certain?"

"No."

"Doesn't make much sense, but I'll check with Top. Don't let it bother you, 'cause we've got something more important to worry about. Jimmy Wilkes called this morning to say the preliminary hearing will be sometime in the middle of next week."

"That soon?"

"Things move pretty fast around here. Besides, I imagine he's gotten a lot of pressure to get this over with. Nice of him to call me personally. We need to talk about what we're gonna do. I think Jimmy might still be willing to cut some kind of deal. How about if I see you this afternoon about four?"

"All right. Lester, you don't think my getting beat up has anything to do with the case?"

"No, why would it? Look, should I meet you where you are now or at your hotel?"

"The hotel. I'll be leaving here in a few hours."

"See you later. You take it easy. Bye."

Rosen hung up. No longer did he smell the incense. It had finally burned out, but in its place he inhaled something as distinct—the stale odor of tobacco. Surprising he hadn't noticed it before, despite the incense. On the floor below a chair in the far corner, he saw an ashtray filled with cigarette butts.

Slowly swinging his legs over the side of the bed, Rosen took a deep breath and stood. He walked in minced steps and sat in the chair, groaning as his thighs slapped against the cushion. He picked up the ashtray and counted six cigarette butts; they were labeled "Bushnell," the kind nicknamed "coffin nails" because they had no filters, and each had been crushed about two thirds of the way down, long before it was necessary. There were no lipstick marks on any of the butts, yet Trac was wearing a shade of ruby-red. He wondered if the ashtray's contents were old, from the deceased Nhi or one of her clients, but the odor was too strong. No, they had been smoked last night by someone else who had been in this room, someone Trac had neglected to mention.

Moving back toward the bed, he stood in front of the nightstand mirror to get a better look at his face. As his fingers touched the area below his eyes, they felt something coarse and, looking closer, he saw a burn, almost circular, the size . . . the size of a cigarette tip. Closing his eyes Rosen saw those same specks of light he had remembered seeing last night, only now they weren't innocent flashes, but the burning ends of cigarettes moving toward him and away, each time a little closer, until wincing he opened his eyes and caught his breath, trying to remember more, to remember whom. Unable, he lay back in bed and, despite the flashes of light behind his eyelids, fell into a deep sleep.

When he awoke, Rosen saw on the night table a new white paper bag, whetting his appetite with the smell of hot grease. Trac sat in the chair near the ashtray and held what looked to be a long slender guitar. She was polishing the instrument with a chamois, working so carefully that she didn't notice him watching. The first Christmas card Rosen had ever seen depicted the Madonna bending swanlike over her child; Trac was like that now. A devout Jew believes in the essential goodness of man, and looking at Trac that moment made it very easy for Rosen to believe.

"It's beautiful," he said.

She looked up. "It's nearly one. Have you been asleep all this time?"

"Almost. Collinsby called just after you left. Then I fell asleep. I must've slept straight through till now."

"Good. How do you feel?"

"Better. In a few days I'll be good as new. That's a beautiful instrument."

She smiled. "A *vo de cam*—the three-stringed guitar of my people. I needed one for an upcoming museum exhibition on the music of Southeast Asia. A family friend who lives down the block brought this from Vietnam. He was one of the boat people. He carried a guitar across the ocean instead of an extra sack of rice and almost starved to death. You should hear how he plays." She strummed the instrument, sending a murmur into the room like a breeze rustling through chimes.

"Can you play?" Rosen asked.

She blushed slightly and nodded.

"Please."

Pausing a moment, Trac's fingers returned to the vo de cam, playing a sad melody. She began to sing a Vietnamese song in her soft voice, flitting around the music like a butterfly in a field of flowers, a caress all the more desirable because it was so elusive. He felt the same stirring as when, earlier that morning, his fingers brushed against her leg. No, that was not what he needed—not now with the trial coming up and questions that wouldn't wait, some involving Trac. Did not the Talmud state that women were to be seated apart from men in synagogue so as not to distract them from the worship of God? No, that was not what he needed, yet she sang so sweetly and it had been such a long time.

"I've put you to sleep?" she asked, having finished her song.

"No, no. It was beautiful."

"I thought you only cared for jazz."

"You remind me of Lu. The same instrumental quality of your voice, the same . . . sadness. What was the song about?"

"It's from my country's greatest poem, 'Kim Van Kieu,' about a young woman who becomes a prostitute to save her family's fortune. After fifteen years she meets her childhood sweetheart in a temple. Despite all that has occurred he still loves her and asks for her hand, but she refuses, not wanting to bring him dishonor."

Trac sang a portion of the song and translated, " 'Should you look for a flower when its season has passed, so you will draw attention to my shame, and hate will replace the love in your heart.' " She sang more. "He told her, 'the mirror of your soul is clean of all the dust of the world, and the years have only deepened my love.' But in the end she convinced him. Not like the movies here with their happy endings. My people are not used to happy endings." Trac looked down at the instrument. "This was my sister's favorite song. I would play while Nhi would sing." She strummed softly a few more chords and lapsed into silence.

Rosen said, "You two were very close."

"We were once, but when I went away to college, she drew closer to my brother Van. Whenever I came home on vacation she remained distant. You know how sisters are supposed to have their own little world where they share secrets about their dreams and love. In our house my brother held Nhi's confidence. They would whisper to one another, stopping abruptly whenever I entered the room, as if I were a stranger. It had been over a year since I entered this room. Not until after she . . . after she died."

She set the vo de cam gently against the wall and moved to the chair beside the bed. Opening the bag of food, Trac smiled. "I've been talking while you must be starving. I hope you like it. I wasn't sure what to get."

"Some Vietnamese delicacy, no doubt."

She took out the sandwiches. "A megaburger from the Sultan of Sandwich on the corner. Here's a Benzai Shake and some french fries as well."

He laughed. "Is this the kind of stuff you eat regularly?"

"Not really. I prefer pizza and tacos."

"No rice or fish?"

"You mean soul food? Yes, when I have time to cook. I used to take back jars of *nuoc-man*, a fermented fish sauce—it's the one smell that dominates all others in this neighborhood, but the neighbors in my apartment complex complained about the odor. Thus went a bit of my ethnicity. Mm, it's still warm," she said, biting into her sandwich.

As they drank their shakes through carnival straws, Rosen thought this was the closest he had ever been to a date at a fast food drive-in. In his old neighborhood there was a McDonald's he had to pass every day on his way home from cheder, and often his eyes wandered to the parked cars with the boys snuggling close to their girlfriends while sipping through the same straw. He would often carry that image the next day as he bound the phylactery around his forehead to keep the thought of God before his eyes. It was a sort of blasphemy, one of his first, and a sin not so much because it had occurred but that he did nothing to prevent it.

"I'm glad you have an appetite," Trac said. "That's a good sign."

He watched her cheeks pucker while she sipped her drink. One of her legs rested against the bed very very close to his hand. He had wondered what the boys' hands were doing after disappearing below the steering wheel.

She continued, ''You know a great deal about my family background, but I know nothing of yours.''

He shrugged, looking at his hamburger. ''There's nothing to tell. Nothing that would interest you.''

''Were you one of those typical suburban kids spoiled rotten by his parents?''

''I thought all Orientals were supposed to be demure and never ask personal questions.''

''You forget what an American I've become. We live in a democracy, where everyone has an equal opportunity to embarrass himself. Come on.''

Rosen looked at her, and she smiled at him the way girls smile at their boyfriends. ''All right.'' He put down the sandwich. ''What do you want to know?''

''Your family?''

''There's so much you won't understand. I don't mean to sound patronizing, but you must know how it is. Unless you've lived through something . . . well, you know.''

''Fair enough.'' She settled back in her chair, the milkshake resting on her lap.

''You keep talking about how you had to assimilate into the American culture. We have more in common than you think. I had to assimilate too.''

''I assumed you were born here.''

''It's not a matter of geography but of time. I was born two hundred years ago. For me Chicago might just as well have been a Polish shtetl— village. My grandfather died a few years ago still thinking the Tsar ruled Russia. I never heard him speak a word of English, nor did he understand how the twentieth century differed from the nineteenth. I'm sure he had no idea of atomic energy, and cars—they were what sinners rode in on the Sabbath. He often said that God made eyes for one reason only, to study Torah, the Law. As he became older, when he wasn't bent over Torah, he would cover his eyes with a rag so as not to waste their energy. Growing up, I sometimes had the feeling that we were a colony of Martians living in the midst of these earthlings with their strange passions and mindless energies. We might just as well have been Martians the way people looked at us, the long black gaberdines, earlocks below the ears, and always holding our books as some men might embrace their lovers."

He stared at Trac, waiting for her to say something, but she only looked back at him, her eyes very soft.

"You told me about the rituals surrounding your sister's funeral. You thought you might amaze me." He gave a short laugh. "Do you know how many commandments I had to follow? Six hundred and thirteen. I'm not talking about the run-of-the-mill not killing or messing with your neighbor's wife or stealing an apple from the street vendor. I'm talking about your basic Leviticus —when to wash; when to work; when to pray; how to act with your parents, your wife, your children; whom to avoid; when to light one candle; when to light two candles."

He held up the small bit of hamburger that remained. "And eat, that's a whole ball game by itself. This 'terefah' . . . this hamburger . . . I never had one until I went away from home. What do you expect, a rabbi to stand in the slaughterhouse and bless the cows on their way to McDonald's? To have two order windows—one for meat and one for milkshakes? Besides, you couldn't drink your milkshake until four hours after eating the hamburger."

Rosen felt himself breathing heavier; he was sweating under his shirt, and his face was hot.

After a long drink, he cleared his throat. "I'm sorry. I didn't mean to ramble."

Trac leaned forward in her chair. "When did you . . . leave all that?"

A sick smile briefly crawled across his face. "You never leave something like that, not really. I was sent away. My father wanted each of his sons—there are three of us—to uphold the faith without deviation. Only then might each of us become a tzaddik, a righteous one. You see, my people have their stories too. One of them, which my father devoutly believes, is that God allows the world to exist only because there are thirty-six just men on earth, the tzaddikim. That's one reason it's such a sin to kill anyone—the person might be a tzaddik keeping the earth going for the rest of humanity." He shook his head slowly.

"And you didn't live up to his expectations?"

"When I was fourteen I made friends with a Jewish boy down the block. His family was very modern—they believed God was some kind of wind-up clock in the sky. I started spending a lot of time over there and pretty soon became a secular addict. First eating a piece of chicken that wasn't kosher, then having it with a piece of buttered bread on the same plate. I became interested in baseball, went to a few Cubs games instead of study sessions with the rabbi. When my father found out, he didn't say much, just asked me if I wanted to repent. I wanted to talk, but for him this was not a subject for discussion. It was one of those 'yes' or 'no' questions in which that one word is the first step in a direction from which you can never turn back." He shrugged. "Well, that's about it."

"What do you mean? What happened?"

"He sent me to one of our cousins, a wealthy

contractor who was also an unrepentant. When I went to live with his family, the first thing I did was to cut my two curls. For so long I had thought of them as chains and wondered what I would do if I ever became free. When I saw them lying in my hands, I felt so naked that I stayed in my room for the whole day. I suppose that's the way I've always felt since that day, a little naked. And all for watching the Cubs, as if they weren't punishment enough.''

"So you became a lawyer," Trac said. "Perhaps you didn't fall away as far as you thought. Your life as a child was bound by laws, and so is it now. Have you really changed that much?"

"One difference, one important difference!" He caught himself and lowered his voice. "I'm a defender. You see the difference? I defend those accused of breaking the law. I make certain their right to be heard is respected. Even a scum like Basehart has a right to make his case." Rosen leaned back and stared into his cup.

"I understand. Do you ever see your father?"

He continued staring, almost in a trance.

"Nate?"

"He's a . . . very busy man. So much to look after, the moral fiber of the world. No, he's much too busy."

"Perhaps you judge him too harshly. He must have a father's love."

Rosen muttered, "A love that kills."

They lapsed into silence, until Trac said, "But you have your daughter."

He smiled. "Yes, Sarah."

"She must be a wonderful girl."

"I haven't shown you her picture, have I?" He took his wallet from his back pocket, opened it to the photograph, and passed it to Trac. "It's about

six months old, before her mother had Sarah's
hair cut. Over my protests, I might add. Let me
clean all this up."

While Trac looked at the photograph, Rosen
stretched his limbs stiffly, gathered the wrappers
and walked slowly to the wastebasket in a corner
of the room near the ashtray. He felt a little better.
Bending to drop the papers into the garbage, he
noticed the latter was filled with crumpled tissues.

"She is beautiful," Trac said. "I see the resemblance between the two of you, especially around
the eyes."

"Not now, I hope," Rosen replied touching his
bruises. "You have a cold?"

"No. Why do you ask?"

"All this Kleenex. Looks like someone's been
sick."

"I don't know about that. The wastebasket was
filled when I arrived. It hasn't been emptied since
. . . since Nhi was here."

"Maybe she had a cold."

"Nhi? I doubt it. None of us, Van included, ever
got sick, except for Van's appendectomy last year.
Van used to say that even American doctors
would grow poor if they had to depend on us for
a living. Why do you ask?"

"No reason I guess." But as he put the wrappers into the wastebasket, he removed one of the
soiled tissues, rolling it into a small ball and slipping it into his pocket.

"Same for those cigarette butts?" he asked.

"Hmm?"

"I haven't seen you smoke. These butts must
be from before."

"I suppose so."

He turned and saw that her hands were gripping the sides of her chair. "What do you mean? You should know."

"I suppose so. How do I know? The police coming here day after day. Some of them were smoking. They probably . . ."

"Sure."

"I don't see why this is of any importance." Her knuckles whitened.

"It's not. You know how lawyers and cats are—always curious. Sorry if I've upset you."

"Upset? I'm fine." She tried to smile. "Come sit down. You look very pale."

He returned to bed and sat against the pillow, while Trac brought a fresh pan of water from the bathroom sink. Taking the cloth she dabbed his eyes which caused him to wince and draw back. She moved closer to examine the wound and, in doing so, her hair brushed across his cheeks and he inhaled the warm musk of her perfume. His arms encircled Trac who let her body be drawn over his; Rosen felt both heartbeats quicken as they kissed. Gone was the pain that racked his body. Gone too were doubts and duty and even the great Eyes of God—all pushed aside by the urgency of his hands and mouth, while Trac murmured something deep in her throat and helped him with her clothes. Her skin was incredibly smooth as his mouth followed the line from her shoulder to her small firm breasts. Wrapping around each other, man and woman reveled in the original sin, their bodies moving with the same abandon the ancients displayed before Baal. In his final shudder Rosen lost all shame but only clung tighter to her until she cried out then lay back panting, her hand wandering aimlessly across his back. When he finally drew away she pulled him back, and this time it was her mouth and hands that moved with such abandon, drawing his blood, his very soul into her.

Sometime later Rosen became aware of his surroundings. They lay together, arms and legs entangled, and at first he wasn't sure which were his. Stretching his limbs he watched curiously certain sets of fingers and toes move.

Trac stirred, her eyes fluttering open, and smiling she snuggled closer. "Is there anything I can get you?"

Clearing his throat Rosen replied, "No, thanks. I seem to be feeling much better."

"You certainly weren't acting like a sick man."

They both laughed, she moving to rest comfortably in the crook of his arm. They lay quietly for the next few minutes until Rosen asked, "Do you know what time it is?"

"My watch is on the chair. Let me see." As she reached over him, he saw tiny discolorations on the inside of her forearm. His body chilled, and he pushed away from her arm.

"Two thirty," she said. "Why do you ask?"

"No reason, I guess." Indeed he hadn't known why, but now the marks on her arm brought him back, and he heard the clock inside his head start ticking again. It was ticking for Basehart—Rosen never heard it sound so distinctly, and he saw each second mark as clearly as the needle tracks on her arm.

He moved away from her and sat up.

"What's the matter?" Trac asked sleepily.

"Nothing. It's just that I'd better be going. I have to meet Collinsby at four. Lester said the grand jury might hear Basehart's case in a few days."

"Will my parents or I have to testify?"

"Maybe, but it's not the same as a trial. The

grand jury only needs to find sufficient evidence for Basehart to stand trial for your sister's murder. With the gun and Basehart's background, even if the Commonwealth's Attorney ate his cereal with vodka, he'd be able to persuade the grand jury to bind the accused over.''

"Do you really think Basehart is innocent?"

He sighed, rubbing his fingers against his temples. "I don't know. Right now I don't really think much about anything." He stood and steadied himself.

Trac put a hand on his arm. "Do you have to go? Maybe stay a little longer."

"I've got some other things to do."

Her eyes narrowed. "Like what?"

"What do you mean?"

"I want you to be careful, that's all. I'm worried about you."

He bent to kiss her. Afterward he dressed and took his jacket from the chair.

"When will I see you again?" she asked.

Pulling a hand into his pocket to find his car keys, Rosen felt the wad of tissue. "I'm not sure. Soon." He walked to the door.

"Don't forget me," she said.

"Not a chance."

Chapter 10

FRIDAY AFTERNOON

"Don't feel like answerin' any more damn questions. How 'bout you lettin' me outta here, and I get us a couple women?"

Tilting back so that his chair balanced precariously on two legs, Basehart squinted across the table at Jimmy Wilkes and laughed sharply. The interrogation room seemed even hotter and closer, the prisoner's odor permeating the warm dank air. It sickened Wilkes, as did everything about Basehart.

"How 'bout it, Jimmy? Bet you ain't had a good lay in years. Sounds like a pretty fair deal to me."

Swallowing hard Wilkes said, "You haven't heard a word I've been saying. The grand jury's scheduled to convene next Wednesday. Once it finds reason to bind you over for trial, with all the publicity there's not much I can do for you. But if you clear your conscience and confess now, we could avoid the death penalty."

Basehart's chair fell forward with a bang. "Death penalty! You ain't cookin' me! How many times I gotta tell you, I didn't kill no Slant woman!"

Wilkes shook his head wearily.

"Where's my lawyer? Ain't I supposed to have a lawyer here when you're askin' all these questions? Yeah, sure, I know my rights—you're just

tryin' to trick me. Where the hell's my lawyer!''
Basehart looked wild-eyed past Wilkes to the door
then crumpled back in his chair, legs drawn up
so that his arms curled tightly around them, hiding his face except for the eyes which darted everywhere until finally closing tightly.

Despite his contempt, Wilkes felt a stirring in the
pit of his stomach. ''I called Lester Collinsby. He
said he'd try to get down here. As for Mr. Rosen,
I left a message at his hotel. Of course, you
needn't make a formal statement without your attorney present. It's just that I want to give you
every opportunity to help yourself before it's too
late.''

He had done it again, Wilkes thought to himself, pressing a fist against his lips. Saunders
would've gone for the jugular, jumping all over
Basehart with the gallows rope in his hand until
the poor bastard begged for a chance to confess.
That's what Edgar Simpson called ''the killer instinct.'' So what did Wilkes feel for his prey—pity.
Pity for the accused and, at that moment, for himself as well. And how did Basehart react to his
kindness?

''Shit. You're just tryin' to trick me.''

Wilkes stood. ''I don't think this is doing either
of us any good. I'll talk to Mr. Collinsby, and if
he so advises and you accept, we'll meet sometime before the grand jury. For your sake, I hope
there's enough time.'' He turned to leave.

Basehart shouted, ''I ain't scared!''

''Then you're even crazier than most people believe.''

Wilkes reached for the doorknob, when it
opened from the other side, and Rosen walked in.

''Where the hell you been!'' Basehart demanded, pounding his fist on the table.

"I've been thinking of you too, Edison." He held out his hand to Wilkes. "I'm Nate Rosen. We met a few days ago, in this room as a matter of fact. I'm helping Lester Collinsby defend Chuckles here."

"Of course. It's nice to see you again." He couldn't help staring at the bruises on the other man's face.

"Why don't we sit down."

Wilkes returned to his chair. Rosen sat between the two men and took out a pen and notepad.

"What the hell happened to your face?" Basehart asked. "Looks like some dog's been usin' you for a bone."

"A few guys worked me over last night at Top o' the Evenin's nightclub."

"Why?" Wilkes asked.

"I don't know. They didn't take any money. Whoever it was really enjoyed their work."

Basehart laughed. "That's what ya get for hangin' 'round some nigger bar."

"Please, not so much compassion, Edison. Your heart's already too filled with the milk of human kindness."

"Did they hurt you badly?" Wilkes asked.

"Only when I laugh. Which is a real danger representing Edison with his rapierlike wit."

"Shit," Basehart drawled.

"See what I mean. Glad I brought my notebook."

" 'Bout time you showed up."

"Sorry, I was busy. I made a quick stop at the post office then came right over. What's up?"

Shaking a finger at Wilkes, Basehart shouted, "What's up is that he wants me to say I killed that Slant!"

"Well?" Rosen replied.

"Huh?"

"Tell the man."

"I'm gettin' pretty goddamn tired a' tellin' everybody I'm innocent."

"Then let's try something new. Why don't you tell us why your buddy Billy Lee Pelham didn't provide you with an alibi? In fact, he may be your ticket to the chair."

Basehart wrung his hands and looked at the floor.

"Well?" Rosen demanded.

The prisoner's words were slightly muffled, "Don't know."

"Maybe I have the answer. Maybe it's because you weren't with him at the time of the murder. Maybe Pelham doesn't want to perjure himself and be your accessory to murder. Why should he get his brains fried over scum like you?"

"Damn you!" Basehart tried to continue but only managed a gurgling deep within his throat.

"What's the matter, Edison, catfish got your tongue?"

Wilkes cut in, "That's enough, counselor. Don't you think you're going too far?"

"I'm the one who's had to listen to all his lies. I'm the one who got beat up. If it wasn't for him I'd be in Chicago helping my daughter celebrate her birthday, surrounded by family and friends." To Basehart, "But you wouldn't know anything about friends, would you? Not with someone like Pelham as your pal."

Basehart muttered, "Well, mebbe . . . mebbe Billy Lee ain't such a friend after all."

"Apparently not."

"No, I mean . . ." He eyed Wilkes suspiciously. "He got to be here?"

Rosen clicked his tongue disgustedly, but

Wilkes said, "Of course not. You have every right to consult privately. Mr. Rosen, if you'd like to meet with me tomorrow, I'm sure it could be arranged."

Yawning, Rosen shook hands with Wilkes. "Thank you."

As he closed the door behind him, Wilkes heard the other lawyer say to Basehart, "This better not be wasting more of my time."

Canary was waiting for him in the parking lot, leaning against his car and blowing a chain of oblong smoke rings into the sky, continuing even after Wilkes stood patiently like a schoolboy in front of his teacher. Finally the cigarette was finished; the policeman obliterated the butt with his foot and grinned. "Did you make him spill his guts?"

Wilkes ignored the sarcasm. "He hasn't changed his story at all. If anything, he's even more adamant about his innocence."

"Like a dying fish wiggling on the line. I seen a hundred others just like him. He'll crack."

"Did you get the search warrant?"

Canary lit a cigarette and took a few drags before replying. "Yeah, Judge Spencer loved having his golf game spoiled. We'd better turn up something. Let's go."

Canary eased himself behind the driver's seat, but Wilkes hesitated, looking back toward the courthouse.

"What's the matter—forgot something?" the detective asked.

"Wait a few minutes."

"Huh?"

"We may have some company."

"Company? This ain't no damn party."

"Wait," Wilkes said, surprised at the firmness of his command.

Canary grunted. "While we're waiting, I have some information you wanted. Checked with the bank where Basehart does his business. The bait and tackle shop isn't owned by him. It's under the name of his organization, Guardians of an Undefiled Nation. The balance of the mortgage, almost six thousand dollars, was paid off last year in cash. Basehart and Pelham brought the money in together and said somebody donated it to their cause."

"Who was the generous donor?"

Canary shrugged. "They didn't tell the bank. Guess we'll have to ask them. Basehart's personal account is just under five thousand dollars. Small deposits and withdrawals over the last few years— nothing special. Funny thing is that Pelham has about twice as much in his personal account. Not bad for someone who earns a living as an assistant worm digger." He lapsed into silence, working on a series of perfectly round smoke rings.

After a few minutes, Rosen walked from the courthouse, his legs taking the steps gingerly as he reached the sidewalk that led to the parking lot. Pausing to wipe his forehead with a handkerchief, he continued slowly onto the blacktop, stopping at a dented Dodge a few spaces from Canary's car.

"Your car's beat up worse than you!" Wilkes called out.

Rosen nodded wearily and opened the door.

Wilkes quickly walked to his side. "I take it your client is still asserting his innocence."

Rosen nodded.

"Look, Mr. Rosen, I'm not asking you to reveal what Mr. Basehart said in confidence, but if there's anything you're at liberty to share, I think we might help each other get at what we both want."

The other attorney smiled. "What's that?"

"The truth—is Basehart innocent or guilty?"

Closing the door Rosen said, "The truth? If you can find it in this town, you should take out a patent. I've just had another go-around with my client and yet another truth."

"Does it have to do with Billy Lee Pelham?"

"Uh huh." He paused. "You said something about a quid pro quo."

"Yes."

"Well, since we're in the South, I'll remember my manners. You go first."

Wilkes said, "I've obtained a search warrant for Basehart's bait and tackle shop. That's also where he and Pelham share living quarters. It was simply to seek additional evidence against your client, but if he really is innocent and Pelham is somehow implicated, we may find something to help your client's case."

"Sure. And how am I supposed to be certain that this evidence, which unties your neat little conviction, appears in court? You wouldn't mind if I went along for the ride, would you?"

"I was just going to suggest that."

Rosen stared at him. "All right. Let's go."

As the two men walked to the squad car, Wilkes said, "Quid pro quo. I'd like to know what Basehart said about Pelham. It could help in our search."

Rosen replied, "He's not so sure about his good friend anymore. For several months Billy Lee's been sneaking off now and then—never says where. At first Basehart thought it might be a woman, but Pelham usually brags about that sort of thing. Also he's been getting the feeling that Pelham's trying to take over his precious Guardians of an Undefiled Nation. They've had a few arguments about it lately, even a fistfight. Pelham takes the men drilling on certain nights but won't say where."

"How does that fit into the murder of Nguyen Thi Nhi?"

"If I knew that, I'd be on my way home."

They reached Canary's Ford where the policeman sat impatiently, one arm hanging over the window and flapping like a seal against the car door, while the other worked a cigarette in and out of his mouth.

"You remember Mr. Rosen," Wilkes said. "He's assisting in Basehart's defense."

The policeman grunted and looked straight ahead.

Rosen leaned against the car. "I'm sorry about what happened between us last Monday. Probably my fault."

Wilkes continued, "I've invited Mr. Rosen to join our search of the bait and tackle shop."

Passing the cigarette from his right to left hand, Canary flicked a long ash out the window. "This is getting to be a regular party."

Rosen watched the cigarette dangle from the detective's hand. "That's a real killer. Extra long with no filter. What kind is it?"

"Bushnells, a local brand."

"Pretty popular around here?"

"Old men and kids. It's what boys start out with—makes you a man if you don't choke first. After that, only a few of us keep on. Sort of a badge of honor, you might say. Besides, I like the way I can work the smoke in my mouth, sort of like taffy." Inhaling, he blew a giant smoke ring which paused momentarily like a halo around Wilkes's head. "Wanna try one?"

"No thanks. Just curious."

"Well, then, let's go."

Wilkes sat next to the detective, while Rosen leaned against a corner of the back seat and carefully stretched his legs. He groaned softly.

"You all right?" Wilkes asked. "We could stop at your hotel if you need anything."

"Thanks, but I'm fine." Rosen snuggled deeper into the corner and closed his eyes. "Wake me when we get there."

The car slipped easily through traffic and soon passed the downtown area. The three men rode in silence, Canary idly puffing a cigarette, Rosen dozing in the back seat, and Wilkes watching the city break into open land covered with rows of tobacco plants, their broad leaves hanging heavily in the listlessness of late afternoon and causing him to yawn at their monotony. For a moment a dozen images flashed behind his eyes—Basehart, Edgar Simpson, Saunders, Collinsby, and the murdered woman among others—but he shook his head until his mind cleared of everything but the color of the tobacco plants. Each one was green and moist with heavy nodding leaves, and so Wilkes too closed his eyes, the last thing he remembered until feeling his shoulder nudged.

"All right, boys, naptime's over." Canary's voice.

Eyes fluttering open, Wilkes turned to wake Rosen but found him staring down the road.

"You planning to surprise Pelham?" Rosen asked.

"Yeah," Canary drawled. "Billy Lee just loves surprises. Besides, I can use the exercise."

They stepped from the car and walked slowly

along the shoulder, the two lawyers following the policeman's waddle, Rosen wincing with an occasional sigh. As they neared the shop, Wilkes thought at first it was empty; neither Pelham's truck nor any other vehicle was in the driveway. Everything was still, a picture postcard of a cottage, except that the flowers in the window pots were beginning to wilt. So, it must have been Basehart who tended them so carefully.

Suddenly three men bolted from the garage at the end of the driveway and ran toward the back of the house.

"Hold it, Billy Lee, Rupert, Burl!" Canary shouted, unbuttoning his suit coat so that his holster showed, the handle of his gun glinting in the sunlight.

The three men stopped dead in their tracks, whispered a few words to each other, and grudgingly walked down the driveway to the storefront. Pelham was wiping his hands with an oily rag, which he stuffed into his back pocket. The six men met on the front stairs, Rupert and Burl sitting on the top step while their friend swung into his hammock, propping his head with a tattered pillow so he could view the proceedings like some hobo Caesar.

"Afternoon, Lt. Canary," Pelham said with a toothy grin. "Didn't expect you. Maybe we should fix some tea, boys." Rupert grimaced, his lower lip showing a scar from the cut Canary had given him a few days before. "We were busy out in the garage," Pelham continued, "workin' on the truck. Havin' a helluva time. Carburetor's leakin' oil like a Dago."

The policeman asked, "Where were you off to in such a hurry just now?"

"Why, Rupert just remembered his favorite cartoon show's on, that's all."

"You don't say. Now what's that?"

Rupert's lips curled into a smile. "Porky Pig." The smile faded quickly under the policeman's gaze.

"What you all doin' here anyway?" Pelham demanded. "Man's got a right not to be exposed to all this police harassment. I ain't sure I like this." He jabbed a finger into the air. "Ain't sure I shouldn't get me a lawyer to protect my rights. Then maybe you all'd leave me be."

Now Canary was smiling. "You want a lawyer? Well, this is your lucky day." He nodded at Rosen. "This here's one of Edison's attorneys. You ain't been properly introduced. This is Mr. Rosen, all the way from Washington."

Pelham bent forward in his hammock and looked Rosen up and down. "Nah, Lieutenant," he finally said, "nice joke . . . you're jokin', ain'tcha?" When Canary shook his head, Pelham continued, "I'll be. You see what jail can do to a man, boys. Must addle your brain. Why else would ol' Edison get himself a Hebe lawyer? That's rich—Edison Basehart bein' defended by a kike. What're all the loyal members of the Guardians of an Undefiled Nation gonna think?"

Rosen kept silent, his face impassive, but Wilkes said, "None of that, Pelham. Hate's already caused the death of one woman. This town doesn't need you or your friends stirring up any more."

"I ain't stirrin' up the hate. It's them."

"Who?"

"Them that's comin' here where they don't belong. First the Slants and now this here Hebe. Nobody told him to come here anyways."

Rosen asked, "How do you know?"

"Huh?"

"As far as I know, you haven't seen or spoken to Basehart since his arrest. How do you know he didn't send for me?"

Pelham scratched the stubble of his beard.

"How do you know that Basehart didn't suddenly undergo a religious experience in prison, in which he threw off all his hatred and bigotry, as one would a set of dirty clothes, and now stands naked and joyful in the sunlight of pure innocence?"

Looking at Canary, Pelham asked, "What the hell's he talkin' about?"

Rosen persisted, "What I'm talking about is that I've been seeing a lot more of Basehart than you, supposedly his best friend. You fish together, beat up defenseless black people together. How come you haven't visited him? It's been nearly a week."

"I been busy, not that it's any a' your business."

"Sure So busy fixing an oil leak that you can't see your best friend. That is, of course, unless he's not your best friend, unless there's a reason why you want him in jail, something you're hiding that might implicate you and the other members of your gestapo boy scouts in the murder of Nguyen Thi Nhi."

"Sh . . . Sh . . . Shit!" Pelham's lips exploded. "You got no call to say any a' that!"

"No proof, you mean."

"Yeah, that's right, no proof."

Wilkes stepped forward and demanded, "Where did you get the money to pay off the mortgage on this place?"

"It was a gift from someone who don't wanna be recognized for his generosity. Let's just say,

one a' the last true-blue Americans left. You
know, there's still some a' them around.''

"Did he also pay for your new pickup?''

Pelham shifted uneasily in the hammock. "The
truck's part a' our organization. Sure we get do-
nations. Just like the Red Cross. Yeah, that's right
. . . why don'tcha go bother the Red Cross instead a' messin' 'round here?''

Canary leaned against the railing. As was his
custom he first finished his smoke, crushed the
butt with his foot, then spoke. "That's why we
came out this afternoon, Billy Lee, to look around.
You wouldn't mind if the three of us stepped inside for a couple a' minutes and took a . . .''

"The hell I wouldn't! This here's still a free
country, and a man's home's his castle. I know
my rights. Now, Rupert 'n Burl, you just get inside 'n tend to your chores . . . know what I
mean? As for you three, get off this here property,
or I will get me a lawyer and sue the . . . what
the hell's that?''

Pelham's friends moved slowly toward the front
door, while the detective took a document from
his inside coat pocket.

"This is a search warrant," Canary said. "Gives
us the right to enter your castle even without your
permission.''

Pelham pushed himself from the hammock and
moved between the door and Canary. "Not till I
see it's what it says it is. Boys, get goin'!''

Rupert and Burl dashed through the doorway;
Rosen ran after them, pushing Pelham aside with
a groan. Wilkes followed, as Canary stuffed the
search warrant down the bib of Pelham's overalls.
Wilkes entered what served as the shop, its walls
neatly lined with rows of fishing rods and a
counter filled with shelves of lures. Sprawled on

the floor against the counter, Burl moaned while holding his head. Past him, through the door behind the counter, Wilkes heard a loud gurgling. Running into the next room, he stopped suddenly and blinked hard.

The room was small and windowless, illuminated by a naked bulb dangling from the center of the ceiling over a small table, while along the walls were shelves filled with stock, assorted rod and tackle. Papers were scattered on the table, several having fallen on the floor, and several more stuck in the mouth of Rupert who was bending over the table and retching. Rosen stood beside him with a hand on his shoulder.

Gasping for breath Rupert sucked in deeply, the air whistling through his stuffed mouth, then began to swallow the papers, only to have Rosen punch him hard in the stomach. The lawyer prepared to strike again, when Rupert held up his hands and reluctantly spit out the papers. The last few documents were spotted with crimson; Rupert's cut had reopened. Ignoring the injured man, who slunk into a far corner, Rosen flattened the papers and read them carefully.

"Look at this," he said to Wilkes.

Canary entered the room followed by Pelham, who cried out and ran to the table, trying to gather the papers and shove Rosen aside. He tripped, however, while Rosen grabbed his arm and threw him to the floor. Sputtering in anger Pelham crawled back to the table and lunged for the papers, the lawyer once again pushing him aside. They continued grappling, until the detective lumbered forward and put his hand over both of theirs.

"That's enough, boys. You all can play some more later, if you've a mind to. Now let's see what we got here." He took a few of the sheets, sharing them with Wilkes. "What do you make of them?"

Wilkes studied the papers. "They're part of a ledger. Looks like a crude sort of accounting. Columns listing businesses and money collected on a monthly basis."

"And the businesses?"

He read them more carefully. "Vietnamese. They're all Vietnamese businesses down in the Paddy. What are you doing with this list, Pelham?"

"None a' yer damn business." His eyes darted around the room.

"It's a shakedown list, isn't it," Rosen said.

"It ain't nothin'!"

Wilkes said, "We've checked with your bank. You have almost ten thousand dollars in an account. That's a lot of money for someone without a steady job."

"Earned every penny of it fair 'n square."

"How," Canary asked, "digging worms?"

"Runnin' this store. Doin' odd jobs here 'n there. Now I ain't sayin' no more 'cept to leave me be. Ain't done nothing wrong."

"What about this list of names and businesses?"

Pelham folded his arms tightly and remained silent.

"That's good, Pelham," Rosen said. "You'd better practice keeping silent. And you'd better look for a lawyer. I think you're going to need one real soon."

"The hell I am. Now gimme that." He reached for the papers on the table, but again his hand was pinned down by Canary. "C'mon, lemme go!" he cried out, squirming like a mouse in the mouth of a snake.

"Mr. Rosen, take a look at his hand," the detective said. "That interest you any?"

Pelham's knuckles were badly skinned.

Canary asked, "Where'd that happen, working on your truck?"

"Yeah," he replied quickly. "I mean . . . I don't remember."

"Pretty bad scrape. Looks like you mighta been in a fight . . ."

"Or maybe beating on somebody," Rosen cut in. "Like me."

"Don't I wish," Pelham snarled.

"Why, Billy Lee," the detective said, "I do believe you did beat up Mr. Rosen. Not by yourself, of course. That's not your style, a fair fight. But maybe with the help of Rupert n' Burl. What do you think, Mr. Rosen?"

Rosen took a step toward Pelham and smiled. "I think we should lock him up in the same cell as Edison Basehart. Maybe he could get Pelham to give us some honest answers."

"That's a wonderful idea. Sorry I didn't think of it first."

Pelham blanched and slunk into a chair. "I . . . I ain't sayin' nothin' more, 'ceptin' I wanna see a lawyer."

"C'mon, let's all of us go downtown."

Pelham cringed. "Why can't you just . . . why don't you all . . . !"

Rosen put his hand on Pelham's shoulder. "I think we've kidded him long enough, Lieutenant."

"Huh?" Canary said.

"Sure. We all know there isn't enough evidence for me to file charges for assault. He'll probably have a dozen witnesses claiming he was somewhere else at the time. And the papers we've found prove nothing—at least not yet. They don't directly involve him with Nguyen Thi Nhi's murder, which is why you obtained your search warrant in the first place. Not that we can't search the rest of the premises.''

Wilkes and his two companions searched the rest of the house carefully—through the two bedrooms, kitchen, and bathroom—but found nothing other than piles of dirty dishes and even larger piles of dirty laundry. Only inside the garage, which must also have served as a meeting room for G.U.N., was there anything that could have been considered incriminating, and that applied equally to Basehart as it did to Pelham. The walls were covered with posters of a colonial soldier brandishing a musket with various slogans, such as ''Keep Our People Pure'' and ''America—One God, One Color.'' Stacks of pamphlets, some of which had turned yellow, littered the garage floor, acting as blotters for paint and oil cans. Among several mechanics' jumpsuits hanging in an open closet were a few colonial costumes, similar to those in the poster, only streaked with grease.

Wilkes bent and, picking up one of the pamphlets, read the first page.

''What will it be like, a few years from now, when the last white Christian takes his last few breaths of his native land? Seeing his government run by niggers, his stores by kikes, and his farmland, the good earth God and his ancestors bequeathed him, turned into rice paddies by a bunch of Slants whose morals are as crooked as their eyes. Will he close his eyes and die quietly or, taking a deep breath, will he reach for his rifle and take a few of them with him? Thank God, it's not too late. The Guardians of an Undefiled Nation . . ."

He glanced at the next few pages, his stomach recoiling at the words of hate, at the utter ignorance which could lead to anything, even murder. That poor woman. He wondered why there hadn't been others. Dropping the pamphlet Wilkes looked for a place to wash his hands and saw Canary puffing impatiently on a cigarette.

"Nothing else worth bothering about," the policeman said.

Rosen asked, "You didn't see anything that might be used for rigging an explosive?"

"No, why should I? We don't blow the fish out of the water in these parts. Why you want to know that?"

"No reason."

"Well, Jimmy," Canary asked, "do I haul in Pelham or not?"

Wilkes glanced at Rosen, who shook his head.

"No, Lieutenant. As Mr. Rosen said, there's nothing we can hold him on."

"O.K., but I'm taking these ledger sheets with me. I think they'll come in handy." He left the garage and walked down the driveway, a series of smoke rings trailing in his wake.

Rosen moved beside Wilkes. "Better leave Pelham free for now. I've got an idea."

"You'll tell me about it eventually, Mr. Rosen?"

"All in good time, Mr. Wilkes. All in good time."

THE
SECOND WEEK

Chapter 11

Judge Spencer asked the bailiff to refill his pitcher of ice water. It was the second time that morning the judge had kept the courtroom waiting, and while doing so he ran a comb through his thinning hair. He was a man known to be as committed to the law as he was to his own appearance, and these proceedings gave him special concern. It was the first time anyone, even old Francis the bailiff, could remember a packed room for a preliminary hearing.

Wilkes looked back from his seat at the prosecution's table and was surprised by all the unfamiliar faces. There were at least a dozen reporters; three in the front row, just behind him, were sketching courtroom scenes. Wilkes saw his likeness in several of the drawings and wondered how his wife and daughters would react seeing it on TV. He almost smiled, until noticing Nguyen Thi Trac sitting in the back, the only Vietnamese in the room. Their eyes met momentarily, and his face grew warm. Looking away he saw his boss, Edgar Simpson, back from vacation, who grinned and made a jab with his fist the same way a manager encourages his boxer before the final k.o. Wilkes remembered his father and Simpson talking about Joe Louis. "That nigger knew what to do—a man can't hurt you if he's on his ass."

That's where Basehart was, on his ass, and

there wasn't much Rosen or Collinsby could do
for their client. Wilkes had seen to that, but then
a five year old could have done as well. He had
merely placed the evidence before the jury, beginning with the murder weapon found near the
victim's apartment—Basehart's gun with his fingerprint on it. That in itself was enough to bind
over the accused for trial. The rest was frosting,
including witnesses who heard Basehart on various occasions threatening Vietnamese store own-
ers and Exhibits D through G, an assortment of
hate pamphlets written by Basehart against the
"Slants," each one more virulent than the other.
Finally, there sat Billy Lee Pelham in the witness
box waiting patiently, like everyone else, for Judge
Spencer to get his second pitcher of ice water so
that the hearing could proceed.

After taking a long drink and patting his lips
with a handkerchief, the judge tapped his gavel
and drawled soft as a melon, "Gentlemen, let's
proceed. Since Mr. Pelham has already been
sworn in, you may begin your questioning, Mr.
Wilkes."

Hearing the scratching of the sketch artists grow
more frenetic, Wilkes approached the witness.

Pelham had groomed himself for the occasion,
greasing back his hair so that it curled behind his
ears. He wore an old brown suit short at the
sleeves and ankles, a string tie neatly poking out
his adam's apple, and a grin he must have saved
only for his biggest fishing stories.

"Mr. Pelham," Wilkes began, "you're pres-
ently living at the bait and tackle shop operated
by the defendant, is that not so?"

"Yes, sir."

"And you are a member of the organization Mr.

Basehart heads, the Guardians of an Undefiled Nation?"

"A colonel . . . a full colonel."

"I take it that you and Mr. Basehart are friends, as a matter of fact, the best of friends."

Pelham shrugged. "We fished outta the same hole, chased women . . ."

"And are politically active together."

"Huh?"

"You believe in and work for the same cause."

The grin slowly faded, pausing on Pelham's lips in the thinnest smile. "Whatcha gettin' at?"

"I merely want to establish that you and Mr. Basehart, besides being friends, share the same political views, so you would have no desire to incriminate him."

"Oh. Just wondered where you was headin'." The grin crept back onto his face.

"Now, Mr. Pelham, on the night in question, you and the defendant . . ."

"Objection, your honor," Rosen said.

"Hmm?" Judge Spencer inquired.

"Mr. Wilkes has asked the witness a question and not allowed him to answer. I'd like it established for the record that Mr. Pelham is every bit the insensitive racist bigot my client is."

The judge scratched his head, while motioning with his gavel to the witness. "Oh, all right. Better answer the question."

"Huh?"

Rosen said, "That you and Mr. Basehart felt the same way toward the Vietnamese immigrants."

"Hell, yeah. I mean . . . yes."

Judge Spencer sighed. "Proceed, Mr. Wilkes."

Wilkes looked back at Rosen, who was studying a packet of papers on the table, then returned to the witness. "On the night Nguyen Thi Nhi was murdered, you and Mr. Basehart began the evening together, is that right?"

"Uh huh." Pelham shifted back in his chair and crossed his legs. "We went out fishin' most of the day. That's what we usually did on Sunday, the store bein' closed. Cooked our catch for supper, that with some beer was real nice. Afterwards we talked 'n played cards till 'bout eleven. Then we turned in."

"What did you talk about?"

"Y'know, different things."

"Fishing?"

"Uh huh."

"Women?"

His grin broadened. "Yeah. There's this one waitress down at . . ."

"Did you talk about politics? More specifically, about the Vietnamese in Musket Shoals?"

"Yeah, that too. Edison got pretty hot under the collar 'bout the Slants. Said he wouldn't mind puttin' a hole in one or two of 'em. He was pretty drunk, to tell the truth."

"No worse 'n you!" Basehart shouted from the defense table. "And I never said no such thing!" Collinsby put his hand on the defendant's arm.

Judge Spencer tapped his gavel.

Wilkes continued, an eye on the grand jury, "The crucial time to account for is the hours after midnight, the time during which Nguyen Thi Nhi was murdered. Would you tell us please what happened during that time?"

Pelham shrugged. "Like I said, we played cards till about eleven, then went to bed."

"You two slept in the same room?"

He nodded and suddenly held up a hand. "Don't get that wrong. We ain't . . . you know, we ain't . . . Got our own beds on different sides

a' the room. It's just that there's only two bedrooms 'n one's filled up with stock 'n all.''

''I'm not implying anything. What you're saying is that, because you were asleep, you can't
state for certain that Mr. Basehart was in the bedroom all night.''

Pursing his lips Pelham drummed his fingers on
the railing. ''Yes, sir, guess that's right.''

Wilkes paused, waiting for Collinsby or Rosen
to object. Not that there was any real justification
for an objection, but Pelham's testimony was so
damaging, a defense lawyer had to say something, even as a baseball manager might criticize
an umpire's call if only to ''protect his player.''
Finally someone did speak, but not who Wilkes
expected.

''No. No, sir, that ain't quite right,'' Pelham
muttered.

''What's that?''

''I said, that ain't quite the truth, not the whole
truth 'n nothin' but the truth. I already swore on
the Bible. It just wouldn't be right to lie, even if
Edison is my friend.''

Wilkes stared at the witness and saw from the
corner of his eye Judge Spencer lean forward expectantly. He began to speak but paused, trying
to understand what Pelham was doing.

''Mr. Wilkes . . . ?'' the judge began.

As if pricked by a needle the attorney blurted,
''What are you saying? That Basehart wasn't there
at your house all night?''

The silence weighed so heavily in the room, that
Pelham slunk in his chair. ''I . . .''

''Go ahead.''

''I was goin' to take a piss.'' Pelham looked up
at the judge. ''Can I say that in court? I mean . . .
I got up in the middle a' the night, about one, to

go to the bathroom. You know, all that beer. Anyways, when I walked past Edison's bed—I had to pass it on the way to the pisser . . . the bathroom—he wasn't there.''

"You're sure? It was pitch-dark, wasn't it?"

"There's a window, and the neon light from the cafe across the street shines right through. It didn't light up on anythin' but the blanket on his bed.'' He shifted in the chair. "Somethin' else I gotta say. There's a night table by Edison's bed, where the alarm clock is—that's how I knew what time it was. There was also a gun on the table. Edison had been cleanin' it 'n put it there before goin' to bed. Well, when I walked by his bed at one, the gun was gone along with Edison."

"There weren't no gun! That's a damn lie!" Basehart shouted. His thin frame sprang from the chair, almost snapping over the table as his hand reached toward the witness stand. "I'd like ta rattle the truth outta ya!"

The judge rapped loudly, as the court broke into a ripple of murmuring. "The defendant will be seated and remain quiet." Several reporters ran down the aisle and out the door.

"But that son-of-a-bitch's lyin' through his teeth. A man ain't got no right to lie like that, not once he's put his hand on the Bible."

Collinsby helped settle Basehart into his chair.

"It just ain't right," the defendant repeated, banging his knuckles on the table and looking down at his lap.

Judge Spencer rubbed his eyes. "Now let's see, where were we?" His vision drifted up to the ceiling. "Oh, yes. Mr. Wilkes, do you have any more questions of the witness?"

Wilkes knew he should have stopped; nothing more was necessary to establish a reasonable

cause. Even without Pelham's testimony, the gun
was sufficient evidence. All he needed to do was
say "no" and leave the witness to the defense
attorneys. Perhaps it was too easy, perhaps because that was what everyone expected, but
mostly because Wilkes didn't care if he was the
Assistant Commonwealth's Attorney. He thought
Pelham was lying.

"Just a few more questions, your honor." He
stepped to the witness stand, placed his hands on
the railing, and smelled the liquor on Pelham's
breath. "This testimony of yours—the part about
you waking in the middle of the night and about
the gun—you've never mentioned it before when
questioned by the police."

"Uh . . . guess I just forgot about it."

"That's pretty important testimony to have forgotten, isn't it?"

"Well, maybe it was because I just didn't wanna
get Edison in more hot water."

"You sure that's it?"

"Uh . . . yeah." Pelham stroked his chin nervously.

"And you're telling it now because . . ."

" 'Cause I took an oath, 'n it ain't right to lie
in court!"

"You're a liar . . . a goddamn liar!" Basehart
shouted.

"Hell if I am! You're the one who's gonna fry!"
Pelham snarled.

"You son-of-a-bitch!"

The judge banged his gavel sharply. "I've had
enough of that. Mr. Collinsby, you better instruct
your client that the next time he opens his mouth,
he'll be in contempt of court."

"Yes, your honor," Collinsby apologized then

whispered something to Basehart, who made a face and looked away.

Wilkes said to Pelham, "You don't seem to be such good friends, after all. Why's that?"

"Told you, I'm just sayin' the truth."

"You're sure this 'truth' wasn't something you just conveniently invented—"

"Huh?"

"—to get Mr. Basehart out of the picture so that you could take over his business, or maybe become supreme commander of G.U.N., or perhaps there's an even simpler explanation. Perhaps you wanted to remove suspicion of Nguyen Thi Nhi's murder from someone else and lay the blame on Basehart. After all you were roommates, you had the same access to the gun in question. . . ."

"You're crazy!" the witness retorted. "You're a goddamn crazy man!" Looking at the judge he demanded, "Do I hafta answer that? What the hell's he tryin' ta prove anyway? I mean, whose side's he on?"

The judge scratched his head. "I was beginning to wonder about that myself. Mr. Wilkes, are you planning to leave anything for the defense's cross-examination?"

Blinking hard Wilkes took out a handkerchief and wiped his face. "I only want to discover the truth," he half whispered.

"What's that?" Judge Spencer cupped his ear.

Behind Wilkes the press, the townspeople, and Commonwealth's Attorney Edgar Simpson bore their weight upon his back. "No further questions."

"Very well." Judge Spencer nodded at the defendant's table. "You gentlemen have any questions of the witness?"

Collinsby looked at Rosen, who leaned forward. "Just one, your honor. Mr. Pelham?"

The witness nervously scratched his jaw. "Yeah."

"Do you know what your blood type is?"

Pelham stared at the lawyer. "What?"

"I asked, what's your blood type?"

Furrowing his brow the witness thought deeply. After a minute of silence, broken finally by a cough from somewhere in the back of the courtroom, Pelham shook his head. "It's pure white man's blood, if that's what you're askin'."

"No further questions," Rosen said.

Another pause, followed by Judge Spencer scratching his head and asking Rosen, "You don't want to know what his favorite color is?"

"We're finished with the witness," Rosen replied, curling back into his chair.

"Very well, Mr. Pelham, you may step down."

The witness hesitated. "You mean, that's it? I don't hafta answer any more questions?"

The judge shook his head. "Not unless you want to tell us who your tailor is." Spencer smiled at the scattered laughter his comment produced. "You're excused, Mr. Pelham."

Grinning, Pelham eased himself from the witness stand and swaggered down the aisle, stopping to admire one of the sketches a reporter was doing of him.

Meanwhile Judge Spencer felt a few strands of hair out of place and reached for his comb. Checking his watch he said, "It's about noon. Mr. Collinsby, Mr. Rosen, guess we can wait until after lunch for you to begin your defense. Court will recess until two o'clock."

A light tap of the gavel released a cacophony of scraping chairs, feet scuffling along the rows of

the gallery and cameras clicking like the call of
locusts just outside the courtroom door. Framed
in the doorway and waving his hand as if the
ticker tape was falling upon his shoulders, Pelham answered a barrage of questions from reporters. He stopped occasionally to smile for the
cameras.

On the other side of the room Basehart was being led away by a lone policeman, the prisoner so
tired and thin that the handcuffs seemed about to
slide from his wrists. Wilkes shook his head violently. Basehart was as bad as Pelham, yet why
should he feel such compassion for the defendant
as to jeopardize his case and act like a damn fool
in front of the whole town? Why didn't he just
do his job?

"Jimmy!"

Wilkes turned to see Edgar Simpson making his
way through the crowd toward him. The Commonwealth's Attorney was beet-red from his vacation; only the circles around the eyes, where his
sunglasses had been, remained white.

"Great job," Simpson said, shaking Wilkes's
hand.

"Thanks. I'm glad you approve."

"This one's a sure thing, especially with Pelham's testimony. That and the gun, of course.
Wouldn't be surprised if Collinsby and that other
lawyer won't ask to make a deal. Why not? You
got 'em by the balls; all you got to do is squeeze
a little harder. Know what I mean?" He gave a
sharp tug with his hands then laughed.

Wilkes asked, "What do you think I should do
. . . if the defense wants a deal?"

"Like I promised, it's your case. Either way you
can't lose. Cut a deal, and you save the taxpayers
a lot of time and money. Nail Basehart to the wall

and you make a helluva name for yourself. Like I been saying, with the election for Commonwealth's Attorney coming up . . . well, you're not your daddy's son for nothing."

Wilkes looked to the table and gathered his papers into his briefcase.

"I gotta get going now," Simpson said. "Several appointments this afternoon. No need for me to see the rest of the hearing anyway. What're Basehart's lawyers gonna do, stand on their heads and spit wooden nickels? Just one thing, Jimmy."

He took a step closer. Wilkes had been waiting for this and was surprised Simpson had taken so long.

"I know this case is in the bag, but there's no need to feel sorry for the other side. What I mean is, you're used to dealing with corporate cases . . . somebody loses and dips into the treasury to pay a few thousand dollars fine. But here if somebody loses, he gets hurt bad. Just remember, Basehart killed a woman, and in this state convicted murderers can get the death penalty. That's the bottom line. I don't want you to think I'm criticizing . . . not that there's any way you could let this case get away from you." He paused, shaking his head. "I better shut up."

Patting Wilkes on the shoulder, Simpson waved good-bye then joined the rest of the courtroom exiting down the main aisle and through the double doors.

Wilkes saw sunlight push its way past the eager reporters onto the backs of the very last row of chairs and knew he couldn't run the gauntlet of clicking cameras. Looking around the room he noticed an emergency exit near the judge's chambers and hurried through the door. The exit led to a small parking lot behind the courthouse where deliveries were made. Weaving his way through the parked cars, he crossed the street that led away from the main avenue to a labyrinth of side streets.

At the next intersection he saw, about a half block down, a large sign hand-lettered in red, "Giorgio's Pizza," and the picture of a fat mustachioed chef beckoning customers. The last place one would expect to find an Assistant Commonwealth's Attorney, so Wilkes turned to walk down the street, looking over his shoulder once before entering the restaurant.

Lining the walls were a dozen booths, half-filled with working men smelling of garlic and breaking breadsticks over plastic checkered tablecloths. He took the last booth in the corner, just before the kitchen's swishing double doors. Settling back in his seat, Wilkes wanted to forget the trial; he stared through his glass of cloudy water the waitress had brought along with the menu.

She returned a few minutes later, snapping her gum before asking, "Anything wrong?"

"Hmm?"

"The water—you want another glass?"

"Uh . . . no." He gave a half-hearted glance at the menu. "I'm really not very hungry."

A voice behind him asked, "How about splitting a pizza?"

He turned to see Rosen. The defense attorney sat across from him and studied the menu carefully. "I haven't had pizza in a long time. What kind do you like?"

Wilkes stared at the other man, then glanced at the entrance to see if anyone else had come with him. "How'd you get here?"

"I walked, just like you."

"You followed me."

The waitress snapped her gum.

"I wanted to talk to you," Rosen said. "We'd better order. How about mushrooms and onions?"

"Uh . . . all right."

"And two beers—whatever's on tap."

Simpson had said that Basehart's lawyers would come running to make a deal. Wilkes didn't believe Rosen would give in so easily, but he said, "You're going to lose."

Rosen shrugged. "One less nut running around in the world. Funny, but I got the impression in court that you might be more upset with Basehart's conviction than I."

"Why do you say that?"

"The way you attacked Pelham on the witness stand. Basehart didn't need me there with you looking out for his rights. You think my client's innocent, don't you?"

Wilkes asked his own question. "What was that business about Pelham's blood type?"

"Last Wednesday when I was beat up, I spent the night recuperating in the murdered woman's room. I checked her wastebasket, which was filled with soiled tissues. Nguyen Thi Trac said no one else had used the wastebasket since her sister's death."

"Yes, I remember seeing it filled, when Lt. Canary and I first went over the room. The police found traces of cocaine."

"Did you have the tissues analyzed for anything else?"

"Such as?"

"You can tell a person's blood type from his saliva. I sent one of the tissues to a private lab my organization has occasion to use. The results came back yesterday, showing Type O positive. From the autopsy we know that the victim's blood was Type A positive. So is Basehart's. I think whoever had a cold either may have been the killer or witnessed the murder.''

''That's quite a long shot.''

''Not if Basehart didn't do it.'' Rosen leaned forward slightly. ''Like you to do me a favor.''

Rosen tore open a package of saltines and ate one of the crackers. Wilkes knew what the other man wanted.

''I'd like you to find out Pelham's blood type. Also Van, the victim's brother. When I woke up in her room after my beating, I found some cigarette butts. Not Trac's. Maybe her brother finally showed up for a visit. I'd like to find him. Would you do that?''

Wilkes found himself nodding. He was about to say that was standard police procedure anyway, when the witness brought the pizza and beers.

Rosen slid a slice onto his plate. ''I have something else to ask—something more important—but it can wait until we finish lunch. Looks good, doesn't it?''

The two men spent the next fifteen minutes eating, Rosen absorbed in his meal, while Wilkes studied the other man, wondering what the second favor would be. Despite his liberalism, he felt a slight aversion toward Rosen. He hadn't known many Northern lawyers, let alone Northern Jewish lawyers, although he had heard his fill of stereotypes. But it was something more personal about the other attorney. The way Rosen treated Basehart, as if he didn't care whether his client was found innocent or guilty. Understandable for a Jew to hate an anti-Semitic bigot like Basehart, but his reaction seemed more indifference than hatred. What kind of a man was he?

They finished the pizza, and Rosen ordered two more beers. "Wasn't a bad meal. Better than the fast food junk I usually eat on the road. Hope you liked the mushrooms and onions. I don't eat sausage; suppose we could've ordered half and half."

"The pizza was fine. It's against your religion, isn't it, to eat pork?"

Rosen nodded. "Like they say, old habits die hard."

"Are you devout?"

He looked down at his plate. "The Hand of God is on me always."

Wilkes sipped his beer, while Rosen took a long drink.

"Basehart . . ." Wilkes began before pausing to find the right words. "How do you find him?"

"Personally?"

Wilkes nodded.

"I think he's someone the world would be better off without."

"Do you think he's innocent?"

"I don't know. It's possible."

"You're not exactly conducting a spirited defense in the courtroom. I was just wondering . . ." Wilkes left the sentence unfinished.

The waitress brought the second round of beers. Rosen took a drink then asked, "What is it? You think I'm helping strap Basehart into the chair?"

"No, I didn't mean that."

"Look . . . how can I explain this?" He paused, swirling the beer gently in his glass. "There's a story in the Talmud concerning why God began by creating only one man. This was to show that each man is an entire universe and by killing one person, you have in a sense destroyed the entire world. Therefore, to save a life is like saving the entire universe. Even Basehart's life."

"That's a beautiful sentiment, though I don't suppose your client would subscribe to it."

"No," Rosen agreed. "But if difficult for a layman like Basehart, think of the problem for a lawyer being forced to litigate a power exempt from the law." Drinking deeply, Rosen lifted his hand to order another beer.

Wilkes reached absently for a package of crackers. "I don't quite follow you."

Rosen laughed sharply. "How could you? Your God is one of mercy, taking on the world's suffering and offering forgiveness in return. You're like that, Wilkes, the kind who takes the world on his shoulders. Why, you feel so sorry for Basehart, you're doing my job and yours at the same time."

"I know," Wilkes said softly, "no killer instinct."

"But my God comes out of the whirlwind demanding to know how His people could dare judge Him, Who flooded and burned the world when it pleased Him. You asked about my lackluster attitude. I guess it's a carryover from childhood. Hard to fight when the odds are stacked against you."

"Yet you still fight."

"All the way. That's another trait of my people. The worse things get, the harder we cling." He stared at Wilkes. "Like my client is doing right now. Which leads me to my second favor."

"You're sure I'll do you more favors?"

Rosen said, "Someone else wouldn't. Most wouldn't, not with the press coverage this case is getting. But I think you will. Your Jesus-Jeffersonian ideology compels you the same way my . . . adversary compels me. Besides, I've got my own theory about you, Mr. Wilkes."

"What's that?"

"All in good time. Now about that favor. When court reconvenes this afternoon, I'm going to ask that Basehart be released on bail, his five thousand dollar bank account as security. I'd like you to go along with my recommendation."

"He's charged with a capital offense. It's not likely Judge Spencer will agree to bail. That's just not the way things work. Especially, like you say, with all this press coverage."

Rosen said, "Spencer might, if you acceded."

"And if Basehart runs away or kills somebody?"

"He won't. You don't think so either. You just said, 'kills somebody,' not 'kills somebody *else*,' like most people would've said."

Wilkes shifted in his chair. "What's the difference if Basehart is released? Doesn't seem to be anyone missing him now."

"No, quite the contrary. I think someone's very happy with Basehart behind bars."

"The murderer?"

Rosen smiled. "You're sounding like a defense attorney again."

Wilkes began to rise. "I don't think we have anything further to talk about."

"Wait." Rosen stayed him with his hand.

"What have I to do with it! You're Basehart's attorney. Make your proposal before Judge Spencer and let him decide whether or not to release your client. You do it. Start earning your fee!" He spoke the last sentence so loudly, the men at the next booth turned their heads toward him.

"Look, I'm sorry," Rosen said. "I didn't mean anything by it other than a complement." Leaning over his folded hands, he continued, "If Basehart didn't commit the crime, the murderer's still out there and is likely to feel very uncomfortable with Edison walking around free.''

''What's your point?''

''Let Basehart do some of the legwork for us. Pelham's the key to this. He's got to be lying if Basehart's telling the truth. How do you think he'll feel when he learns Edison's out and looking for him?''

''That's just what I'm afraid of. If I become a party to an act of violence on the part of your client . . .''

Rosen hit the table with his fist. ''Now you're sounding like a lawyer! Don't disillusion me. I want to cheat the Great Hangman, you want to do justice, mercy, or whatever. This is the best chance we have.''

Again the use of the plural ''we,'' as if Rosen and he were co-counsels. What was he really thinking, this Northern Jewish lawyer who would be here today and far away tomorrow, leaving Wilkes holding the bag in front of a dozen television cameras? So easy to appeal to a sense of justice, but what did it really mean, when Basehart was guilty at least of the bigotry that caused the woman's death. Even Rosen had said the world would be better off without his client. Wasn't it better than to let each of them—Rosen, Wilkes, and Basehart—play out his assigned role and allow a free hand to whatever moved the wheel of justice? He was the prosecutor, Wilkes had to keep reminding himself, like a child sent to the store to buy one specific item. Yet wherever he was sent, there was always that weather-worn bust of Jefferson at the end of the street.

Wilkes said, ''It's getting late. Court is scheduled to reconvene in a half hour.''

Rosen stood. ''I'll go first. Wouldn't look proper

for us to be walking back to court together.'' He put some money on the table. ''This should cover my share. I don't think either of us should treat the other. Years from now when you're a famous statesman, the waitress might be called before the Senate to tell how I bribed you with beer and pizza. See you in court, Mr. Wilkes.''

As the other attorney left the restaurant, Wilkes sat looking into his beer glass, playing out the upcoming courtroom scene. Watching Rosen stand and request bail for Basehart. Judge Spencer curling his lower lip disapprovingly before looking Wilkes's way for comment. And he. . . ? The reel spun out, leaving only the click-click of the projector, or was that his knuckles rapping nervously on the table?

Chapter 12

WEDNESDAY AFTERNOON

The telephone was ringing as Rosen opened the door to his hotel room. He grabbed the receiver while loosening his tie. The air-conditioning wasn't working.

"Hold on a second," he said, then hurried to open the window. Glancing down the four stories to the street, he noticed a red Jaguar parked near the corner and thought that Collinsby might have followed him from the courtroom after Judge Spencer's afternoon adjournment. Collinsby wasn't in sight, and Rosen remembered the phone.

"Hello. Sorry to keep you waiting."

"This is Trac." Her voice was toneless, as if an automated machine.

"Sorry I missed you. I looked for you after the adjournment—to explain what's been going on concerning Basehart's case. I wouldn't want you to misconstrue what I have to regard as an obligation to my client. Certain things I can't explain, of course, being privileged information, but I do want to talk to you." Rosen had rambled, not saying much of anything; not trusting Trac, he couldn't say anything. Yet he didn't want her angry—not at him.

"I couldn't stay in court, not after what you

did." Her voice so cool, so passionless was worse
than anger.

"You mean about Basehart being released on
bail? It's a duty I owe my client to request . . ."

"I can't talk now on the phone, nor do I wish
to listen to a list of excuses. I'm sure there are
dozens you could give me. We'll talk tonight. Not
in the Paddy. I don't want my parents to find out.
They are already very upset."

"Trac, I had no intention of . . ."

"There's a quiet bar called Ernie's on Stuart
Street, near your hotel. Can you meet me there
tonight at ten o'clock?"

"Sure, but can't you tell me what this is all
about?" There was no response. "Trac?" He
thought he heard a voice at the other end of the
line, a voice that wasn't hers.

She finally said, "I'll see you tonight at ten.
Good-bye."

He kept the receiver to his ear, as if Trac had
not really hung up but was about to say more.
Rosen knew better but still waited for nearly a
minute before putting down the phone. Waiting
in silence had always been one of his worst habits, a sign of fear never outgrown, ever since as a
boy he had hesitated to answer the rabbi's question concerning religious law. Answers he knew,
yet still was afraid.

Rosen finished pulling off his tie then lay back
in bed, reaching for his daughter's birthday card
on the nightstand. More hesitation. Under the
"Dear Sarah" he finally wrote, "I hope this will
be your happiest birthday and that . . ." And
what . . . that he couldn't help their being apart?
That he was very sorry if she had been hurt? That
no matter what had happened between husband
and wife, she was still loved by both?

Looking into the birthday card with eyes first fixed upon the words then closed and turned inward, he thought the answer would come, just as it had when long ago he had studied Torah the same way. But it no longer came for him that way; nothing did anymore. Torah was written on parchment, but Rosen no longer read parchment, hardly even paper. Everything was modern and quick. The speed of light, and it changed. Maybe that was the answer. The computer in his Washington office—if only he put his feelings onto the screen, adding and erasing and rearranging, maybe the machine would help him find the right words. Surely among the million pieces of software, there was a program that could boot up just the right words for any occasion—like what a divorced father should say to his daughter when away on her birthday. Machines held all the answers and, more importantly, didn't make you feel guilty. He would call his office secretary, transmit the information to her. . . . Leaning back against the headboard, he shook his head. Sometimes he was such an idiot.

"I hope this will be your happiest birthday and that . . . I could be there spending it with you. It's unfortunate . . ."

A knock on the door. Putting the card back on the nightstand, Rosen opened the door to a large black man who looked familiar. He wore a blue pullover that seemed too tight for his shoulders and bulging biceps.

Despite his size the man spoke softly. "Mr. Rosen . . . uh . . . I come over here to bring you a message. It's from Top o' the Evenin'. Y'see, he want me come down here to tell you somethin' important."

"You're the bartender at Top's nightclub, aren't you?"

"Yes, sir, that right. They calls me Big Ben. I saw you when you come in that night with that lady, sister a' the dead woman. Anyway, Top want me to tell you somethin'."

"He could've called."

Big Ben shook his head. "No sir. Cops got a way a' listenin' in on the phone. Then maybe Top be in big trouble. He told you before—don't wanna be gettin' in any more trouble with the cops. Maybe they close his place down. You gotta promise, if you talk with the cops, not to tell where this come from. You gotta promise."

"I don't want to cause your boss any trouble. He knows that. Come in." Rosen closed the door. "Sit down and tell me what this is all about."

Big Ben took the only chair in the room, near the open window, while Rosen sat on the edge of the bed. The black man leaned forward, resting his elbows on his knees. "It be like this, Mr. Rosen. Top don't want no trouble, but he said for you to know maybe you was right about that Slant woman bein' killed over drugs. Not that Top had anythin' to do with the mess. Y'see, sometimes Top buys a little shit. . . ."

"Drugs."

Big Ben nodded. "Cocaine and horse . . . heroin. Not that much. Sometime Top do a favor for a friend or some old customer he can trust. Just part a' doin' business, he say."

"Where does your boss get his supply?"

"Different gangs from D.C. They send somebody down with the shit, and Top pays 'em."

"Who? What're the names of the people who bring . . . ?"

"Top don't know."

"The names of the gangs then?"

Big Ben shook his head. "Top don't know that either. Don't want to know. They bad people. Kill for fun. Top just pay for the shit and close his eyes. Best for everyone. Best you not know."

"What's the point of all this?" Rosen asked. "What good does this information do my client?"

"It be about the dead woman's brother, Van. 'Bout a month ago, Van told Top not to buy from the gangs in D.C. anymore. Say he gonna be sole supplier for not just the town but the whole country. Van even had his boys cut one a' the brothers comin' down here to deal. Cut him and took his shit. Real stupid. Van don't know who he messin' with."

"What happened?"

Big Ben shrugged. "You see what happened. No one messes with the brothers. They musta come down here lookin' for Van 'n killed his sister as a warnin'. Sure as hell worked, cause Van ain't been seen since. We think he left town. For good if he smart."

"You and Top know all this for a fact?"

"I . . . look, mister, I just be tellin' you what Top want me to tell you. He doin' this as a favor, cause he promise you he look into any drug connection. This all the favors he be doin', so you leave him be. Now I got to get back. Almost time for my shift, and my Mrs. waitin' dinner on me."

Rosen stared at Big Ben, who lowered his eyes. "Thank Top for me. Tell him I appreciate the information, but I'll need to speak to him personally. I'll try to get over there later this evening."

"But, Top say . . . !"

"Just tell him what I said. Thanks."

Big Ben was about to rise, when the door opened suddenly. In walked Junior Dickerson followed by two other men, each taller and heavier than their leader and wearing, over their beer bellies, T-shirts advertising a local bar. One man's forearm was tattooed with some faded design resembling a dragon. Folding their arms, the two men blocked the door, while Junior walked to the window.

"I didn't hear you knock," Rosen said. "In fact, I believe the door locks automatically."

Junior held up a key on a large ring. "Hotel manager's a friend of mine. Gave me the passkey, because I wanted to surprise you. Surprise!" The two men by the door grinned like idiots.

"What do you want?"

He took out a pack of cigarettes, the local brand Bushnell, and lit up. Looking outside he said, "Nice day. Too nice to be cooped up inside this crackerbox of a hotel room."

Rosen replied, "You're right. I'd hate to keep you and your playmates. Get out."

"No, not just yet. I was thinking about this Negro here. You ought to be outside in the sun, boy, getting a nice tan."

Now the two idiots were laughing, while Big Ben looked down at his shoes. "Don't want no trouble."

"No trouble? Then why'd you come up to see this troublemaker? What's he to you?"

Rosen asked Junior, "Do you know this man?"

"Well, not that I make it a habit of associating with members of the African race, but I run into this boy now and then. Funny we should come to see you, and just who happens to be here but . . . what's your name, boy?"

"Stop it," Rosen said. "You knew Big Ben was here. That's your red Jaguar down the street. You followed me here after court adjourned, saw him come into the hotel and figured it was to see me. No need to play more games, is there? I know we've played some before . . . you remember, don't you?"

"Think I'd forget?" He flashed a smile. "How's your face getting along? Still looks like a coon that's been run over on the road a time or two."

"It's getting better. Thanks for asking. While we're on the subject of health, how's that little medical problem of yours . . . you know, that social disease you were so worried about?"

Glancing at one another, the two idiots shifted uncomfortably against the door.

Junior scowled. "Shut up! You're like some dumb hound that just don't learn. Hey, Carleton, remember that hound we used to take hunting. Kept running up to the gun instead of going after the game."

"Yeah," his friend with the tattoo said, "you finally shot its tail off to teach it a lesson."

"That what I need to do with you, Rosen . . . shoot your tail off till you learn your lesson?"

"Did it work for the hound?"

The smile crept back onto Junior's face. "No. Finally had to kill it. Wasn't good for a damn thing. Just wouldn't learn. Know what I mean?"

Rosen knew exactly what he meant. As if to make sure, Junior nodded to his friends; each clicked open a switchblade and walked a few steps into the room, after the tattooed one slipped on the door's chain lock.

Big Ben clasped his hands. "Look, Mr. Dickerson, I don't want any trouble. Just let me get outta here. Didn't hear nothing. Didn't see nothing. Nothing!"

"Why'd your boss send you up to see this son-of-a-bitch?"

"Top don't want no trouble either. You know that. You know Top. Always mindin' his own business. That the way he be."

"Then what the hell are you doing here?"

"I . . . ah . . . I . . . ?" Big Ben clenched and unclenched his fists while, brandishing their knives, the two men moved closer.

Hands on his knees, Rosen leaned forward on the edge of his bed. He had always lived his life in small spaces, which made him hate being boxed in all the more. All the scars of body and soul were made when he couldn't maneuver; he needed time to think, to move. Time was running out, and so was space. If this was another game of Junior's, that was one thing. But with those knives . . . he had no chance of handling the three of them alone. Not even close. He needed the black man, and that meant taking a chance.

He said to Junior, "Let Big Ben go. He's got nothing to do with whatever you want."

"I'll let him go, as soon as he tells me what he told you. Otherwise, things might get kind of unpleasant for this nigger. Carleton and Dave here might have to work on him like he was a Thanksgiving turkey. Pretty soon folks'll be calling him Baby Ben. How would you like that, Baby Ben?"

"You're bluffing," Rosen said. "You won't do anything to him or me. The hotel manager gave you the key, so he knows you're in here. If anything happens to either of us, there's a witness . . ."

"Old Charlie Hartrey! He can't remember what day it is, let alone who he gave his passkey to. No, old Charlie won't care what the hell happens to you two. Never did before, just as long as we clean up all the blood. Why there was a time a few years back, when another nigger, a salesman from . . ."

"All right, I tell you!" Big Ben shouted, looking up at Junior. "But don't you be calling me 'nigger.' I ain't no one's nigger, y'hear. All Top say was for me to tell this man maybe the dead Slant woman she got killed cause a' her brother. You know how wild that man be . . . crazy with drugs. Lot a' folks after him. Could be somebody after Van 'n shot his sister. Maybe he went away. That all I tell him. That all Top told me to tell him. I swear. Now can I go?"

Junior glanced back at his friends. "Maybe he should stay and watch this lesson about what happens when you go snooping where you don't belong. You niggers are supposed to have more sense. Thought you were taught better than to . . ."

"Asked you not to call me 'nigger.' Ain't got no call to say that. I told you the truth, and now I'm leavin'."

Rosen saw his opening. "Big Ben is right. You shouldn't be calling him 'nigger.' It's about time you and your friends learned the proper way to address an African-American."

Junior snickered.

"You think it's funny that Big Ben wants the same respect as any other man?"

"Shit. You don't know much about folks around here." Junior rubbed Big Ben's hair. "Does he, boy?"

Big Ben pushed his hand away.

"Careful, boy," Junior warned.

"I'm leavin'."

Rosen said, "Junior, don't you know when you've hurt someone's feelings? Why, the next thing you'll probably do is insult the man's family . . . like his mother."

"Sure wouldn't be able to talk about this boy's

father, 'cause I bet Baby Ben don't know who he is. That right, boy?"

The black man began to tremble. Standing, he brushed past Junior. "You best leave my family be."

Junior grabbed his arm. "Sit down, boy. You don't have permission to leave—not just yet. Now, where was I?"

Rosen said, "Big Ben's mother."

"Probably some whore, like the rest . . . Christ! No!"

Junior suddenly flew through the air, hitting the wall just below the window. He had been thrown by Big Ben, who grabbed young Dickerson by the belt and collar, lifted and dangled him halfway out the window. Junior's legs flailed wildly, trying to reach the floor, but he was held like a child in the other man's grasp. Big Ben shook in anger.

"Told you not to talk down my family! Ought to drop you in the street 'n let them scoop you up like a pile a' dog shit! My momma was a good woman and ain't nobody got cause to   . !"

"Christ, don't drop me! Don't drop me! Carleton , . Dave . . . for Chrissakes, help me!"

Junior's friends ran toward the window. Rosen tripped the tattooed one, who cracked his head against the wall and cried, "Damn, I cut myself!" then grabbed at the other man's knife hand, wrestling him back against the bed.

"Call off your goons," Rosen shouted, "before Big Ben gets so nervous he drops you!"

Junior blabbered, as if he hadn't heard, "Jesus Christ, Jesus Christ, shit! Don't drop me! Shit, you son-of-a-bitch! Don't drop me!"

"I said, call them off!"

"Don't no one talk down my momma!"

"Jesus Christ, shit! Help me, Carleton . . . Dave!"

"Call them off!"

"Oww, my hand, I cut my own damn hand!"

"You shouldn't a' called me 'nigger'!"

"Help! For Chrissakes, don't drop me!"

Rosen managed to push the other man on the ground near his wounded friend. "Stay put, both of you, or else I tickle Big Ben and Junior hits the street."

The two men looked at one another then settled back against the wall.

"Now put your knives on the bed. On the bed!"

"All right," the injured man said. "Just tell him to bring Junior back inside. Please, mister. You don't know Junior's daddy. He'll kill us if anything happens to his boy. No shit." They dropped their knives on the bed and backed away.

"Go over to the door."

The two men stood and did as instructed, one wrapping a handkerchief around his wounded arm. Closing and putting one of the switchblades in his pocket, Rosen held the other knife open in his hand. "All right, Big Ben, why don't we invite Junior back into the room. Big Ben?"

He seemed not to hear. Instead, he leaned forward, inching Junior even further out the window, so that only his legs were showing. Legs that no longer were thrashing but hung limply over the sill.

"Ben, bring him in. Do you hear me? Ben!"

"Huh?" The big man blinked, looked at Junior and then around the room. "I . . ."

"It's all right. I think you've taught Mr. Dickerson a lesson in respect. Bring him inside, please."

Nodding, Big Ben pulled Junior in by the collar

like a puppy and dropped him into the corner. Junior's face was an ivory mask, eyes glazed and forehead beaded with sweat, and his pants were darkened around the crotch where he had lost control.

Rosen turned toward the two idiots. "Big Ben is leaving now. He's going home for supper, and I'm sure you two don't want to upset him anymore." They shook their heads as if on springs. "You're walking out with him, and I want to see you in the street standing by the Jaguar. I have some things to discuss with Junior before he joins you. I'm sure he wants a few minutes to compose himself. Go ahead, Big Ben. By the way, you still don't go crazy when inside an elevator?" Junior's friends looked at one another. "Maybe you two should take the stairs. Now get out of here."

Glancing down at Junior, Big Ben said, "Sorry 'bout all this, Mr. Rosen. Every now 'n then, get so worked up I can't see straight. That's why I don't never drink. I didn't want no trouble. Just come up to give you a message. Some folk won't let you be. Ain't it a shame?" He walked past the two idiots and unlocked the door. "Ain't it a damn shame?"

Giving him a good minute's head start, Junior's friends followed Big Ben from the room, closing the door behind them. Rosen watched as the black man walked down the street, shaking his head and muttering to himself. As he turned the corner, the two idiots were just leaving the hotel entrance. They walked quickly to the Jaguar, one getting inside while the other sat on the hood and looked up at Rosen's window.

Rosen closed the second knife and put it away. He brought a glass of cold water from the bathroom, then adjusted his chair so that he sat directly in front of Junior.

"Here, drink this. Go on."

It took Junior a long time to understand. His face was still bone white. Finally he reached up, both hands trembling, for the water. Taking a few sips he spilled half the glass as he placed it on the carpet beside him.

"Are you all right?" Rosen asked.

Junior nodded. "Is he . . . is he g . . . gone?"

"Yes. Did you want me to call him back, so the two of you could finish your discussion about his family tree?"

Junior pressed himself into the corner and shivered. "He's . . . damn crazy. He could of killed me."

"What a tragic loss to humanity that would've been."

"Where're Carleton and Dave?"

"They had to leave . . . something about tickets for the ballet. This gives you and me a chance to talk. These quiet meetings between us are getting to be a habit. Why did you follow me, and why were you so interested in what Big Ben had to say?"

Junior finished the glass of water, wiping his mouth with a shirt sleeve. Some color was returning to his face. "I want to . . . I want to get out of here."

"Why did you come up here in the first place?" When Junior tried to stand, Rosen pushed him back down. "Well?"

"No particular reason."

"You followed me from the courthouse and then saw Big Ben go into the hotel. From the way you two were talking, you knew all along he worked for Top o' the Evenin'. What do you care if the two of us talked?'' He leaned closer. "What does your father care?''

"My . . . father?'' Junior ran a hand through his hair. "You shut up about my father or the both of us will kick your ass.''

Rosen took out one of the switchblades and flicked it open an inch from Junior's face. "I wouldn't take that attitude, or I might become as upset as Big Ben and maybe . . . what's the old saying . . . carve you up like a Thanksgiving turkey. Now, are you going to answer my question?''

"S . . . Shit, what the hell you think you're doing? You don't have the nerve to cut me.''

Rosen let the knife balance in his hand. He thought of what he must look like at that moment; what if his father or daughter could see him. "Forgive me,'' he whispered, closing the knife and putting it away.

Grabbing the windowsill, Junior pulled himself to his feet, and this time Rosen did nothing to stop him. "I knew you were a chicken shit,'' Junior said. "This is the last time I'm warning you. Keep your nose out of everybody else's business. That goes for me, that nigger nightclub owner, and anyone else in this town. Don't even think about seeing my father again. In fact, it'd be a good idea for you to catch the next bus out of here. Tonight. Or else my friends and I might have to come back again, and without that crazy nigger you won't be so lucky next time. You hear me!''

"Get out of here. Just . . . go.''

"I'm warning you, if I have to come back . . .''

"If you do come back,'' Rosen said as he stood up, "change your pants first—''

Junior looked down to where he had dirtied himself. "Shit!"

"—and maybe wear a diaper. Save us all a lot of embarrassment."

Taking off his shirt and wrapping it around his waist, Junior hurried out the door, which Rosen closed and chained. He walked back to the window and watched young Dickerson run across the street to his Jaguar and the two idiots. Sliding behind the wheel, Junior gunned the engine and sped down the street, flipping up his middle finger as he passed the hotel.

Above the street, the sun was drowning in a murky gray sky, and the breeze blowing through the window had turned cold. Rosen felt himself shiver, but it wasn't from the wind. Sitting on his bed he took out the two switchblades and placed them on his pillow, not far from the nightstand where Sarah's birthday card lay. What had he done—taken a knife to a man's throat! It wasn't the possibility of actually using the weapon on a defenseless man, even someone like Junior, that sickened him; the evil was that he had made the threat. To have invoked terror—that was like a prayer to the devil. Long ago his grandfather had warned him of the outside world's corruption, yet Rosen refused to accept that theology. Instead, he grew to believe it was the internal universe of a man that mattered, that one need not be stained with sin even in the world of sinners. Yet, who but a tzaddik could walk without sin in such a place as Musket Shoals? Looking at the knives, Rosen knew he was not a tzaddik.

Chapter 13

No matter how much Rosen traveled across the United States, certain things remained constant. Like the dimly lit taverns where he whiled away the hours until the cash register's final ring. Like Ernie's with its Naugahyde booths, black plastic ashtrays, cardboard coasters advertising a local beer, and the ruby-colored light flickering from neon signs behind the bar. Shifting his weight on the stool, he carefully shelled a peanut and thought, "At least I won't be alone tonight."

It was not quite ten o'clock, the time Trac had set for their meeting, but Rosen had arrived an hour early. He didn't want to stay in the hotel. It was too warm, too close. His breath kept getting caught in his throat, and he couldn't think clearly. Not with the image of Junior Dickerson hanging out the window like a flag in dead wind. Nor with the two switchblades lying on his pillow, ready to flick their serpent tongues and whisper evil. It was hearing their whispering that had made him run from the room, and he hadn't slowed until far down the street.

Taking the first sip of his second beer, Rosen began to feel better and, in fact, was almost enjoying himself. Ernie's was a few blocks from the downtown area; it was small and subdued, a pool table with torn felt taking up one corner of the far wall. A few stools down from him three old men in fishing caps hunched over the bar to concentrate on their drinks and the television up in the corner. That was the best part; the TV was broadcasting a Chicago–Atlanta baseball game.

The Cubs were his team, ever since he rode the "El" to Wrigley Field to watch Ernie Banks and his teammates plagued by fate and misplayed fly balls. More than a team really, a sort of morality tale replayed every year, like Christ's Passion reenacted by that village in Germany. Or Job crying out to the whirlwind, "Why last place again?" The Cubs were leading the Braves by a run going into the eighth inning, but he sensed—among the beer, peanuts, and tense voice of the sportscaster—that his team would clutch under pressure.

Rosen wondered if Sarah was watching back in Chicago. She was as big a fan as he, loving the ball games he took her to whenever he was in town. Her birthday was in three days, and once again he would miss it. He stared at a broken peanut shell, which reminded him of a piece of jigsaw puzzle, the kind his daughter loved putting together. If only he could find the person holding the one piece that would make the puzzle of Nguyen Thi Nhi's murder intelligible. Maybe she was walking through the door that very moment.

"Hello, Trac." He pushed off his stool and indicated a nearby table. "A glass of wine?"

She nodded without smiling and, after he ordered her drink, they moved to the table. He had never seen Trac like this. Her dress was wrinkled and stained with sweat, an earring was missing, and her mascara smeared heavily as if she had been crying. Her eyes, usually so cool, darted between Rosen and the door. Was she thinking of running away or afraid someone had followed her?

"I'm glad you called," he said. "As I said on the phone, I wanted to talk to you. Are you planning to stay in town awhile, or do you have to return to your work at the Smithsonian?"

Trac sipped her wine absently and continued to glance at the door.

"Are you expecting someone?"

She almost jumped from her chair, then stared at him curiously. Her eyes were dilated.

He asked, "Are you hopped up on something?"

It was a long time before Trac's eyes broke away, and she shook her head. Taking a dirty handkerchief from her purse, she wiped her nose and patted her forehead dry. When he reached for her hand, she drew away.

"L . . . Leave me alone." Her arms folded tightly across her chest. "How could you . . . Why did you do it?"

"What?"

"It's a game for you lawyers, isn't it? D . . . Doesn't matter which side you're on, doesn't matter the right or wrong. Only the game."

"You mean about Basehart?"

"Yes!" she hissed. "Why did you let my sister's murderer out of jail?"

"He's only out on bail, and everything he owns has been taken as collateral. Besides, it was the judge who issued bail. Even the prosecutor, Mr. Wilkes, agreed."

"Like I said, your lawyer games."

"Basehart's not going to run away, I promise you."

"What if he goes after my parents . . . what then? Another dead Slant or two. It probably won't even make the front page the second time around. What will you and the Assistant Commonwealth's Attorney say the next time you're sitting around beer and pizza? 'Remember the Nguyens? I must get out to the graveyard with some flowers.' Is that what you're—"

"How did you know I had lunch with Wilkes?"

"—going to say?"

"Who was following me? Or was Wilkes the one being followed?"

"I'm f . . . frightened. I don't want that man out of jail."

"How did you know about my lunch with Wilkes?"

"You've got to have Basehart returned to prison."

"How did you know?"

Closing her eyes Trac collapsed in her chair; her breathing was steady but shallow. Rosen let her alone for the moment, settling back in his own chair while feeling his heartbeat quicken and the inside of his palms begin to sweat. The same reaction as when he was about to cross-examine a hostile witness.

A few seconds later Trac opened her eyes, wincing at the sight of Rosen. "You won't put Basehart back in prison?" she asked weakly.

"I can't. I'm his attorney. Look, I promise he won't harm you or your parents. Besides, I don't think he killed your sister."

"Of course not. You're his lawyer."

"I mean it. I have reason to believe the murderer is someone else."

Slowly Trac straightened in her chair, and her eyes narrowed. "Who do you suspect?" She spoke softly, her words so casual that Rosen was

put on his guard. Then again, more impatiently,
"Who is it, Nate? I have a right to know."

His turn to grow quiet.

"Who?"

He didn't believe Trac as an imploring woman,
like an actress obviously miscast who presses to
the end of her performance. But to what end? The
way her eyes darted nervously, she was on some
kind of dope. It seemed to point neatly to her
missing brother.

Rosen nudged his beer glass toward her.
"Where's Van?"

She stared blankly, while tearing a napkin into
small pieces.

"I think you know where your brother is. I
think you've known all along."

She swallowed hard, choking out the words,
"You're . . . crazy."

Rosen poked his beer glass a few inches further,
and she moved back slightly, her fingers squeezing the table edge.

"Who visited you that night I was laid up in
your room?" He waited for the lie and watched
her body twitch as she said it.

"No one. We were alone . . . the whole time."

"The room stank of cigarette smoke."

"Mine."

"No lipstick marks on the butts. Besides, you
wouldn't smoke Bushnells. I doubt many women
do."

She glared at him. "So you go poking around
in ashtrays."

"Sure. In wastebaskets too. I had a D.C. lab
analyze one of the tissues for blood type. Received the results late yesterday afternoon. The
saliva from the tissue was Type O positive, the
same as your brother. We got his blood type from

the hospital where he had his appendectomy. That's a great deal of circumstantial evidence. That and one thing more."

She tossed her head, her mood suddenly changing to defiance. "What?"

Rosen pushed his drink to the edge of the table. Trac drew back quickly as if the glass were red-hot. "You're doped up on something, and my guess is you got it from your brother. Just like your sister got it from your brother. Isn't that right?"

Eyes widening she shook her head wildly.

"I'm right," he said.

"Damn you."

"He had something to do with your sister's death."

"No."

Rosen leaned forward, just behind the beer glass. "Did he kill Nhi?"

"Damn you!" she screamed, knocking the glass to the floor so that it shattered. She stood and, steadying herself, shouted with tears sliding down her cheeks. "What do you know about Van . . . about anything! You think you're so damn smart playing with other people's lives, but you're nothing . . . an amateur!" Abruptly her voice lowered to a hoarse whisper, "You're the one who's being played with. You think Van . . . Van . . ." Her voice choked on the last word.

Rosen reached for her, but she drew away. Swaying she touched her head, then began to walk away.

"Trac." Rosen grasped her wrist; it felt cold, almost brittle.

Pulling free she stared at him, and her eyes softened. "Stay away from me, Nate. My people have a saying about walking with Death. It takes a long time to realize you too have died. Stay away from me." Turning unsteadily, Trac walked from the bar.

Rosen tried to stand, but his legs were too weak to rise. He could only watch her go, not even attempt to call her back. Gritting his teeth he stared at the doorway, waiting in vain for her to return. He had taken a chance and accused her brother of the murder. Not that Rosen believed it, but he wanted to get Trac angry enough to tell what had happened to Van . . . and what was happening to her. Yet the anger only made her run away and leave him alone.

After a few minutes, he walked to the bar, easing onto the stool, and ordered a beer. The three old fishermen looked away.

Rosen felt he had to say something so, sipping his beer, asked the bartender, "Who won the game?"

"Atlanta. They got two in the ninth."

"Damn. That makes the evening just perfect."

Glancing up at the television, Rosen saw a rerun of an old sitcom. He didn't want to think about Trac, so he watched TV and concentrated on the damn Cubs blowing another one. They, in turn, led him to his daughter, who had probably tuned in the last few innings before doing her English homework. Sarah said she always did her reading last, because if she fell asleep, at least it would be with a good book. He needed to send her present, the ao-dai, tomorrow so it would arrive in time for her birthday.

The present reminded him of Trac and the ao-dai she wore at her sister's funeral. She stuck in his mind, a series of contradictory images—implacable at the wake, tender alone with him in bed, now half-crazed by drugs and fear. What was that fear she would not confide? Rosen brought the beer to his lips and caught sight of a "Special Report" bulletin flashing on TV.

A moment later the screen was filled with flames lapping a small squarish building. Smoke billowed into the night, forming great gray clouds that blocked the stars, but just enough firelight illuminated a portion of the sign above the doorway—a hand holding a top hat. Someone in the bar shouted, "Christ, it's Top o' the Evenin's place!"

A reporter was saying, as firemen rushed past, "Police strongly suspect arson. Apparently the owner, known as Top o' the Evenin', discovered two men near the kitchen entrance in back. After calling for help, the owner was shot. The bartender came with a pistol and exchanged gunfire with the two suspects. Police arrived and killed one of the suspects, the other escaping. Police have not released information on the present condition of the popular nightclub owner, who was rushed about fifteen minutes ago to St. Isaacs Hospital. As you can see, fire has nearly gutted the building. Fortunately the customers fled in time, a few being treated for minor burns and smoke inhalation. We'll have a full report on the eleven o'clock news."

Paying his bill Rosen hurried from the bar, got into his car, and drove toward the nightclub. He couldn't shake the feeling that there was a connection between the fire and Basehart's release from jail. What if Trac was right and Basehart was dangerous? Rosen had used all his guile to obtain the prisoner's release; it would be his hands dipped in blood. What of Wilkes—he had gone along with the bail on Rosen's say-so, a kind of blind trust. More than that, goodness motivated by a sense of justice over any selfish desires. Rosen believed Wilkes to be one of the few truly good men of this earth, and if Basehart had done anything wrong, the reputation of a good man would be ruined. There were few things as precious; Rosen possessed nothing equivalent to justify his own existence. That was why he sped down the highway fast as his clattering Dodge would carry him. To see for himself.

He had worried needlessly about missing the turnoff, because at the intersection a squad car with flashing red lights had pulled onto the shoulder of the highway. A policeman leaned against his car while eyeing the traffic. He raised his hand—Rosen stopped after turning onto the side road—and walked toward the lawyer.

"Nightclub's closed, Mister. Been a bad fire."

"I know. I need to get in there. I'm an attorney in a case involving Top o' the Evenin'." When the policeman frowned, Rosen added, "Is Mr. Wilkes or Lt. Canary there?"

He nodded.

"Check with either of them. I'm sure it'll be all right. I'm Nate Rosen."

The policeman looked him up and down, then, pushing off the door, sauntered to the squad car and made a radio call. A minute later he waved the lawyer ahead and settled back against his car.

Rosen hadn't driven very far, when his eyes began to tear from the acrid smoke. A thick charcoal haze hung in the air, below which were the blackened remnants of Top o' the Evenin's nightclub. The roof had collapsed, taking down two of the sides, the other two bulging obscenely under its weight. Everything had lost its color except a few red sparks that leaped from the ash heap and danced triumphantly until disappearing into the

night air. Firemen were loading equipment into
their trucks, while a team of lab technicians sifted
through the ashes. Lt. Canary and Wilkes stood
near what had been the nightclub's entrance.

Parking his car nearby, Rosen approached the
two men. "I came over as soon as I heard the
news on TV."

He glanced from one man to the other, searching for the slightest sign of reproach. They merely
looked puzzled.

"How come you're here?" Canary asked.

"Why, Top o' the Evenin' . . ." Rosen realized that neither man knew about his meeting
with Collinsby and the nightclub owner nor of Big
Ben's visit to his motel room. For a moment he
considered withholding the information but saw
no purpose in that. Besides, he had already committed himself.

"Top o' the Evenin' said he would try to find
Nguyen Van Van and discover if there was a drug
connection between Van and his sister's death. I
was planning to see Top tonight."

"You sure do get around," the policeman said
lighting a cigarette. "Collinsby put you on to him,
huh. Being Lu's kin, I'm surprised Cowpie didn't
come with you. Think he'd be interested."

"We weren't together this evening. How's
Top?"

Canary gave a slight jerk of his head, and the
two attorneys followed him to the rear of the rub-
ble, where the charred remains of the back door
wobbled precariously. A few yards away lay the
nightclub owner, eyes closed in the peaceful sleep
of death. His body had been untouched by the
fire, but on either side of his breastbone were two
splotches of drying blood, rust-colored upon his

starched white shirt. A plainclothesman was snapping photographs from various angles.

Rosen sagged, hands cupped over his knees, and felt his stomach turn as the sweat slid under his shirt. Wilkes led him away, holding him steady until the waves of nausea passed.

Rosen mopped his face dry. "The newscaster said Top was shot and taken to the hospital. He never mentioned . . ."

"The man was killed instantly," Wilkes replied. "It was Lt. Canary's idea to withhold publicizing the murder."

"Why?"

A smoke ring drifted between them, followed by Canary who said, "We're still looking for one of the killers. Figgered he wouldn't be running so fast if he thought he hadn't done any killing."

Rosen had forgotten about Basehart. Once again his neck grew damp. "The . . . reporter said one of the arsonists was killed. Is that true?"

Canary nodded toward an ambulance nearby and yelled to the driver, "Open the bag, Clint, and let him take a look!" To Rosen, "This should interest you. He was a playmate of yours."

Rosen tried to read Wilkes's face, but the other attorney looked at the ground. Walking to the ambulance he watched the attendant try to open the body bag. The zipper stuck but, after several attempts, he succeeded in unzipping the sack as far as the neck. "Go ahead," Clint said with a halfway grin, "he won't bite you."

Swallowing hard Rosen drew close and peered inside. It was Pelham's friend Rupert, the man he had fought at Basehart's bait and tackle shop. Like Top, Rupert seemed at peace. His death was no loss to humanity, and Rosen wanted to feel the satisfaction of having one less bigot in the world.

Yet his eyes could only see the Torah written across the dead man's face—God would allow no rejoicing over the death of Pharaoh's army, for they too were His children.

"Can I close the bag now?" the driver asked.

Rosen walked back to the other two men. He asked Canary, "You're certain Rupert set fire to the nightclub and shot Top?"

The policeman flicked a long ash. "You see a fox near a henhouse with chicken feathers sticking out his mouth, what do you think?"

"You weren't able to ask him any questions?"

"He didn't feel like talking."

Wilkes said, "He was firing at the police. Lt. Canary killed him."

Rosen looked at the policeman, who stared back with a small smile, then said to Wilkes, "Rupert would've been an important witness. He could've helped Basehart's case."

Canary snickered loudly. "How? You got a connection between Rupert and the murdered woman?"

Rosen felt his face grow warm. "I told you. Top o' the Evenin' was looking into . . ."

"Top's dead. So's Rupert. So what you got . . . nothing."

"If you hadn't killed Rupert, maybe I would've had something."

Canary only grinned.

"What about Pelham?" Rosen asked. "Don't you think he was the other man involved in Top's murder? Have you got him in custody yet, or would that be too much exercise for you?"

Wilkes said, "We've alerted the police to bring him in for questioning, as well as that other one who hangs around the bait and tackle shop—Burl.

There's nothing more you can do here. Why don't you go home and get some rest."

"No, not yet. Is Top's widow here? I'd like to pay my respects."

"I think so. This way."

The two attorneys started back toward the ambulance, leaving Canary puffing contentedly.

Wilkes said, "You may be right about Pelham being involved. This afternoon I ran a check on his blood type, like you asked. Type O positive, the same as Van's and the same as what was found on the soiled tissues. Of course, it's the most common blood type of all. The lab technician said more than a third of the people working in the courthouse, from my boss to my secretary, are O positive. Not very conclusive, but it's something."

He spoke encouragingly, shoring up Rosen's case by knocking away the props from his own. Rosen wanted to thank the other attorney but held back. What if even Wilkes was somehow mixed up in the murders? Rosen was a lawyer even before he was a man, and the one thing a lawyer could never afford to be was a fool.

He said, "Canary was pretty quick on the trigger, killing Rupert."

Wilkes stopped abruptly. "You can't think he had anything to do with the Nguyen woman's death? He may be crude and overbearing, but he's a good police officer. My God, you've got to trust someone."

"Those cigarette butts at the dead woman's apartment were Bushnells, what Canary smokes."

"As do hundreds of other men around here," Wilkes replied, his face reddening. "Guess I'm lucky I don't smoke Bushnells. Excuse me. I have some work to do."

"I didn't mean . . ." Rosen began, but Wilkes was already gone.

Turning, Rosen walked a few steps then stopped abruptly, fascinated by what lay before him. It might have been a painting, the sharp lines falling away in obtuse angles from the center—Lu's large shoulders huddled as she sat upright in a chair, hands held prayerlike before her lips. The bartender Big Ben knelt on both knees and, eyes closed, rested against her, while Top o' the Evenin's walking stick leaned from the ground to her hip. She wasn't crying; her eyes stared at Rosen with a terrible lucidness. Her breathing was so shallow, she appeared motionless.

Approaching cautiously he heard a soft moaning, and it was another moment before he realized the sound was coming, not from Lu, but the bartender. The man trembled slightly, one hand clutching the hem of Lu's skirt, while the other lay open on the ground like a dead animal.

"Lu," Rosen whispered.

She remained still, but Big Ben cried out, "I tried to save him! If I could a' just got there a half minute sooner," he shook his head violently, "I might a' saved him!"

Slowly blinking Lu laid a hand on the man's head, stroking his hair. "Shh, Ben. You did everything you could."

"If I just could a' got there sooner. Top was the best. I tried, Lu, I tried." He cried softly into her dress.

"Shh, I know," she murmured. "Nothing more to do now, Ben. Go on home. Your family must be worried 'bout you." He looked up at her like a sad-eyed dog, and she said again, "Go 'head. Go on home."

"Ye . . . ah," he replied with a cough. Wiping

his eyes with the back of his hand, the bartender got up. "You just call if you need anything. Anything, you hear."

She nodded, more a jerk of her head telling Big Ben to get on with his life. Once again coughing, he turned and walked away.

Rosen approached as close as the bartender had been and knelt beside her.

Her eyes narrowed. "You here to say how sorry you is, I suppose. There'll be lots a' that now. His folk'll be coming up from Raleigh, and his old army buddies from New York. Even his ex-wife, I guess. Everybody saying how sorry they is. I best be getting the house cleaned. My sisters can help with the cooking. Lord, we're gonna need to cook up a mess a' food. Children need new clothes. Henry's suit coat's all patched at the elbows."

At the sound of her son's name, Lu swallowed hard and her eyes grew moist. Clearing her throat she continued, "I know you must be busy, Mr. Rosen. Nice a' you to come by like this."

Rosen said, "Lu, if you don't want to talk now, I understand, but I need to ask some questions. Why did this happen?"

She looked at him strangely. "What do you mean? You don't know much for a lawyer, if you have to ask that question. Like Top used to say, 'Take a miracle for a nigger to die in his bed.' " Her breath caught in her throat. "Old Top . . . he knew."

"You think this happened just because he was black?"

"Reason enough in this world. Besides, that man the police killed. He was a member a' G.U.N. They hated us folks."

"You know about that group?"

"I heard Top mention them on the phone."

Rosen leaned closer. "When?"

"Just the other day."

"When . . . before or after I visited the night-club and heard you sing?"

She touched her forehead. "It was . . . after. Two, three days ago, I think. He was talking to someone, and the name come up. I remember Top laughing. He was talking 'bout G.U.N.-toting cowboys riding horse."

"I don't understand."

"You know . . . Top was talking 'bout horse . . . heroin."

Rosen sat on the ground, arms drawn around his legs, trying to fit the conversation into the puzzle. If Top had been following a lead on the Basehart case . . . he must've been, otherwise why mention G.U.N.? If drugs were involved in Nguyen Thi Nhi's murder, that led away from Basehart and to . . . Van? What about Senator Dickerson and his lovable son, Junior? And of course, the biggest piece of the puzzle—Billy Lee Pelham? Almost certainly Pelham or his friend Burl was the other man helping Rupert, but why? Pelham should have done everything in his power to stay out of trouble until after the trial. It didn't make any sense, unless . . .

"Lu, did you hear Top say anything else on the phone?"

She shook her head.

"Nothing at all?"

"No, not right away. Later after he hung up, he was all grinning. Saying how pretty soon we was gonna have all the money we needed to fix the place up real nice, just like a big city night-club."

"Did he say where the money was coming from?"

"Top was always talking like that. Didn't mean nothing. Nothing at all."

"Did he say?"

"Something 'bout . . ." She paused a moment to think. "It was funny, the way Top said it. Like . . . getting paid not for what you know but for what you don't know. Can you figger that one out, Mr. Rosen?"

"Maybe. It may take awhile, but I think so. Lu, I'm really sorry about Top."

"I know."

"I don't know why Top was killed, but if it had anything to do with the case I'm working on, I promise you that the murderers will be brought to justice."

Lu stared at him for a long time. Her eyes finally softened. "Don't need to trouble yourself none. Don't make no difference anyway. Not too many cared 'bout Top."

Rosen repeated what he had said once to Wilkes. "Each man is a universe unto himself. The murder of any man is like destroying an entire world."

Lowering her head Lu murmured, "My world, my world."

He listened to her grief lap against him, wave upon wave, each one carrying the piece of Top's death into the puzzle and turning it, turning it, until it almost fell into place.

Chapter 14

THURSDAY MORNING

Feet propped upon his desk, Wilkes thumbed through the report of Top o' the Evenin's murder. Twelve hours had passed, yet there was still no progress in the investigation. He tossed the file aside. Everything was unraveling. Both Pelham and Basehart were still missing, and the trial was set to begin next week.

There was a knock at the door. Wilkes brought his feet down as Martha walked into the room.

"Mr. Simpson just buzzed," she said. "Wants to see you in his office now. He was most insistent."

Frowning, Wilkes asked, "How did he sound?"

"Not good. You'd better get in there pronto. Wouldn't hurt to run a comb through your hair." Martha fixed his tie and, as he walked past her, squeezed his elbow. "Go get 'em, tiger."

Although he tried to maintain a smile after leaving the office, it weakened then disappeared as Saunders, perched atop his secretary's desk, looked up from a report.

"Hi, Jimmy. Haven't seen much of you lately."

Wilkes nodded. "What's that you're reading?"

"What? Oh, this . . . it's the report on the death of that nightclub owner. You know Edgar's assigned me to the case."

"Any leads yet?"

Saunders grinned wide as a crescent moon. "We're working on it. We'll catch him."

"You realize there's probably a connection between Top o' the Evenin's death and that of the Nguyen woman. The suspect killed by Canary was a member of G.U.N. and a friend of Billy Lee Pelham. Have you found Pelham yet?"

The grin remained plastered on Saunders's face. "Now, Jimmy, you wouldn't be trying to tell me my business? If Edgar thought there was anything to your theory, he'd have assigned you to this case instead of me. Ask him yourself. You're going into his office now, aren't you? By the way, since we're on the subject of missing persons, have you located Edison Basehart? Interesting tactic, letting an accused murderer out on bail. I must admit, that strategy would've never occurred to me. Of course, if he runs away, that saves the state the time and expense of a trial. Very considerate of you."

Everything Saunders had said was true. Yet, damn it, there was a connection between the two murders. Wilkes wanted to say so but kept silent. His face growing warm, he could almost feel Saunders's teeth picking at his bones. Both cases had become big news, giving whoever became the media's "star" prosecutor an inside track to Edgar Simpson's job. It was the kind of game his rival loved—turning the law into a blood sport.

With a slow shake of his head, Wilkes continued to the other end of the office.

"He's expecting you," Simpson's secretary said with her usual smile. "Go right in."

Seated behind his desk, the Commonwealth's Attorney was bent over a stack of papers. Without looking up he motioned for Wilkes to take a seat opposite him. It took several minutes for Simpson to stop shuffling papers and scratching with his pen. After finishing, he paused to clear his throat.

He tapped his pen on the stack of papers. "Go on a week's vacation, and spend a month to catch up." Taking off his glasses, he rubbed his eyes. "Damn it all. Five months to go until retirement, and all hell breaks loose. Can you understood that, Jimmy? Ever since me and your daddy started out together, this county's been stuck in God's back pocket, the biggest thing maybe Mel Turner shooting off his friend's head for messing with his wife. Now this, with me having only five months to go. What the hell's happening, Jimmy? Just tell me that. What the hell's going on with the Basehart case?"

Wilkes felt like a little boy in the principal's office. He shifted in his chair and folded his arms tightly across his chest. "The case is much more complicated than it first appeared."

"Such as?"

"What happened last night—the murder of the nightclub owner Top o' the Evenin'. I think it's connected with the Nguyen woman's death, the one killer being a member of G.U.N. and . . ."

"Yeah, I hear you." Simpson pointed a finger. "You better hope you're dead wrong."

"Why?"

"Because if there is a connection, that leads right back to Basehart. He's the chief suspect, and he hasn't been seen since he got out. No, let me rephrase that—since *you* let him out. Of all the jackass . . . !" Leaning back Simpson continued, "If it wasn't for the memory of your daddy . . . How you could've let Basehart go when you held him between your fingers like a tick. He only needed just a little bit of squeezing. Why did you

let him out on bail, Jimmy? If I could just understand that."

Wilkes wondered what to say—that Basehart
might force Pelham to reveal the truth, or that
Rosen simply had asked him for a favor. Simpson
wouldn't understand, because he was right; it
didn't make sense. "I thought at the time it was
the right thing to do."

"And now?"

"Now . . . I don't know."

"Well, Jimmy, I know. This afternoon you're
going to ask Judge Spencer . . . beg if you have
to . . . that Basehart's bail be revoked and he immediately be brought into custody."

"On what grounds?"

"You're smart enough to think of something."

"Maybe in light of the second murder . . ."

"Christ, don't mention that!" Simpson thun-
dered. "The newspapers are already hinting the
two murders might've been done by the same
man. If we ever admit that could be true, that
after we released Basehart he went out and killed
someone else . . . first a Slant and then a nigger
. . . hell, Jimmy, those out-of-state reporters are
gonna have a field day. They'll make my last few
months a dark swamp for me. And you—you
might just as well pack up Ellie and the kids and
move to Alaska, because it won't only be your
political career that's ruined. You see Saunders
strutting like the cock who just chased his last rival out of the henhouse. He knows you're halfway gone and that gives him a pretty clear shot
at my job. You better get yourself together, boy.
Find Basehart and get that conviction. Believe me,
I know about these things. You're running out of
time."

As Simpson spoke, sweat broke out on his forehead, and the fingers of both hands appeared knotted together. Wilkes clenched his fists—to have caused so much grief to his father's friend, a man who had almost been a second father.

"Edgar, it may be that Edison Basehart isn't the murderer."

Simpson stared at him in disbelief.

Wilkes persisted, "Basehart's attorney, Nathan Rosen, has another theory which is very plausible. It's based on a possible drug connection including the dead woman's brother, Nguyen Van Van, who's been missing ever since his sister's murder. Pelham may also in some way be involved. That's why this murder of the nightclub owner could be a lead to solving the first killing. We know that the victim, Nguyen Thi Nhi, was a drug addict. According to his police record, Top o' the Evenin' had been arrested twice on suspicion of drug dealing. So you see, it could tie together."

Simpson's eyes grew wide, while his whole body trembled. He tried to speak, but the words gurgled in his throat. Wilkes moved toward him, when Simpson lifted a hand.

"You're . . . you're out of your head." He took a few deep breaths before continuing. "Look, I expect Basehart's lawyer to come up with some wild theory to get his client off the hook—hell, that's his job. You don't blame a man for doing his job. You're supposed to be the prosecutor, remember? I'm sure that organization Rosen's working for pays him a pretty penny to wiggle his clients off the hook. He sure don't need any help from you, but I do. Hear that, Jimmy, I do. Let's get this over with. You find Basehart, convict him, fry him, and send this Rosen back North with his tail between his legs. You do that, Jimmy, for me, for your family, for yourself. You don't really have any choice. Just get some of that killer instinct!'' He jabbed with his fist. ''Know what I mean!''

Sighing deeply Simpson leaned back in his chair and mopped his face with a large handkerchief. His hand was still trembling when it drew the cloth away and rested on the table. Wilkes waited to speak, not wanting to set off the other man again. That and because he wasn't sure what he could say. Like a quarterback calling his own game suddenly receiving plays from the bench, what choice was there other than to swallow your pride and take the orders? Of course, this wasn't a game and it wasn't a case of pride but of justice at least that's what Wilkes had been telling himself all along. That's what it was—justice, wasn't it—and not merely trying to do things his own way? Regardless, Simpson was now calling the plays, and as the old saying went . . .

''You're the boss,'' Wilkes half whispered. ''Is there anything else you want me to do?''

Simpson seemed not to be listening. His eyes were half-closed.

''Edgar?''

''Hmm?''

''Is there anything else you want me to do?''

''Uh . . . no. We'll let Canary and his men bring in Basehart, then you just go for the conviction. With any luck, this whole mess'll be forgotten in a couple of months.'' He brightened a little. ''A conviction, the right kind of publicity, and who knows, you might wind up sitting in this chair after all. Now wouldn't Saunders shit a few bricks over that.''

Looking down at his hands, Wilkes chose not to reply. He was very tired, like he used to feel after playing football in the heat and mud. The point at which winning or losing didn't matter. He wanted to be alone swimming in some cool quiet place.

Clearing his throat Simpson nervously thumbed his stack of papers. ''You can't believe how glad I'll be to get this job off my back. The day I retire I'm going down to the river, just above where the Paddy is. Hope the fishing's still good. Your daddy and me used to go there as kids. Remember, we took you and Tad there to fish when the two of you together could hardly hold a pole. Them was the days. Everything was simple—you had your whites and blacks and they never mixed. Oh, you might step out to a colored whorehouse now and then, but a white man, he stood for something in those days.'' He squinted at Wilkes. ''I suppose you don't know what the hell I'm talking about. How could you? Your daddy, now I could've talked to him. He'd have understood.'' He shook his head. ''Ah, get outta here.''

''All right, Edgar.''

Wilkes walked from the room. Turning once he saw Simpson bent over the papers but distracted, his pen held like a conductor's wand waiting for the orchestra to come to attention.

He passed quickly through the lobby, stopping at his secretary's desk for messages. She handed him two, both within the last fifteen minutes, from Nathan Rosen.

''He asked that you call him immediately. Said he had some important news for you.''

Holding the message between two fingers as if contaminated, Wilkes entered his office and sat behind the desk. His hand paused an inch from the telephone, while he thought of all the reasons for not calling. In his mind Wilkes heard Simpson

recount them—his duty, his career, and that in
some way he was a disappointment to his father's
memory. What good was a law degree without
someplace to show it off? No, Simpson knew all
the right things to say.

Wilkes slowly pulled his hand away, when the
buzzer sounded from Martha's desk. "It's Mr.
Rosen again," she said. "Line one." He stared at
the blinking light, his hand still suspended in
midair, until Martha again said, "Jimmy, line
one."

"Yes, yes!" he snapped, then shook his head.
As his father would've said, a leopard can't
change his spots. He lifted the receiver to his ear.
"Hello, Nathan." Why did he use the lawyer's
first name?

"Hello, Jimmy. Glad I caught you. Hope you
haven't eaten lunch yet."

Instinctively Wilkes checked his watch; it was
11:45. "Uh, no."

"Good. Can you get right down to Lois's
Cafe?"

"Where?"

"Lois's Cafe, where the discriminating truck
driver eats. Opposite Basehart's bait and tackle
shop."

"Yes, I know." He remembered Canary's two-
chili lunch. "Is it really necessary?"

"Yes, it's necessary. I wouldn't ask if it
wasn't." The excitement in his voice, barely sup-
pressed, was infectious.

Still, Wilkes remembered Simpson's warning.
"I don't know. I've got a full calendar. And
there's some bad news for you. The Commonwealth's Attorney wants Basehart's bail revoked.
I'm afraid this afternoon I'm going to have to . . ."

"Forget about that for now, and just get down

here. I think I'm onto something. Something that will help us out."

"I . . . uh . . ."

"And, Jimmy, bring some bicarbonate of soda. This chili's a killer." Without waiting for a reply, Rosen hung up.

Cradling the receiver, Wilkes let out a low hiss. "Damn." He had committed himself once again, and Rosen knew all along it would be that way. He had once again used the word "us" . . . "help *us* out a lot," as if they were co-conspirators. Now another rendezvous at lunch, chili instead of pizza, but the same result no doubt. Wilkes would be sucked deeper into the swamp, and this time not even Simpson would bother to throw him a rope. And for what? Wilkes snickered. He had no time to soul-search; his good friend Nathan was waiting for him. Whatever else, he had to keep that appointment.

The drive along the ocean was difficult, with the waves kicking up angrily as if they too had something negative to say. The sun was interrupted by a series of clouds, each one larger than its predecessor, while the wind slapping against his face smelled of rain. Rolling up the window, he stepped on the accelerator and rushed past seagulls picking their way through the rocks to find shelter from the coming storm. He switched on a rock-and-roll station, the one his daughters listened to, and tried to hum along. Anything not to think about where he was going and its implications.

Twenty minutes later Wilkes turned into the diner's parking lot and pulled between two semis. Rosen was waiting in a window booth, his spoon scraping the bottom of the chili bowl. Wilkes sat across the table and raised his hand to call the waitress.

"No time now," Rosen said, glancing at the window. "I hope we're not too late." Again he looked across the street, this time resting his gaze on the bait and tackle shop.

"What is it?"

"Take a look. How good of a detective are you?"

Wilkes concentrated on Basehart's store but saw nothing out of the ordinary. The shop's door and windows were closed, unusual for the middle of a business day but understandable given Basehart's circumstances. Although the grass was getting long, everything else looked as he had seen it the week before, maybe even prettier, the tulips in the window boxes blooming in brilliant reds and purples.

"I don't see anything different. Well, the flowers are out."

"That's it!"

"Hmm?"

"The tulips in bloom. And last week they were beginning to wilt."

"Yes?" Wilkes was growing irritated.

"Last week the flowers weren't blooming—no rain this past week—and now they are. Why?"

"Somebody watered them." Suddenly Wilkes understood. "Basehart?"

"That's my guess. I can't imagine Pelham or his pals puttering around the tulips."

"So, Basehart's been back to his home. Wish I could've found him before Top o' the Evenin's murder."

"I think he still might be there. I walked by the shop just before calling you. The window boxes were still wet from where the water had splashed.''

''You knew he'd be here?''

Rosen shook his head. ''I came out to ask a few questions and hoping to find Pelham. The waitress was helpful. She said this morning a red Jaguar parked in Basehart's driveway for a short time.''

''Did she see who was driving it?''

''No. She noticed it about ten, and fifteen minutes later it was gone. I've got an idea about the driver, but we'd better check on Edison first.''

''How do you know Basehart didn't go away with the car?''

Rosen stood. ''The water hasn't evaporated off the window boxes yet. They were probably watered during the last hour. I've been watching the shop since then, so Edison's in there. Unless he sneaked out the back.''

Wilkes followed his companion to the cashier then through the doorway. ''Why did you bother to call me? Why are you sharing this—after all, if we find Basehart, I'm going to insist he be returned to jail. I told you, his bail's being revoked.''

Rosen smiled. ''Any number of reasons—we lawyers always have a pocketful of arguments, don't we. First, you're not after Basehart; you want whoever's really the murderer. Second, I owe you a few favors. You went to bat for Edison on the bail issue, and I think it's paying off. And finally . . .'' He stopped to run across the highway just ahead of an oncoming truck.

''Yes!'' Wilkes shouted as he hurried after, catching up on the edge of Basehart's driveway.

''In case we have to break in, I can tell the police I had the law backing me.''

While Rosen walked up the driveway to the front door, Wilkes hesitated like a schoolboy watching his friend play hookey to go fishing, torn between what was right and a great adventure. Like most schoolboys he chose the adventure.

"Anyone answering?" he asked after joining Rosen.

"No." Rosen knocked a second time but again no response.

Wilkes peeked through one of the windows. "I don't see anyone. Something's on the floor though." He peered into the darkened room, his eyes following something long and thin from below the counter into a back room. "Looks like a garden hose. Probably what Basehart watered the plants with. Maybe you should knock again."

"No, you knock. I'm going to check around back." Rosen disappeared around the corner.

Wilkes rapped on the front door until his knuckles ached. Then he waited quietly, an ear cocked until he was sure of a noise within one of the back rooms. He started for the window, when the door suddenly opened wide.

Teeth clenched, Rosen stood in the entrance. Silently he led Wilkes into the bait and tackle shop. A thin layer of dust covered the shelves; the floor was dirty and wet with the coils of a tangled green garden hose, neither end visible. Someone's suitcase lay open near the hose, its contents strewn about the floor. A partial set of footprints led toward the back room, where Rosen leaned against the open doorway, his jaw still set tightly.

"Did . . . did you find Basehart?" Wilkes asked.

Pushing off the doorframe, Rosen beckoned. Wilkes followed him inside to a small room, where light from a hanging bulb filtered through the dust. The room where he and Canary had watched Rosen rough up the now deceased Rupert. Wilkes remembered the scene so clearly, it was a long time before he realized that the body slumped in the corner under a pile of rods and reels was not Rupert's.

"Is he . . . ?" Wilkes began but could not finish.

"Is he dead?" Rosen echoed. "No. Is he Basehart? No. Someone far more deserving."

As Wilkes stepped forward, his foot caught on the garden hose. Following it like a path, he came at last to the end, a heavy steel nozzle lying in a reddish puddle, the same color as the head of the man beside it. Bending closer he recognized Billy Lee Pelham hunched in a fetal position, the body rising fitfully as air wheezed through his nostrils.

"Do you think he's hurt badly?"

Rosen sat on the edge of the table. "It'll be a long time before he plays the violin again." He gazed at Pelham. "Like sharks smelling blood, eating one another."

"You'd better phone for an ambulance."

Rosen made no move to call, although the telephone was on the table near him.

Wilkes persisted, "He could be seriously injured. Maybe a concussion. You really ought to telephone . . ."

"Basehart did this. He must've been boiling mad when he heard what Pelham said on the witness stand. Couldn't wait to get his revenge."

"You're certain it was Basehart?"

"Who else would beat Pelham to a pulp with a hose nozzle then take the time to water the plants? It was my client all right. I'm surprised he left this guy alive. If only Pelham could tell us something. I'd give a lot to know where Basehart's off to."

Wilkes asked, "How do you think it happened?"

"The back door was unlocked. I found some muddy boot marks outside the doorway, big ones the size Basehart would've made. He probably came in, surprised Pelham in the front, beat him with the hose—there're a couple hanging behind the counter—then decided the plants needed watering. After finishing his gardening chore, Edison dragged Pelham, the hose still wrapped around him, to the back room. Afterward he ducked out the back way. That's why I didn't see him leave."

"Maybe it happened the other way around. Maybe Basehart was already here, and Pelham walked in on him."

Rosen shook his head. "I checked the suitcase. It was Pelham's—his bankbook's in there as well as what're probably his only pair of clean socks. Looks as if he was getting ready to leave town."

"He probably knew what would happen to him once Basehart was released on bail." Wilkes looked down at the injured man, and a wave of nausea came over him. "I'm responsible for this."

Rosen clicked his tongue in disgust. "Don't waste your sympathy on either of them. This is what we've both been after . . . to make something happen. Well, something's happened."

"Not this. Is justice served when something like this happens? My God, Nate, we're practically standing in the man's blood!"

Rosen gave a hard laugh. "My God," he repeated the phrase slowly, relishing the sound of the two words. "Do you know what you're saying, Jimmy? The same thing Job cried out, only to have the whirlwind whisper back, 'Have you an aim like that of God, Let loose the fury of your

wrath; tear down the wicked and shatter them.'
Prostrate yourself, Jimmy, like Job did before it's
too late. No, God's reasons are obscure, beyond
the comprehension of mere mortals—just ask the
six million killed by Nazis with the same mental-
ity as Basehart or this goon here. It's not for us to
judge. Let's just try to win this one for the good
guys.''

Staring at the injured man, Wilkes shook his
head. "No, not this way. Are you going to call
the ambulance or am I?''

"All right," Rosen replied, reaching for the
telephone. He suddenly whistled softly, his finger
poised to dial.

Wilkes grew impatient. "Well?''

"Look here.''

Wilkes walked to the table and followed Rosen's gaze to an open telephone book. The letter
"C" lay exposed, from "Cl" to a portion of "Co,"
and his eyes skimmed the columns looking for a
familiar name until he exclaimed, "Collinsby!''
Immediately he remembered what the waitress
across the street had said. "Collinsby," he repeated, turning to Rosen. "He's got a red Jaguar.
Maybe he came here looking for his client, Basehart.''

"Maybe. Anyways, it gives us another lead.
Why don't you call your friend and ask why Pelham or Basehart would be interested in his phone
number.''

Wilkes dialed Collinsby's office number. A
woman's voice answered. "Lester Collinsby,
Attorney-at-Law. May I help you?''

"This is Mr. Wilkes from the Commonwealth's
Attorney's office. May I speak to Mr. Collinsby?''

"I'm sorry, Mr. Wilkes, but he's not here just
now. May I take a message?''

"What time are you expecting him?"

"I really couldn't say."

"This is important."

The sound of pages flipping. "I am sorry, but his appointment calendar is open for this afternoon, and he made no indication as to when he'd be returning. I'll give him your message as soon as he comes in. May I take your number?"

"When did he leave the office today?"

"Oh, quite early. About nine thirty."

"Was anyone with him when he left?"

"Why, no."

Wilkes was about to hang up, when Rosen put his hand over the receiver's mouthpiece. "Ask her if anyone else called Collinsby during the last few hours."

Wilkes posed the question, to which the secretary replied, "Well, an insurance investigator called regarding a case we've been working on. Then there was one gentleman . . . I don't know why I use the word 'gentleman' . . . he was very gruff. Wanted to know . . . no, demanded to know where Mr. Collinsby was. Wanted to see him 'right now.' He was very rude."

"Did he leave his name?"

"I asked, but he just growled a few insulting words and slammed down the receiver. I don't mind telling you my ear still has a slight ache from the noise. I'm sorry I can't be of any further help, Mr. Wilkes."

He gave the woman his number and hung up.

"Where do you think he is?" Rosen asked.

"I have no idea."

"Collinsby's home phone number and address are listed below his office. I wonder . . ." Rosen dialed Collinsby and let the phone ring for a long time before putting down the receiver. "No answer. I don't like this."

"Me either. If Lester's involved, that means Basehart could be after him too. Look what he did to Pelham. My God, Pelham!" Quickly Wilkes dialed for help. "The ambulance should be here in a few minutes."

Rosen said, "Pelham was trying to get away, maybe even out of town. Collinsby might have the same idea."

"Why would Lester be involved in all this?"

"Good question. When we catch up with him, maybe he'll tell us. You better go over to his apartment. Hate to think of him lying there in the same condition as Pelham."

"All right. Are you coming along?"

"No. I don't know Collinsby very well, but if he wanted to hide, there's one place he might go to. I'll check that out. I'll call your office later, and we can compare notes." He pushed off the table. "You'd better wait for the ambulance. I'd have a more difficult time explaining this to the police." He looked down at Pelham whose breathing had grown steadier. "Looks like he'll be all right. Like the old saying goes, 'Only the good die young.' See you later."

Wilkes remained seated until he heard the front door click. It was only then that Wilkes realized he didn't know where Rosen was going. He wanted to tell him to be careful, for they weren't opponents after all but allies searching for simple justice. Looking down at the injured Pelham and with the ambulance siren ringing in his ears, Wilkes knew he was going to need all the allies he could muster.

Chapter 15

THURSDAY AFTERNOON

It had been five years since Wilkes visited Collinsby's apartment. That last time they had sat on the floor and shared a bottle of scotch, while the movers carted away all the furniture, part of Lester's divorce settlement on his second wife. Wilkes supposed that high school friends naturally grew apart over the years, but he had always felt guilty not keeping in touch. While his own career had plodded along, Lester's had soared like a series of forward passes into the end zone, each knocked down at the last moment. His leg injury denying him a pro football career, the position with a high-powered law firm he just couldn't handle, the beautiful wives who expected too much—all of which brought him back to his small office, small apartment, and the few clients who still remembered good old "Cowpie." Yet, he always managed to dress well, and he always drove a red Jaguar just a year or two old.

Collinsby's apartment was in an old respectable three-story building near the courthouse and across the street from a school playground. Wilkes walked through a courtyard arranged around an artificial fountain and filled with mothers wheeling baby strollers, while their toddlers straggled behind like ducklings. Women and children seemed to flicker in the sunlight. Looking up

Wilkes saw a series of dark clouds pass overhead. Probably more rain.

He rode the elevator alone to the third floor. The corridor was empty except for a janitor on a ladder changing a light bulb at the end of the hall. Collinsby's apartment was second on the left, and Wilkes knocked so loudly that the janitor turned his head. No answer. He knocked again, waited, then tried the doorknob which was locked.

"Sounds like no one's home!" the custodian shouted. "Guess that's why the telephone was invented!"

Taking out his wallet, Wilkes signaled for the man to come over. Shaking his head, the janitor climbed down the ladder and walked slowly toward him.

"I didn't mean anything by that, Mister."

Wilkes showed his identification. "I'm with the Commonwealth's Attorney's Office. I have official business with Mr. Collinsby and need to get into his apartment. I'd like you to use your passkey to let me in."

The janitor stared at the identification then looked Wilkes up and down. Stroking his jaw he said, "I don't know. Ain't you supposed to have a search warrant?"

"This is an emergency. If you prefer, I can call the police and have them come over."

"No, no, the manager wouldn't like that—all those red lights and sirens." He took one more look at the identification card. "Guess it's all right, you being kinda like the police. Besides, I'll be outside here in case . . . Well, I'll be here."

Taking the passkey from the chain on his belt, he unlocked the door and stepped aside as Wilkes walked in. Wilkes shut the door, which almost hit the janitor's face as it closed.

He stood in the corridor that led to the living room and called, "Lester!" The word sank into the apartment's deepening silence. He walked slowly down the hallway, stopping to look into the kitchen. At the table was a single place setting which probably had been used for breakfast; there were bread crumbs on the plate, a knife streaked with jelly, and a nearly empty coffee cup.

The living room was not at all as Wilkes remembered. A bookcase covered the wall to his left, gray leather couch and love seat rested at the opposite corner below a long picture window, and to his right a teak wall unit encased a stereo system, large color television, and VCR. In front of the couch was a glass-topped coffee table, where a recent legal journal peeked bashfully through an assortment of sports and girlie magazines.

Wilkes looked outside into the courtyard. The sky had darkened, but the mothers continued to stroll with their babies in the playground across the street, as older children scampered home from school, a few boys using the baby carriages as an obstacle course. Playing games, calling to one another—so much joy in the world. So much joy in the world, and Collinsby's bedroom still needed to be checked out. He delayed for several minutes, watching a game of baseball begin in the playground and remembering how Tad, Lester, and he used to play ball as kids, coming home sweaty, bruised, and exhilarated, waiting only for the next day and the next game. Now the next day was something only to be feared, and there were no more games.

Wilkes was about to turn away when he noticed, not far from his own parked car, an old Ford the same model and color as Lt. Canary's. Someone was sitting inside, although Wilkes saw only an arm emerge to stretch beside the door as if holding a cigarette. Drumming his fingers on the sill, he thought of running downstairs to see if the driver was Canary. If he was, then what—bring the detective back here, to show him what? The bedroom hadn't been searched. Better wait, at least until Wilkes had cause to call the police. He took two steps from the window when it struck him—why would Canary be watching Collinsby's apartment? There was no reason for the detective to be there, no cause for suspicion, unless he knew what Rosen and I know. But how could he, unless . . . ? Again Wilkes looked outside; the car was still there, and the arm.

A hallway led to the apartment's single bedroom, but he walked into the bathroom first. It smelled musty, and the inside of the shower curtain was slightly damp. Above the sink the medicine cabinet door was ajar. Opening it wide, he scanned the shelves but found only a half-empty bottle of aspirin. No toothbrush or toothpaste, no shaving cream or razor, no deodorant—as if Collinsby, too, had packed to take a trip.

He approached the bedroom, hesitating for a moment, then walked through the open door. The room was dark, the blinds drawn on the large window to his right, but his hand found and flicked on a light switch. A bed, a low chest of drawers—upon which his right hand rested—and a double-doored closet running the length of the wall to his left filled the room. Headboard and drawers, like the living room wall unit, were teak and looked expensive, as did the deeply piled carpeting. The bed was unmade, blanket slipped halfway onto the carpet, and on one of the pillows was another girlie magazine.

Wilkes went to the chest of drawers, some of

which were half-opened, put his fingers on the
top handle but again hesitated, feeling cheap and
dirty. Shaking his head, he opened the drawer
and saw Collinsby's underwear, as well as an
open box of condoms. He quickly glanced through
the other drawers—pajamas, socks, handkerchiefs, a bottle of whiskey, an old family album—
before banging them shut. He was disgusted with
himself but still noted that the sock and underwear drawers were half empty, suggesting that
Collinsby had taken off. Where and, more importantly, why? What had he to do with the death of
Nguyen Thi Nhi?

Wilkes walked around the bed to the closet,
sliding open the left-hand door very slowly, half
expecting Collinsby's body to drop to the floor.
When it didn't, he leaned against the closet frame,
half-smiling at his own fear. He thumbed through
Collinsby's clothing. There were four suits and
twice as many sport coats; the tie rack was an
endless rainbow of silken colors. Several hangers
and shoe racks were empty. Opening the right
side of the closet, Wilkes saw a collection of sport
shirts. He reached in to feel the material.

A hand sprang from behind the shirts and
grasped his wrist. Clothes tumbled out the closet
followed by another hand holding something that
glinted hard. Wilkes fell back against the bed, his
attacker on top of him, the knife glancing Wilkes's
left wrist, cutting the cuff and leaving a streak of
blood.

Wilkes grabbed for the knife hand. Looking up
half-dazed, he saw his assailant was Pelham's
friend Burl, squat like a cockroach and wheezing
from the struggle and his own fear. Wilkes caught
hold of the other man's arm and felt the panic
shivering through Burl's body as he tried to

wrench free. He did momentarily, the knife slashing down again, this time Wilkes blocking Burl with his own forearm, droplets of blood from his wounded wrist speckling the air.

Burl stood then hesitated, his chest heaving, sweat dripping down his face, and his eyes looking wildly from the bed to the door. He turned to run, but instead of letting go, Wilkes grabbed at the man's legs, bringing him down hard and hearing a low moan muffled by the fall. Wilkes hovered on his knees over his attacker, ready to grab the knife when Burl got up, but the other man didn't rise . . . didn't move. Instead, the carpet on either side of his belly began to darken and grow wet. Wilkes watched the blood ooze, then fighting back his own light-headedness, he turned over the body.

The blade had been driven to the hilt up through the abdomen, as if Burl had committed hara-kiri. His hands trembling violently, Wilkes felt for the pulse that was no longer there. Burl's eyes were open, his lips parted almost into a smile, as if it were all a joke.

Wilkes drew away from the corpse, scooted back onto the bed, and leaned against the headboard, folding his arms tightly to stop the shivering. He stared dumbly at his wrist. The wound still didn't hurt, but finally he took out a handkerchief and bound it tightly. He forced himself to think about the case . . . the case. How did Burl get in, what was he doing here—waiting for Collinsby or looking for something? Wilkes tried to think. The drawers had been opened; if Burl had been looking for something, what? Wilkes knew Lester Collinsby well enough to realize if the man had been doing something wrong, he'd hide it well. That's the way he was as a kid. Wilkes glanced at the girlie magazine and remembered what Lester had always done as a boy with those magazines. Not stuff them under the mattress— that was too obvious—but slit an opening into the box springs and hid them there, keeping the opening shut with a piece of electrical tape.

Wilkes swung his legs over the bed and, looking down, his eyes locked on the dead man's face. No longer grinning, Burl's lips were slack and rubbery as a bass that had flopped onto a boat. Easier to think of him as a gutted fish. Or a cold-blooded killer who probably helped murder Nguyen Thi Nhi and Top o' the Evenin'. This is what the State of Virginia did to murderers. Wasn't an executioner an officer of the court just as was an Assistant Commonwealth's Attorney? Wilkes felt dizzy again, took deep breaths until the fire behind his eyes cooled and his head cleared. No—better to think of the dead man as a gutted fish.

Looking at his shoes, Wilkes dropped to the floor, brushed aside the blanket, and slid underneath the bed. He ran his fingers in concentric circles toward the center, until one hand touched something smooth, a piece of tape. Carefully tearing away the strip, he reached in and removed two manila folders, one thin and the other very thick.

He placed each folder gently on top of the bed. The thin one looked new and was labeled BASE-HART. Opening the folder Wilkes found a copy of the police report of Nguyen Thi Nhi's death, Basehart's previous arrest record, notes of Basehart's hearing, and a list of phone numbers, two of which he recognized—the Commonwealth's Attorney's Office and Rosen's hotel. There was nothing extraordinary about the file; it was what any defense attorney would have gathered. Why had Collinsby hidden it so carefully?

Wilkes turned his attention to the other folder, creased and torn, across which was written DICK-ERSON. It contained nearly one hundred sheets of paper, records covering cases over the past six years. The defendants were petty offenders accused of disturbing the peace, vandalism, assault and battery, and burglary. Burl was included; three years before, Collinsby had defended him for breaking the windows of a Vietnamese storekeeper in the Paddy. Pelham and Rupert were mentioned for similar offenses. Wilkes wondered if other defendants listed in the file were also members of G.U.N. Collinsby had given each case an account number beside which was an amount, generally between five and ten thousand dollars. On the folder's inside back cover, a stapled sheet listed all the account numbers in chronological sequence, fourteen in all, which totaled slightly over one hundred thousand dollars. There was also a shorter list, beginning six years ago, noted as "Yearly Retainer." The sum had begun as $5,000 and was now $10,000. That made the grand total $141,000, all for defending a few petty hoodlums.

Studying the material more closely, Wilkes noticed that all the victims of these crimes were Vietnamese living in the Paddy. Nowhere in the files did he find the name written on the tab of the folder, Dickerson. In one of the headboard cubbyholes was the local phone directory. Wilkes opened it to the "D"'s and found the name of State Senator Dickerson. It was ridiculous to think . . . He checked the phone number against the list of numbers in the Basehart file and came up with a match. So, Senator Dickerson had paid over $140,000 to provide for the defense of an organization of racial bigots.

Wilkes tried to recall the Senator; they had met briefly at some official gatherings. Dickerson cut an elegant figure, patrician in the manner he greeted and dismissed people, like one of the great colonial leaders whose portraits adorned the walls of the statehouse. They had conversed once . . . something about a bill delaying farm foreclosures. The discussion had turned to Jefferson, and Dickerson said something about the great man being naive, speaking as if Jefferson was a contemporary political rival. Wilkes had found the Senator's ego amusing. He no longer thought it funny.

Returning the papers to their respective folders, Wilkes carefully placed them together. Obtained without a search warrant, the material probably could not be used as evidence, but he refused to seal the folders back into the box springs as if they had never been discovered. He had to see Dickerson immediately.

The Senator's number in the directory was that of his headquarters; his home phone was unlisted. Wilkes checked his own pocket directory (he remembered writing it down once—as Edgar Simpson had said, the Senator was a good man to know) and dialed the number.

"Good afternoon, Senator Dickerson's residence." The voice was young and female.

"This is the Commonwealth's Attorney's Office. Is the Senator in?"

" 'Fraid not. He's been over at his yacht since this morning. Don't know when he'll be back. Can I take a message?"

"No, no message."

Wilkes hung up, lifted the phone again, and, index finger wavering, began to dial the police, when he slammed down the receiver. Crossing to

the window, he opened a small crack in the blinds
and watched mothers gather their children as the
first raindrops splattered upon the sidewalk.
Down the street that old Ford was still parked
with the large arm resting outside the car window. If Canary was the man watching Collinsby's
apartment, Wilkes need only signal him to come
up and take over the investigation. After all, they
were on the same side, weren't they? But, still,
why was the policeman out there? Burl had gotten into the apartment somehow. The police had
passkeys. What if Canary had come with Burl
and . . . ? Wilkes closed the blinds. If a state senator was involved, anyone could be.

Returning to the bed, Wilkes called Rosen's hotel room but received no answer. He dialed his
own office, getting his secretary Martha.

"Has Mr. Rosen called and left a message?"

"No, no calls. Mr. Simpson was looking for you
earlier this afternoon. He wants to see you as soon
as you get in. He's out of the office now. And
Murray Saunders has been hopping like a jaybird
between his secretary's desk and mine. He's
watching me right now."

Wilkes thought for a moment. "Leave a message for Mr. Simpson. Tell him I'm going over to
Senator Dickerson's yacht."

He heard her scribbling. "All right," Martha
said, "I'll give this to his secretary. Is that all?"

Wilkes checked his watch. "It's nearly four. I
want you to leave the office now, and if anyone
asks why you're quitting early, make up some excuse. Say you've already cleared it with me."

"Jimmy, are you all right?"

"I want you to drive to that burger joint on the
edge of town by St. Vincent's Hospital. Where
your son used to work."

"What's wrong? Will you please tell me what's wrong?"

"I'll meet you there in twenty minutes. And don't tell anyone, I mean anyone, where you're going."

He peeked out the window and saw through the drizzle that the car was still there. Unbuttoning his shirt for a moment, he slipped in the two folders, tucking them securely under his belt, returned the phonebook to the headboard, and smoothed the bedspread, the entire time avoiding the corpse on the carpet. After stopping in the bathroom to dress his wound and wash the back of his neck with cold water, Wilkes left the apartment, closing the door behind him.

The janitor was standing nearby beside his ladder. "You were in there for a long time. Too bad Mr. Collinsby never showed up."

Wilkes swallowed hard and steadied himself. "You didn't see him leave this morning, did you?"

"No, I was cleaning a drain that backed up on the second floor. Never saw such a greasy ball a' hair."

"Did you see anyone else visit him?"

"No, like I said . . ."

Wilkes rode the elevator to the lobby but, instead of leaving through the front entrance, took the back stairs to an alley where the garbage was picked up. Weaving his way through the dumpsters, he looked over his shoulder to make sure he wasn't being followed, crossed the alley, and ran through the rain to a busy street. From a corner drugstore he phoned for a taxi, and fifteen minutes later he was inside the hamburger stand. While waiting for his secretary, he phoned Rosen's hotel room, but again there was no answer.

A few minutes later, Martha joined him in the booth. Taking out and folding the two files in half, Wilkes stuffed them into her handbag while removing her car keys. He gave her a ten-dollar bill.

"I'm going to borrow your car this evening. Take this for cab fare home."

"What happened to yours?"

"I'll explain later. The information I put into your purse, take it home and hide it. If anything happens to me . . ."

"My God!"

"If anything happens, xerox copies at the public library and mail them anonymously to every newspaper in the state. Say they're from Lester Collinsby's files."

"Jimmy, will you please tell me what's going on? I've never seen you like this before."

He held his breath for a moment before continuing. "And telephone the police—don't give your name. Say there's a man dead in Lester Collinsby's apartment." He watched Martha put a hand over her mouth in horror. "Don't you understand? I've finally got the killer instinct."

Chapter 16

THURSDAY AFTERNOON

Having left Wilkes in the bait and tackle shop, Rosen drove back along the coastline. His rental car sputtered against the wind whiplashing from the ocean, while overhead the gathering clouds brooded like old men. Just before reaching the outskirts of Musket Shoals, he turned onto the narrow road that led to what had been Top o' the Evenin's nightclub.

The building was completely razed. Only a few blackened timbers leaned drunkenly in the wind, that and the sign—a tilting top hat—which someone must have stuck back into the ground. Parking nearby, Rosen walked among the ruins. The long bar had collapsed into a wall of liquor, bottles breaking against one another so that in the intense heat the brown, amber, and white shards were fused like a stained-glass window. Tables and chairs had disintegrated, as had the great piano on the platform; only the ivory teeth remained, grinning wickedly from its grave. All the rest was dust and ash, destroyed as utterly as God once destroyed Sodom and Gomorrah.

No one was around, but a quarter mile beyond the nightclub stood a shantytown of about a dozen shacks. Rosen walked across the field to where three naked black children were playing in a stream.

"Your mother or father home?" he asked.

The eldest one, a boy of about five, pointed to the second shack. "My daddy's workin'. Momma's home. You from the police?"

"Thanks," he said smiling and walked up to where the boy had pointed.

Before Rosen could knock, the door was opened by a barefoot woman in a tattered dress. She looked him up and down. "You from the police?"

"No. I guess you must've got a lot of them out here because of the fire and shooting."

"You with the newspapers?"

"No. Actually I'm looking for Lu, the woman who sang in Top o' the Evenin's nightclub."

"Top's wife. What you want with her?"

"I'm a lawyer. I need to ask her a few questions, that's all. I mean her no harm."

"She been through a lot. Don't need no more grief."

"I promise you, I only mean to help her."

The woman stared at him. "Well, you probably find out where she live anyway. Go back to the highway 'n take it to the end by the ocean, only 'bout a mile or two down. Turn left. She in a white house with green trim, got a picket fence all 'round it."

"Thanks very much."

"Don't you be botherin' her with too many questions. She been through a lot."

"I won't. You seem very fond of Lu."

"Yeah," the woman said, her right arm akimbo. "She 'n Top been mighty good to all us folk. My Huddie used to work at the club helpin' tend bar 'n such—good tips. I know this here don't look like much, but we was savin' somethin' for the first time ever, enough maybe to buy us a little house. Now my Huddie's lucky he can get a job cleanin' out the McDonald's. Yeah, Top was the best. He was even promisin' Huddie 'n the others a nice bonus.''

"I'd like to have had him for a boss," Rosen said grinning. "Did Top say why he was giving out bonuses?"

"Ah, Top was always doin' nice things like that." She was also smiling.

"Any special reason this time?"

"Somethin' 'bout havin' some white fella by the . . ." Her smile suddenly vanished. "Say, why you want to know this?"

Rosen shrugged. "Guess that's what being a lawyer's all about—asking questions. Thank you." He returned to the car, glancing back once before he got in. The woman was still staring at him.

Driving down the highway until it ended, he turned onto the road paralleling the ocean; a cool breeze pattered against his face. The view was stunning, the threat of rain darkening the sky to crimson and making the sun's rays cut like daggers through thickening clouds. So absorbed in the sky, he almost missed the house but saw the picket fence in time and turned through an open gate into the driveway, pulling up beside a row of daisies.

The house was really a cottage, one of dozens along the shoreline, most of which were retirement homes or rental property. Like the others, Lu's home was well-maintained, the trim freshly painted and the lawn immaculate with flowers bordering the fence. Rosen approached the front door, knocked several times but got no answer. He was about to return to his car, when he heard singing from the backyard. No mistaking Lu's voice, as she half-sang, half-hummed "Mean to Me."

There was a small vegetable garden in a far corner of the backyard, where she was kneeling with a hand spade, her back to him, working the dirt between two rows of tomato plants. She was wearing an old housecoat with a bright blue floral pattern and a blue scarf wrapped tightly around her head. Beside her sat a little girl who bore a striking resemblance to Top o' the Evenin', her head a bit large and her eyes dark and piercing. As the girl tugged on her mother's housecoat, Lu turned and smiled.

She wiped her hands and walked to him, the girl clinging to her skirt. "Hello, Mr. Rosen, nice to see you. This here's my daughter Becky. Child, say hello to Mr. Rosen." The girl turned her face away.

Rosen laughed. "That's my usual effect upon women. She's very pretty."

"Thank you. She take after my Top. Yeah, every time I look at her . . . Wish you could meet my boy Henry, but he's in school. C'mon inside. I'll fix us some lemonade."

"I don't want to take you from your gardening."

"It ain't going nowhere." She looked at the sky. "Besides, seem like it be raining any minute now. Just let me go inside for a minute to clean the place up." She went through the back door, her daughter scurrying after, never letting go of the robe.

Rosen wandered to the garden, kneeling to examine the rows of tomatoes, beans, and squash. His ex-wife lived in the suburbs now and had a garden; she was always offering him zucchini the size of bass violins whenever he visited Sarah. One of his favorite photos was of him with Sarah in the garden bending over the lettuce and acting as if he really knew what he was doing. He remembered that day and the good feeling of working with the earth. The feeling of roots.

"C'mon in!" Lu called from the doorway. After he walked inside, she added, "Sit yourself down. Nice cold glass a' lemonade on the table."

Her kitchen was clean and tidy, except for the dishes in the sink, probably from lunch. Rosen noticed two coffee cups among the plates.

"I hope I'm not disturbing you," he said.

"No, we could use the company. Becky 'n me been working all day. Ain't that right, child."

The little girl sat across the table, her mouth on the lemonade but her eyes staring up at him. Lu sat down heavily between them. "Whew! Guess I didn't know how tired I be. This is nice, ain't it." She drank deeply.

"No one came by at all today?"

Lu shook her head. "Tonight I'm expecting a houseful . . . the wake." She looked away.

"You have a beautiful home," Rosen said. "I've always dreamed of owning a cottage by the ocean just like this. I noticed there were a few houses in the neighborhood for sale. Would you mind if I took a walk through your place, just to get an idea of the general layout?"

Becky's eyes grew wider, and she looked up at her mother, who replied, "Why, Mr. Rosen, I'm ashamed to say that, even with family coming to town for the funeral, I ain't had the will to really clean the place up. It's not fit for company, and I don't feel right showing it. But you come back another time 'n I'll give you a real king's tour. How's that?"

"Sure. I didn't mean to inconvenience you." He watched the little girl stare into her lap, then asked Lu, "How have you been getting on?"

Her heavy shoulders shrugged.

"That's a stupid question. I'm sorry."

"No, no." She smiled. "I appreciate your concern. It's just . . . Top was always saying things like, 'if something should happen to me,' or 'when I die,' kinda preparing me for this. We had the house paid off last year—took almost every cent we had—cause he didn't want me 'n the kids to worry 'bout a place to live. He even had a life insurance policy I didn't know about. That was Top. Lots a' people had the wrong idea 'bout him—thought he liked to drink 'n run around. That's 'cause he liked to tease folks, but he was just having his fun. Top was as big a family man as you'd ever meet."

"You're all right then financially?"

"Like I said, the life insurance policy will sure help out. Maybe I'll be going back to work. One a' our old customer's a booking agent. Say he could get me some work in Richmond 'n Charlottesville. My sister'd stay with the children. Hate to leave them 'n my garden, but a woman's got to earn her keep. You know how it is. Besides, Top always say I should be singing in the big time. He always knew best. Always."

The three of them drank their lemonade, the little girl continually glancing at Rosen, looking away as soon as their eyes met.

"Lu, last night you and I had a brief conversation about a phone call you overheard—Top saying he was going to make some big money. Do you remember that?"

"Becky, best you go outside now," Lu said.

Reluctantly the little girl finished her lemonade, slipped from her chair, and walked from the house.

"Mr. Rosen," Lu said after her daughter had

losed the door, "I don't remember much a' anyhing about last night."

"Of course. What you said was . . ."

She held up her hands. "I don't remember othing 'bout no telephone call."

"Then why did you send your daughter from he room?"

She smiled. "If I ever get in trouble, sure do vant you for my lawyer."

Rosen rattled the ice in his glass. "About that elephone call." When she did not answer, he ersisted, "I told you before, if we're ever to discover the truth about your husband's death, ou're going to have to confide in me."

Her smile faded. "Why you here, Mr. Rosen? Vhy you really here?"

"I think you know. In fact, I think you know a ot of things that might help clear up this whole ness—Top's death, Nguyen Thi Nhi's murder, nd a lot of disappearances."

"Disappearances?"

"First the Nguyen brother Van, who's been issing since his sister's death, then Basehart— o one knows where he's gone since he was reased on bail. And now your cousin, Lester."

"Les . . . ter?"

"He's not at home, and his secretary doesn't now where he is. I think he's hiding. I'm not ure why, but if he's involved in any of this, it's robably a good idea. They're bad people—two urders and they almost beat me to death. Who nows what's happened to Van and Basehart?"

"You . . . you don't think Basehart did all is?"

Rosen shook his head and shifted back in his hair. "Basehart's just a fly stuck on some flypaer. We all know that—you, me, and Lester. It's the spider I'm after. I wish you'd trust me, Lu. I feel partly responsible for Top's death. I'd like to help Lester too, because I think he's caught between the police and the murderer—a rock and a hard place. I'm sorry for both of you."

He started to get up, when Lu grabbed his wrist. "You hold on now 'n give me a minute. Got to go into the bedroom. Be right back."

She walked through the kitchen's swinging doors, and while pouring another lemonade Rosen thought he heard two voices in another part of the house. Checking his watch—it was just after three, he was about to call Wilkes. Before he could phone, Lu returned and nodded.

They sat quietly and waited. There was a certainty in Lu's manner—she was so still—the way a parent acts when calling a child to account for some wrongdoing. A minute later Rosen heard a man walking through the house, the alternating light-heavy steps of someone who has a bad leg.

Collinsby sat wearily in Becky's chair, his eyes staring into the table. He looked terrible—hair tousled, shirt wrinkled and stained with sweat, and the breath whistling in and out of his lungs.

Rosen waited for the other man to gain his composure, but instead Collinsby began to tremble and wring his hands.

"Lester," Rosen said softly, touching his shoulder. "Lester."

Collinsby slowly raised his head, his red eyes squinting behind a series of dark circles. Rosen smelled liquor on his breath.

"Lester?"

Lu took Collinsby's hand. "Go 'head, Lester. You got to tell somebody. Maybe Mr. Rosen can help."

Collinsby licked his lips then shook his head.

'Too late. Nobody can help me now. It's too late. 'm done for. I tell you, I'm done for.''

"Just like Nguyen Thi Nhi?" Rosen asked.

"Yeah, just like her, I guess. Look"—he seized Rosen by the lapels—"maybe I could get out of own for a few weeks. Lu's got family in Charleson I can stay with.''

Removing the man's hands, Rosen said, "You an't run away forever. You've got to come home ometime.''

Collinsby lapsed into silence.

Rosen spoke softly. "Lester, you know the story n the Bible about Jonah? God ordered him to reach His word, but Jonah felt inadequate so he ried running away. What happened—he was wallowed by the whale. Guess that goes to show ou can't really run away. Like Jonah, you've een called to speak the truth, and that's something you've got to do. What happened?''

Collinsby raised his hands helplessly.

Rosen said, "Why don't we start with you ropping off Billy Lee Pelham at the bait and ackle shop this morning, so that he could pack o leave town. What's your connection with im?''

Crinkling his brow, Collinsby shook his head. 'I don't know what you're talking about, Nate. 've been here since early this morning.''

"If you're going to lie . . .''

"I swear I'm telling the truth. Ask Lu.''

She nodded solemnly.

Rosen said, "The waitress in the diner across rom the bait and tackle shop saw a red Jaguar arked in Basehart's driveway this morning. Vhere's your car?''

"One of Lu's friends is repainting it another olor, one that's not so easy to notice. Besides,''—

he said the next words through clenched teeth—
"I'm beginning to hate the color red."

"This isn't a very big town, and the only other
red Jaguar I can think of belongs to that charmer
we met on the boat, Junior Dickerson."

Biting his lip, Collinsby looked down at the table.

"Go on, Lester, tell him," Lu said.

He sighed deeply. "All right. I'll tell what I
know, Nate, but you got to believe me that I don't
know everything."

"Do you know who killed Nguyen Thi Nhi?"

"No. Not for sure that is, but I have a pretty
good idea." He paused to look around the room.
"It might've been Junior. Like I said, I don't know
for sure . . ."

"Wouldn't put it past him," Lu said. "Wouldn't
put anything past that boy. When the Lord
wanted to make something wicked, He mixed up
all the evil He could find 'n came up with Junior
Dickerson. Never saw him do a thing that wasn't
low-down 'n hurt somebody."

"Sounds as if you knew him pretty well," Rosen said.

"Not 'cause I wanted to. He 'n Top used to do
business pretty regular down at the club."

"Drugs?"

She nodded. "Not that I liked it, but I ain't
talkin' down Top now. He always said it was hard
enough for a black man to earn any kind a' dollar,
he didn't have the luxury to care if it was clean
or dirty. And every penny a' that money went for
the business or the children."

"So your husband supplied Junior with drugs.
Where did Top get the stuff?"

"Some from a friend he knew in Baltimore."

"Not from the gangs in D.C.?"

"No, he never wanted to fool with them. Too dangerous. That part don't matter anyway. Most he got through that Vietnamese, the dead woman's brother."

"Nguyen Van Van?"

"Yeah. That Van—he a real match for Junior. Like two rotten peas in a pod, one more slimy than the other. All started 'bout three years ago. Junior come into the club with one a' his tramps and began ordering everybody 'round like he was a king. He tells Top that anybody that black oughta have some joints around. So Top had him tossed out. Two days later a couple guys beat Top bad, cracked two ribs."

"Sounds familiar," Rosen said.

"One a' Junior's favorite games. That next week Junior come back, go into the back room with Top 'n buy some joints. Put in a bigger order for the next week. Like a kid, the more Junior got, the more he want. Guess the boy started dealing the stuff to his friends. Next it was heroin 'n then cocaine. Top was scared, Mr. Rosen, he done time before and if he got caught dealing drugs. . . . He told Junior 'n the boy just laughed. Said better Top be in jail than dead. Junior said not to worry, that his old man the Senator had fixed it with the cops, that he had a big cop in his pocket. So what was Top . . . ?"

"Did Junior ever say who this cop was?"

Lu shook her head. "That boy appeared to own everybody 'n everything."

"Do you know, Lester?"

"No, but I don't doubt it. I handled cases for some of Senator Dickerson's roughnecks, and there was always evidence against these men disappearing from the police property room. It was just a little too convenient."

"Well, that where Van come in," Lu said. "He had it all, like he was a walking drugstore. He'd come in all the time, listening to the music 'n joking with Top. That's where Top used to get his joints."

"What was Van's source?"

She shrugged. "Said he had his own sources, his 'soul brothers' back where his family come from. Wherever it was, he sure could get everything anybody wanted."

"So Top would use Van as a supplier for Junior."

"Yeah. After awhile Top figgered the best way to get himself out was to bring those two together. That was a night—having two snakes under the same roof."

"About how long ago was it?"

She tilted back her head for a moment. "Must be 'bout two years ago. It was in that corner booth, near where the piano used to be, so I heard most a' what went on, 'n what I didn't hear Top told me later. Junior was bragging 'bout what a big shot his daddy was, how he owned this 'n that—talking 'bout owning not just things but people. Talked 'bout all them things his daddy bought him, like a new red sports car every year. Oh yeah, he really love that color red."

Collinsby struck his fist against the table.

Lu continued, "Van just sat there 'n smiled like a cat who just swallowed the mouse. Real smooth, that one—all sugar 'n honey. Said he could get Junior anything he wanted—not just drugs but women too. Junior said he was tired a' white and black women, wanted something else. You know what Van went and did—Lord help me but this is the truth—Van said he could get any Slant . . . *he* used that word . . . any Slant woman Junior wanted. Then Junior, like he was testing him, asked if Van had a sister. Van smiled back nice as you please and said sure, that she was real pretty too. Then they shook hands 'n left the club together.''

"Van's sister, Nhi?" Rosen asked.

"Uh huh—thought that might interest you. I read in the paper they found some heroin in her room. Like I said before, wouldn't surprise me one bit to find out that Junior killed that woman.''

Rosen shifted back in his chair. "I'd like to believe it, knowing what a lovely boy Junior is, but why would he do it? What's his motive?''

"Why do a hunter shoot a deer? 'Cause he like to.''

Rosen thought for a moment then shook his head. "Tell me about the phone call you overheard—the one in which Top mentioned G.U.N.''

"Like I told you before, don't rightly know what it was all about. It was after you asked Top to look for Van I begged him not to get mixed up in all this. He told me not to worry, that he already knew the answer, that Teddy John told him the day after the murder.''

"Who's Teddy John?''

"He work down at the yacht club. Takes care a' the boats. I know what you thinking—you wanna talk with him—but you can just forget it. Day after Top died, Teddy John sent some flowers with a note saying he was leaving town for good. Probably in Texas by now.''

"What did he tell Top?''

"Something he saw the night a' the murder. Top wouldn't tell me what, said the less I knew the better off I'd be. All he said was that he was gonna fix it so's we'd be on easy street the rest a' our lives.'' She looked at Collinsby for a moment.

"I think he was talking to Junior Dickerson. Don't know anyone 'round here who he could try to tap for that much money."

Rosen asked, "Did either of you know that, on the afternoon of his death, Top sent his bartender to see me?"

They glanced at one another then shook their heads.

"Big Ben told me some story about Van being involved in a gang war with drug dealers from D.C. and that caused his sister's death. It was all made up to keep me from digging into Top's scheme to blackmail Dickerson."

Collinsby trembled. "If Junior ever found out that Top was talking to you . . ."

"Maybe Junior does know. He interrupted my conversation with Big Ben. He probably knew everything. Got Big Ben so angry, he almost threw Junior out the window. Do you think he had Top killed?"

Hesitating, the other lawyer suddenly snapped, "Yeah, I think he had Top killed."

"Do you have any proof?"

"Like Lu said, just knowing Junior is proof enough. He's the connection, the link between drugs and G.U.N. That's why it's no surprise that Rupert and probably Billy Lee Pelham killed Top. You see, the Guardians of an Undefiled Nation are nothing more than Senator Dickerson's private army. Their whole purpose isn't just random violence against the blacks and Vietnamese. It's all planned very carefully to keep everyone in line."

"You're saying it's political."

Collinsby nodded. "Twenty-five years ago when Dick Dickerson first started out, there weren't any problems. Musket Shoals was about half white and half black. Lot of white folks owed his daddy, an ex-mayor, favors and the blacks just kept quiet and did what they were told. Dickerson went on to become State Senator and a mighty big man around here. He bought a lot of people." Collinsby stopped, licking his lips, and poured a glass of lemonade.

Rosen said, "I'm surprised he never tried for anything more, like Governor or U.S. Senator."

"That's what he'd like to have done, but he was smart enough to know if he ever went for something that big, his finances would never stand public scrutiny. Instead he made Musket Shoals kind of his personal kingdom."

"So G.U.N. became a means of protecting his kingdom."

Collinsby nodded again. "You see, things began to change. The civil rights protests in the Sixties got a lot of black folks registered to vote for the first time. There was even talk of running a black candidate to oppose Dickerson, but the man's car was firebombed and he was killed. Police said it was probably the Klan, but no one ever found out the truth. Things quieted down a lot after that. But now with the Vietnamese moving in, the whites make up a minority of the population. It may not be too long before the blacks, the Vietnamese, and those whites who can't stomach Dickerson get together and kick him out of office. Once that happens and they begin to look into his finances, he'll be on his way to jail, or worse."

"That's where the Guardians of an Undefiled Nation come in."

"Yeah. He's been using them for the past few years to keep the Vietnamese in line. They're new, so he figures they're the easiest ones to scare. He gets the votes of those who've become citizens and 'voluntary contributions' from those who own businesses down in the Paddy. The G.U.N. members do all the collecting and take care of any 'disagreements.' I'm on the payroll too. Dickerson hired me a few years ago to defend any of those G.U.N. creeps caught vandalizing or roughing up a Vietnamese. Paid me well to keep my connection with him quiet. Even gave me Junior's cast-off sports car, like I was a beggar.''

Rosen shook his head.

"What's the matter!" Collinsby demanded. "Don't you believe me?"

"Sure. That explains the ledger sheets I found at the bait and tackle shop. It's just that I'm disappointed in Edison Basehart. I thought he was a bucket of scum but at least one with principles. To find out he's just a cheap thug. . . .''

"No, no.'' Collinsby shook his head. "Basehart wasn't in on any of this. He's been blind as a bat all these years. Thought he was running the last stand for America, when behind his back Pelham's been taking orders from Dickerson.''

"He's been duped all these years?''

Collinsby looked down at the table. "Guess a lot of us believe what we want to believe, like me thinking I was just defending some penny-ante offenders who had a right to a lawyer like anybody else.''

"You said you don't think Basehart killed Nguyen Thi Nhi.''

"When Dickerson called me to take the case, he said to make sure Basehart was convicted. I think Junior shot the woman while looking for Van. Van probably shortchanged him on a drug deal, and Junior came after him. If you find Van, I bet that's what he'll tell you. If Junior and his boys didn't already find him.''

"And so they framed Basehart. Pretty neat."

"Yeah. It got Junior off the hook and put Pelham in charge of G.U.N. I don't think he liked always going behind Basehart's back—got too complicated."

Pushing his chair from the table, Rosen stood.

"Where're you going?" Collinsby asked anxiously.

"To the yacht club. If this Teddy John saw something, maybe someone else did as well."

Collinsby's voice trembled. "You're not gonna tell anybody where I'm hiding, are you? If Dickerson or Junior finds out where I am, I'll be next, sure as the sun rises."

Rosen remembered his Talmud. " 'Shall I say: throw a stone at the one who has fallen?' " He stood at the doorway. "One last thing. This top cop you mentioned—the one who fixed everything for Dickerson. Sure you don't know who he is?"

Collinsby shook his head. "But he's got to be pretty important. I'd be careful about calling the police, if I was you."

"Sure."

Lu and Collinsby holding hands warmed him, and the Talmud came to mind once more, that deeds of loving-kindness are equal to all the commandments of the Torah. However, opening the door he thought of his destination—Dickerson and Junior—and braced himself as if the wind through the doorway had blown from the damp cold netherworld where Nguyen Thi Nhi and God knows how many other of their victims wandered restlessly, waiting for justice to be done.

Chapter 17

THURSDAY EVENING

As Wilkes drove along the shoreline, droplets of rain grew into a steady patter upon the windshield. Although only late afternoon the sky had darkened as more clouds, thick and smokestack-gray, rolled inland, reminding him of the day he was assigned to the murder case. Not even two weeks had passed, yet long enough to leave one life behind, as a snake crawls out of its skin then curiously gazes at what once protected it. He had seen Death lying in its crimson pool, more real than anything he had ever known, terrifying and exciting him. Office politics and the constant haggling with corporations seemed as insignificant as the broken coffee grinder at home, for today he was looking for a murderer. Today he would do simple justice.

His secretary's car began the long private lane leading to the Tyler Yacht Club. Black pavement ahead shone smooth and hard, and the trees on either side were groomed so precisely into a bower they appeared artificial. Only the ocean was real, the tide beginning its evening ritual of return, lapping the shoreline below him, as Wilkes drove the last ribbon of road that dipped toward the clubhouse.

Stopping directly in front of the building, he rolled down his window and beckoned to the doorman who huddled under a narrow canopy. Reluctantly the man ran to the car.

"Yes, sir, can I help you?" he asked, turning up his collar.

"Is Senator Dickerson inside?"

"He was here for lunch but left about three. He was dressed for sailing. You might try the docks."

Wilkes continued to the parking lot and pulled into an open space. There was something familiar about one of the parked cars he had just passed, a Dodge with a dented fender; walking back he recognized it as the rental Rosen was using. It was locked, Rosen's briefcase lying closed on the passenger side of the front seat. Leaving the car, Wilkes splashed across a few shallow puddles and hurried up the steps of the clubhouse.

He walked through the restaurant to the bar but didn't see the other attorney. Sitting on a stool, he ordered a sherry to take away the dampness and described Rosen to the bartender.

"Matter of fact," the bartender replied, "somebody come in a half hour ago who looked like the man you're talking about. He asked about Senator Dickerson and his son."

"What did you tell him?"

"Hadn't seen the Senator since before lunch. I suggested he go down to the harbormaster's office and ask there."

Wilkes still felt chilled but realized it wasn't only from the weather. He glanced at the well-dressed "patrons"—civilized men who seemed so uncivilized to him now, like gorillas wearing cravats. Like Dickerson.

Wilkes stepped into the rain and scooted down the slick sidewalk to the marina and a small blockhouse with a shingle reading, "Ye Old Harbor Master, Terence Monroe, Esq." Pushing open the door, he nearly bumped into a massive wooden desk cluttered with charts and official forms. Sitting in a captain's chair was a stout middle-aged man, red beard salted with gray, whose huge forearms moved crablike over the papers.

"Mr. Monroe?" Wilkes asked.

The harbormaster squinted up at him and shook his head. "Monroe died over ten years ago. Nobody bothered to change the sign. I'm Hugh Douglas. What can I do for you, Mr. . . ?"

"Wilkes. I'm with the Commonwealth's Attorney's office. I need to speak with Senator Dickerson. Do you know if he's down here right now?"

Douglas craned his neck to check the clock on the wall, then scraped away a few of the papers until he lifted one between his two hands. "The Senator notified me he's going out at six for an evening cruise—very romantic at that time with the sun setting. Yeah, he's a big one for setting suns. Of course, with this rain he may change his mind. There's no danger, mind you, but with the rain and clouds—well, not much of a mood." He winked. "Know what I mean?"

"Then Senator Dickerson should be on board his yacht making ready to leave."

"Unless he changed his mind. It's the *Richard III*, second boat down."

"Has anyone else been asking about the Senator?"

Douglas shook his head.

"Seen any strangers this afternoon?"

The harbormaster sifted his hands through the piles of papers. "Been inside most of the day. Got to catch up with this week's paperwork."

"I see. Thanks for your help." Wilkes was about to leave, when a thought struck him. "Can club

members take their boats out anytime they want—
in the middle of the night, for example.''

"When you're rich, you can do anything you
damn well please. As long as the weather's all
right and you notify this office when you're leaving and where you're going.''

Wilkes gave Douglas the date of Nguyen Thi
Nhi's murder. "I'm interested in the hours between midnight and six A.M. Did Senator Dickerson go out at that time?''

"Let's take a look-see.'' Opening a drawer from
the cabinet behind him, Douglas thumbed
through the files. "My assistant's on duty during
the graveyard shift, but he would've logged any
departures. Ah, here's Dickerson.'' He opened
the file and placed it on his desk. Flipping back a
few pages he stopped abruptly and gave a short
laugh.

"Find something?'' Wilkes asked.

"Might've known it.'' Douglas lifted the sheet
of paper. "It's half filled out. No departure information. Only a return time—three fifty-four A.M.''

"You were laughing.''

The harbormaster smiled. "Don't mind that.
Just a kind of in-joke here at the club. See, the
form's signed by Richard Dickerson II.''

"His son?''

"Yeah. Actually he lives on the yacht and kind
of comes and goes as he pleases. Junior's not the
type to care much about forms. Half the time he
takes off without telling us. All we can do is clock
the time he arrives. Like this.''

"Nothing unusual about the trip?''

Again Douglas smiled. "With Junior Dickerson,
guess you could say the unusual is the usual.
Know what I mean?''

"No, I . . .'' Wilkes hesitated, not wanting to

waste any more time. He simply nodded.
"Thanks for your help."

Despite the weather he walked slowly onto the
pier, past a darkened boat, to Dickerson's yacht,
Richard III. Its deck lights were off, but climbing
halfway up the boarding ramp, Wilkes saw light
leaking through the open cabin doorway. He
walked around the deck, noticed nothing unusual, and approached the door, when suddenly
the boat came alive. A loud clattering as the an-
chor was raised, followed by a deeper rumbling
from below, the engine warming in preparation
for an evening voyage. He hesitated in front of
the cabin, unsure whether to go below, call out
for Dickerson, or leave to notify the police—when
the decision was made for him.

Footsteps coming from below, growing louder
as they climbed the stairs toward him. Wilkes
ducked behind the cabin just as a man emerged
through the doorway and walked quickly to the
ramp. Wearing a red-hooded windbreaker, he released the mooring cables and was about to draw
in the ramp.

Stepping around the cabin to stand between the
man and the doorway, Wilkes shouted through
the patter of rain, "Senator Dickerson!"

The man whipped around and took a step forward. He was not the Senator but much younger
with a face white and smooth as an egg, and his
smile, when it came, was crooked as a crack in
the shell.

Wilkes asked, "You're . . . Senator Dickerson's
son, aren't you?"

The young man blinked once, and his eyes grew
wide. "More company."

"I'd like to speak to your father. I'm James

Wilkes from the Commonwealth's Attorney's Office."

Junior moved toward the cabin. "Go ahead. He's in the second room downstairs." He shouted through the doorway, "Daddy, we got more company!"

Wilkes didn't like turning his back on Junior, but he had to see Dickerson and he had to know what had become of Rosen. Passing the young man, he walked down the passageway.

At the bottom of the stairs was a small dimly lit room containing a bar, its two counters forming a square with the wall. On the countertop Wilkes saw a length of rubber tubing and an empty syringe caught within its folds, while at the opposite wall a half-opened door led to another room, where light shone but there was no sound. "He's in the second room," Junior had said. There it lay just beyond the open doorway and so, glancing at the syringe, Wilkes pushed off the bar and walked through the door.

The sharp light blinded him for an instant until, blinking his eyes, he grew aware of a gun pointed directly at his chest. Senator Dickerson held the weapon, his hand trembling almost as much as his voice. "Anyone else with you?"

Shaking his head Wilkes looked past Dickerson into the room. Its built-in leather cushions bordered four walls cluttered with framed photographs of Dickerson glad-handing state and local politicians. The faces on the walls didn't interest Wilkes, but those below, gathered in the far corner, did. Rosen sat on a cushion, legs drawn up below his chin; his right hand rested on the shoulder of a woman huddled on the floor, her body shivering. She was Vietnamese, and Wilkes was certain he recognized the face, despite deep lines under her eyes and the twitching. She looked at him vacantly, as sick people do, and he realized the syringe in the other room had been for her, that perhaps death was flowing in her veins. The word "death" triggered his memory, for suddenly he saw the resemblance to the murder victim and knew this was her sister, Nguyen Thi Trac.

There was one other. Edison Basehart lay a few feet to Rosen's left, his long frame stretched across six feet of cushion, and his head resting on a wadded towel. Basehart's eyes were fixed upon the ceiling, while on every exhalation he moaned softly like a broken accordion. Only when the head turned slightly did Wilkes see a trickle of blood gleam for a moment before disappearing into the towel. He made a move toward the injured man, only to feel the Senator's gun barrel jammed between his ribs.

Dickerson stepped back, the gun still trembling in his hand. Taking a deep breath he waved the weapon toward Basehart, saying, "Go ahead and join him." Eyeing the Senator, Wilkes sat between Rosen and the injured man, while Dickerson continued, "We've been expecting you . . . Dickie and I. In . . . in fact, when Mr. Rosen came on board, we thought it was you. M . . . My, it's been a busy afternoon, first with Basehart coming after me. That Pelham has a big mouth. Apparently Edison persuaded him to reveal my part in this affair and where I could be located. By the way, how is he . . . Pelham?"

Watching the gun Wilkes replied, "The paramedics took him to the hospital. His condition had stabilized by the time he left the bait and tackle shop. You were expecting me?"

Dickerson said, "Too bad. We may have to deal

with him later. That Pelham . . . a moron. Goes
to show that good help is hard to find. Make
yourself comfortable . . . Jimmy, isn't it? I have a
good memory for names and faces—couldn't have
lasted all these years without one. I knew your
father when you were a little fellow . . . see my
picture up there with him. Last time you and I
met was . . . ah yes . . . last year at Congressman
Howell's fund-raiser. Your wife is a pretty little
blond. See what I mean." He nodded toward the
other attorney. "Mr. Rosen and I met recently, on
this boat as a matter of fact. He was rude to my
son, for which he was taught a lesson in manners
by several of Dickie's friends. With the beating he
took, I thought he'd have packed and scurried
back North. It would've been better for everyone
if he had. Would've saved us all this unpleasant-
ness."

The yacht lurched forward then settled into a
steady motion, while the motor buzzed more
loudly. Wilkes started to stand, when Dickerson's
gun pointed him back to his seat.

"Dickie's taking us on a little ocean cruise. I'm
sure you've wanted to know how the other half
lives. Sit back and enjoy it, at least for the time
being."

Flashing a grin Dickerson sat midway along a
wall perpendicular to the others, crossing his legs
and placing the gun beside him on the cushion.
The farther from shore his yacht moved, the more
relaxed he became, whistling "Alexander's Rag
Time Band" while keeping time with his foot.

Basehart moaned loudly and shifted, so that the
towel tumbled from his head and hung loosely to
the floor, dried blood criss-crossed upon the cloth.
Wilkes gathered the towel, tucking it gently under
Basehart's head.

"Thank you," Dickerson said. "I would've hated for his blood to stain the cushion. It's real leather."

"This man needs a doctor," Wilkes said. "The wound hasn't closed. My God, he could bleed to death!"

Dickerson's grin widened. "Don't worry, he won't bleed to death. He won't have time."

"What do you mean?"

"Trac, tell Dickie that everything's secured here, and ask him to join us as soon as we're far enough at sea." Gazing at the floor, she didn't seem to hear him. "Trac, do as I say. Now!"

Rousing herself, the woman struggled to her feet and swayed unsteadily. She held a handkerchief in one hand, using it repeatedly to dab her wet eyes. She moved a few steps from the wall and said to Dickerson, "It's time, it must be time already."

"Why, how would you know, dear? You don't have a watch, and there's no clock in . . ."

"I know!" She rubbed her arms and wrung the handkerchief between her hands. "Junior promised me another. . . ." She stopped suddenly, glancing at Rosen.

Dickerson finished her sentence. "Another injection. That's between you and Dickie. I never interfere with his little amusements. Now you go and find out how long he'll be. Who knows, maybe he'll have that little surprise for you."

Lowering her head, Trac walked toward the door. As she passed the Senator, he stopped her with his hand and reached under her skirt to caress her legs.

"Lovely," he murmured while stroking her thigh. To the others, "You know, I never had much use for these people. But there is something about their women, a certain childlike submission, a willingness to give anything for a piece of candy." His hand moved between her legs, and she stiffened. "Like Trac here—willing to give anything for the right piece of candy. Isn't that right, dear?"

She stood passively, allowing Dickerson's hand to do what it pleased, until the Senator grew weary of his game. Slapping her on the buttocks as a signal to go, he smiled. "Yes, at least they're good for something." When no one smiled back, he licked his lips. "I'd like a drink. Trac . . ." He turned to see she had already gone. "Seems I'm the bartender today. Either of you gentlemen care for a cocktail? No? Well, I'll be in the next room, and the door is open. Let's all act civilized—just remain where you are. If you'll excuse me for a moment."

Holding the gun stead in his hand, Dickerson walked into the other room, every few moments glancing through the doorway. Wilkes took the opportunity to slide along the cushion, until he was beside Rosen.

Wilkes touched his arm. "Nate." Receiving no response, he repeated the name. Rosen finally turned to stare dumbly at him, and that stare more than anything else terrified Wilkes. Feeling his forehead break into beads of sweat, he swallowed hard and whispered, "Don't worry, Nate, we'll get out of this. For God's sake, the man's a state senator."

Rosen shook his head slowly. "Hitler ruled a nation. Don't you understand? Can't you feel it in the air? I've felt it once before, at the trial of some Klan members accused of blowing up a black church and killing two people. They were guilty, but an all-white jury acquitted them. All of them, jurors and the accused, laughed about the verdict in the courtroom, a few feet away from the families of those who had been murdered, families who had been raised as Christians believing that in the end good overcomes evil. But we know that's not always true, Jimmy. You do feel it, don't you, the clamminess in the air. Just as the mystics described evil . . . the absence of God's light. That's what we're feeling—not just dampness, but the absence of God's light. I can see it on your face, dripping from your forehead."

"And what does it mean," Wilkes hissed, "that we too are supposed to march quietly to the gas chamber? Is that what your God is telling us to do?"

Rosen stared straight ahead. "My God," he whispered, "My God."

"What have they done to the woman?"

His jaw set tightly for a moment, Rosen asked, "How did you know to come here?"

"I went to Lester's apartment, and . . ."

They had no further opportunity to speak, for the Senator returned with a highball in one hand and his gun in the other.

Clinking the ice in his glass, Dickerson took a long drink. "Nothing like a nice pick-me-up. I heard you two muttering while I was at the bar. Go ahead with your conversation, just as if I wasn't here. I want you to be as comfortable as possible until . . . until your voyage is over."

Rosen leaned forward, arms resting on his knees. "Which is going to end sooner than yours, isn't it?"

Dickerson giggled nervously into his drink.

Wilkes said, "Are you mad? You can't simply kill three people in a small town like ours and expect to get away with it. How could you possibly explain it? I mean, our cars are in the parking lot. I spoke to the doorman at the club. I had a conversation with the harbormaster, and he knows I went to your boat looking for you."

"Yacht," Dickerson said. "Never call a yacht a boat. That's like referring to a Cadillac as a jalopy. As for your question—am I mad? Of course not. A madman is a radical, wanting this or that and acting irrationally if he can't have it. On the contrary, I've always been a conservative. I simply wish to keep what I've earned for myself and my son—what every working man wants. When someone threatens to come between me and mine, I act. You can understand that, Jimmy. You're a family man."

"What are you talking about? Look at all the families you've intimidated, even destroyed."

"Such as?"

"We know all about how you've used the Guardians of an Undefiled Nation to abuse the Vietnamese."

"Not just goons like Pelham," Rosen said. "Your own son loves to get his hands dirty . . . another one of his games. Like bombing the grocery store next to the Nguyens to keep the people in the Paddy afraid. To keep them from talking."

The Senator shrugged. "No one was hurt."

"Let's talk about what happened to Nguyen Thi Nhi. She was murdered."

Dickerson stared at Rosen then burst out laughing. He had to wipe tears from his eyes before regaining his composure. "Excuse me, but I'd forgotten all about the Nguyen murder, and now for you to get it . . . how would Dickie put it . . . assbackwards. Yes, it is funny. You see, we had nothing to do with her death. Oh, we knew about it," his eyes twinkled, "almost as soon as the law did."

Wilkes said, "But you're framing Basehart . . ."

"The circumstances surrounding that were . . . serendipitous, you might say. It was time to get him out of the way. Sooner or later even someone as stupid as Basehart would discover what G.U.N. was really being used for and perhaps give us trouble. Besides, by doing the real murderer a favor, Dickie and I guaranteed any future brushes with the law will either be ignored or expedited in our behalf. Haven't you guessed what I mean? Someone who could've walked into the police property room and removed one of the weapons confiscated earlier from G.U.N., a gun that still had Basehart's fingerprints on it. Someone you've been working with very closely."

The Senator was about to continue, when the yacht's engine slowly lost power, the buzzing fading to a low hum before growing silent. Wilkes felt the vessel drifting, gently rocked by the waves. Even Dickerson was affected by the motion, for the gun relaxed slightly in his hand, while his head tilted back to rest against the wall, eyes half-closed. Wilkes thought this might be his best opportunity to grab for the weapon, but shifting his weight to the edge of the cushion, he felt Rosen's hand grip his arm and, turning, saw the other man shake his head.

Rosen whispered, "Listen."

Wilkes heard someone clatter down the stairs, and a few moments later a glass shattered in the adjoining room, followed by Junior swearing angrily. Dickerson's eyes fluttered open. "I'll have the usual, son! Sure I can't get you gentlemen anything?"

Rosen said, "You mean a last drink to go along with a last cigarette."

"I like a man with a sense of humor. Oh, but here they are already."

Trac staggered in, carefully balancing a drink with both hands. Sweat dripped from her forehead, but she blinked the moisture away, not daring to take a hand from the glass. She walked slowly toward Dickerson, her entire being concentrated into her hands and feet.

Dickerson said, "How nice of you, my dear, but I would like it before all the ice melts. Hello, Dickie!"

Junior sauntered into the room, a gun in one hand and drink in the other. He had unzipped the windbreaker halfway, revealing a Redskins T-shirt. Wind and rain had turned his face florid, and a cigarette dangled from his lips.

"How's she doing, Daddy?"

"So far, good enough to be in the circus."

Putting the cigarette out in his glass, Junior took a syringe from his shirt pocket. "I told Trac if she wanted a reward, she couldn't spill a drop."

His smile was so cold that even his father grew nervous asking, "Hadn't we better get on with it? There's still a lot to do tonight. When we return, we have their cars to dispose of."

"Another minute or two won't make any difference."

His father yielded, and so they watched Trac's progress, which only made her more nervous. Finally, tears in her eyes, her hands reached Dickerson's, but as the glass was being exchanged a few drops spilled. She turned wild-eyed to Junior. He slowly shook his head.

"It wasn't my fault!" she sobbed.

He returned the syringe to his pocket. "You

lost. Better luck next time." He lit another cigarette.

"It wasn't my fault, please!"

Dickerson's eyes darted from the prisoners to his son. "*I* spilled the drink. Give her what she wants, and let's get on with it."

Junior approached Trac and his father. "That just wouldn't be right—you know, rules are rules. But maybe if she earned it." He looked at Rosen. "Hey, kike, how do you like your girlfriend now? I know you screwed her. I told her to do it, to keep tabs on you."

Rosen looked at Junior's cigarette; it was dark brown, a Bushnells. "You were in her apartment when I was unconscious. Those were your cigarette butts."

"Yeah, I wanted to see how good a job my friends had done on you. And I wanted to use your face for an ashtray." Junior took Trac by the arm. "How was she anyways? Not much I guess. Only when you get them hopped up on something are they any good. Like now." He looked at Trac. "Why don't you show him what you really can do."

"No, please," she whispered. "The shame."

Junior laughed. "Nothing left for you to be ashamed of." He threw Trac forward. She fell on her knees in front of Rosen, to whom Junior said, "Maybe it ain't a whole last meal, but at least it's an appetizer."

She looked back at Junior for a moment, saw he would not relent, then keeping her eyes downcast, fumbled for Rosen's zipper. Rosen grabbed her hands, twisted them away, and their eyes met. For the first time that evening his face softened, but she backed away, arms tightly pulled across her chest, her body trembling from pain and humiliation. Rosen glared at Junior, who lost his smile while nervously fingering the trigger.

Dickerson stood abruptly. "Time to get on with it." Aiming his gun alternately between Wilkes and Rosen, he said, "The two of you carry Basehart on deck. Go on."

Wilkes checked the injured man's head wound and pulse. "He seems worse. He shouldn't be moved."

A smile crept back onto Junior's face. He took a few steps forward, pointed the gun at the injured man's head, and fired. Basehart's face jerked as if suddenly awakened then fell forward awkwardly, a large hole just above the right eyebrow.

As the gunshot exploded, Wilkes shrunk back terrified. When the bullet's reverberations died away his hand reached timidly toward Basehart's face and came away with blood. Feeling the great cold creeping up his body, he fought against the trauma he was falling into. He thought about his children, about a picnic they had gone to where he had spilled ketchup all over himself. His vision was blurring, and what Junior said at that moment wasn't discernible. He couldn't slip away now.

"What's the matter," Junior was saying, "you don't look so good. Can you make it upstairs, or we gonna have to carry you too?"

With great effort Wilkes stood, propping one hand against the wall while waiting for his head to clear. He was still facing away from the body.

"C'mon!"

Wilkes turned to look at the dead man. Basehart's face was already drained of color, its eyes dull and cold. Rosen had taken hold of the dead man's feet and waited patiently, his face as devoid of expression as the corpse's. Fighting down his queasiness, Wilkes lifted Basehart by the shoulders, but the head fell back to allow a rivulet of blood to collect on the cushion.

"No, no, you're making a mess!" Dickerson shouted. The Senator had gathered several towels, some of which he used to support the dead man's neck. He used the others to mop the cushions and floor. "We can't leave a trace for the police . . ." His voice trailed off, as he grew more absorbed in his task. "Th . . . There. I think that'll do it. What do you think, Dickie?"

"Just dandy," Junior replied. "Let's go."

Junior went first, backing up as he led them through the two rooms and up the stairs. Holding Basehart's feet Rosen came next, also facing the rear, followed by Wilkes cradling the dead man's shoulders, and finally Dickerson, who bent every few steps to wipe the floor of blood. Somewhere behind them was Trac. Wilkes couldn't see her but was sure that was on whom Rosen's eyes were fixed.

Struggling up the stairs Wilkes followed Rosen through the narrow doorway into the darkening twilight. Rain continued to drum upon the deck from a sky devoid of moon or stars. Junior had put his hood back over his head and indicated for the two attorneys to place Basehart's body down next to the railing. Having done so, they moved away to sit against the cabin wall, sheltered from the rain by a low overhang, and watched Dickerson wiping up after them. The Senator looked nervously along the deck for traces of blood, walking back and forth in minced steps.

Junior said, "Get over here, Daddy. The rain'll take care of anything you missed."

Dickerson nodded yet took one final look before

joining his son. A moment later Trac stumbled through the doorway, shivering as the rain swept against her face and, looking from one pair of men to the other, moved reluctantly to Junior's side.

Junior laughed. "What's the matter, Slant, your boyfriend over there not good enough for you anymore? Go ahead and sit with him if you want to."

Trac shook her head and leaned over the railing, her hands sliding back and forth across the smooth cold metal.

Stuffing the gun under his belt, Junior lifted Basehart by one arm until, gaining leverage, he pushed under both arms to balance the body precariously against the railing, its head cocked as if waiting for some question to be answered. After pausing a moment to catch his breath, Junior shoved the corpse over the side. The body barely made a splash as it slid under the water.

Drawing out his gun, Junior looked at the two attorneys. "Next?"

Wilkes shook his head. "How can you possibly hope to get away with this? How can you explain the disappearances of three men?"

Dickerson said, "We won't have to. After all this is finished, Dickie and I will return to the club and, using your keys, he takes your car up Ocean Drive while I follow in mine. We send the car over the cliff into the ocean—it's a dangerous night for driving, so dark and wet and slick. If the police inquire, I just say that you two gentlemen came here to ask some political questions concerning my views on the Guardians of an Undefiled Nation and then left together. A tragic accident."

"And if they find our bodies riddled with bullets?"

Dickerson laughed. "Out here? No, no, the

ocean can keep a secret. Believe me, we know from experience.''

Wilkes leveled his gaze from son to father. ''The night of Nguyen Thi Nhi's murder, you took your boat out. You killed her brother Van and dumped his body into the ocean, just like you did Basehart. Just like you plan to do with us.''

''That's not quite accurate. Van came to us that night badly wounded and frightened half to death, for he had just walked in on his sister's murder and was himself shot running away. Since Dickie and he were business associates of sorts, I suppose he felt we would shield him from the killer. He died of his wounds on board. What could we do without implicating ourselves? So we dumped the body. Somehow that nigger nightclub owner found out and tried to blackmail me. Can you imagine that? I did have him eliminated. But Van—you can't hold us responsible. Even Van's sister understood after we explained it all. Didn't you, Trac? Trac!''

She turned to face them; her brow furrowed trying to remember what he had said. She nodded, begging Junior, ''Give me it now! I can't stand it!''

The Senator continued, ''See what I mean—a totally amoral people. It was her own brother who turned Trac and her sister onto drugs, then sold the women. Trac tried to run away from it all, but she made a mistake. When her sister died, she came back. I guess Dickie's charm was too much for her. And the other one, a little whore too.''

''Why was she killed?'' Wilkes asked.

''For love. Yes, that's right. Because a fool who should've known better wanted her. And now I own that fool for the rest of his life.''

Dickerson fingered his gun and was about to

continue, when Rosen said, "Give it to her, Junior."

Junior squinted through the rain. "Huh?"

"Give Trac her fix, or did you throw that overboard too?"

Dickerson's son took the syringe from his shirt pocket, while Trac moved toward him.

Rosen asked, "Are you going to kill her too?"

Junior looked the woman up and down. "I think she's already dead."

"She's a witness, son," Dickerson warned. "She'd be the only one standing in the way of you succeeding me. The money, the power, the prestige, all for you. Let's not jeopardize . . ."

"She's not gonna be just a witness, Daddy. She's gonna do the job." To Rosen, "Get up, kike. You're next."

Rosen stood and took a step forward. Junior's arm encircled Trac, bringing her body next to his and facing the lawyer. Holding the syringe in front of her, he placed her right hand covered by his on the gun, her finger on the trigger. Trac's eyes were fixed on the syringe.

"Go ahead, honey," Junior cooed, "just pull the trigger and all that sweet sweet shit goes into your arm."

"You never give me . . ." she began to whimper.

"This time for sure, honey. This time for sure."

"That's right, Trac," Rosen said. "Then you can dump me over the side just like Junior did to your brother, and I can join the spirits of Van and your sister walking the earth demanding observance, listening to Van whisper in your ear how your family is lost forever, whispering, 'the shame, the shame.' "

"Go on, honey, go on!"

"The shame."

What happened in the next few seconds Wilkes couldn't quite follow, because of the rain, the darkness, and because of the great void through which he had to squint to see any goodness. What he did see was Trac turning on Junior, her right hand twisting the gun toward him while her left struggled for the syringe. A series of shots were fired, and arms entangled with the weight of Junior's body slumped against her, they fell overboard.

A long moment of silence followed, then Dickerson let out a primordial scream, a howl hurtling itself through the rain until at last dying in the distant wind. He rushed to the railing, leaning over dangerously, peered into the ocean and called his son's name over and over. Rosen was directly behind him; one slight movement of the lawyer's hand would have sent Dickerson into the same black abyss, but instead he moved beside the older man and chanted softly in Hebrew. Rising to his feet, Wilkes walked to the the other side of the Senator and took the gun from his hand as easily as if from a child. Below them the ocean had healed its wound and undulated softly like a sleeper disturbed but for a moment, then once again oblivious. To Dickerson's sobbing, Rosen's chant of mourning, or the spirits of Junior and Trac rising to begin their journey, a journey beyond justice and shame.

Chapter 18

FRIDAY MORNING

All night the rain never quite stopped, the sky glazed gray so that, had Wilkes not known the time was 8:30 A.M., it might as easily have been twilight. He pulled into his reserved spot in front of the county building—the first of his colleagues to arrive—and hurried inside, holding back a sneeze until he passed through the doorway. Blowing his nose gingerly, he took the elevator to the second floor, passing the empty reception area before going into his office. His head throbbed from the cold, lack of sleep, and from the thought of what he had yet to do.

Night had passed slowly with enough events to fill a week. Neither Basehart, Trac, nor Junior surfaced, and Dickerson had collapsed into a state of incoherence, oblivious to everything except the ocean, his eyes searching the water while his hands gripped the railing like talons. Having remained in that condition when the yacht returned to shore, he was placed in custody. Wilkes had not yet formally charged Dickerson with any crime, and the police involved in the Senator's detention were sworn to secrecy. Dropping Rosen at his hotel, Wilkes had driven home to change clothes and catch a few hours' sleep—not even telling his wife what happened—and here he was at the office as on any working day.

Settling back in the chair, he closed his eyes and massaged his temples until the pain deadened; his breathing was slow and deep. The county once hired a psychologist to lecture on stress, and she had suggested a person pretend to be somewhere quiet and peaceful. As was his custom, Wilkes thought of the weathered bust of Jefferson but only became agitated. It was easy to believe in the strength of a republic, as long as it was an ideal shelved in the library between the Revolutionary War and the Constitution. But when the leader became Dickerson, not Jefferson, and his followers not the Minute Men but Pelham's Guardians of an Undefiled Nation—what was left to believe in?

Wilkes heard the doorknob turn. Before opening his eyes he pulled out Dickerson's gun and pointed it at the intruder.

"Jimmy! For God's sake!"

He focused past his throbbing temples and dropped the gun onto the desk. Martha ran to his side.

"Jimmy, what's happened to you? You look half dead. I couldn't sleep all night. I wanted to call you but was afraid of upsetting Ellie. My God, what happened?"

Wilkes ran a hand through his hair, trying to collect his thoughts. "Those files I gave you . . . did you hide them like I asked?"

"In a drawer under my corsets. No one'd ever look there."

"I want you to get them."

"Now?"

"Yes. A couple things first."

"Let me put on some coffee. I think you could use it."

"First I want you to call downstairs to the squad

room. Lt. Canary's scheduled to come on duty at nine o'clock. Leave a message that I want to see him as soon as he comes in. Immediately. Then cancel all my appointments this morning."

She asked, "What about your appointment with Judge Spencer?"

"What?"

"You had a ten o'clock appointment with Judge Spencer to request that Edison Basehart's bail be revoked. Remember how insistent Mr. Simpson was."

He stared past her, seeing Junior throw Basehart's body into the ocean, and struggled to keep the edge from his voice. "Cancel the appointment, and let Mr. Simpson know that I've canceled."

"All right, Jimmy. Anything else?"

"Coffee. Then bring me those files from home. Don't worry, I'm fine. I just have to get through this morning."

She left the door ajar, so that he heard her brew the coffee, telephone his message for Canary, and greet the other secretaries as they came in to work. The coffee smelled good when Martha brought it to him.

"Sure you're all right?" she asked.

Wilkes nodded. "See you later. Leave the door open."

Closing his eyes he sipped the hot black coffee and listened to the office awaken to the ringing telephones and opening and closing of the outer door. His environment—where he had worked daily for nine years—but this was the first time he had really been aware of it, like a lumberjack stopping to listen to the sounds of the forest. It comforted him, the same way Martha's coffee had, but he knew it wouldn't last. This world which he had always considered reality would never again be quite so firm, not after the rain and the ocean.

A loud tapping on the door. He opened his eyes and was ready. "Yes?"

Edgar Simpson.

Wilkes checked his watch; it was just nine o'clock. "You don't usually arrive this early."

"What's this about you canceling your meeting with Judge Spencer? I told you I want Basehart's bail revoked. I mean it, Jimmy."

"There's no need to see Judge Spencer."

"No need!" Simpson's face turned crimson. "I just told you . . ."

"Basehart's dead."

"What?" The color drained from his face. "What did you say?" His hand fumbled until guiding him to a seat opposite Wilkes.

"Basehart's dead."

Wilkes recounted last night's events, ending with Senator Dickerson's detention. While listening Simpson sank deeper into his chair, and at the end he could only whisper, as if afraid someone else would hear, "Dickerson in jail?" Wilkes remained silent, watching the other man run his hand through his hair, still not comprehending. "Are you telling me that he and his son killed all those people?"

"Not everyone. Not the Vietnamese woman, Nguyen Thi Nhi."

"Do you have any idea who did? Has Dickerson told you?"

"No. He's in some kind of catatonic state. When he comes out of it, I don't think he'll give us any trouble. His son was probably the only person he really loved. When Junior died, there was not much point going on."

"Yes," Simpson said softly, "I know. When Tad died in the war, I . . ."

"I asked Lt. Canary to come up here." Simpson seemed not to hear, so Wilkes repeated the statement.

"What do you want Canary for?"

"The man who killed Nhi was connected with the police department—Dickerson did say that much. Someone who knew the Paddy, had been there before, who had known both Nguyens—Nhi and her brother Van."

"You mean it had something to do with drugs—this Van was a drug dealer, wasn't he?"

Wilkes stared at his boss.

"Wait a minute. Are you trying to tell me that Canary's involved in this, that he was working with the Senator? With Van and drugs?"

Again Wilkes remained silent. Simpson took the gun from the desk, turning it over in his hands while examining it closely. "Whose is this?"

"Dickerson's. It could have been the murder weapon, but then I wouldn't be here talking to you."

"My God, Jimmy, I didn't . . ." He stopped abruptly.

"Why don't you say it, Edgar?"

Simpson looked down at the gun.

"It was you," Wilkes said. "You killed Nguyen Thi Nhi."

He waited for the other man's angry denial, but Simpson sat quietly, his hands resting on the weapon. Only his eyes looked expectantly, almost eagerly, for Wilkes to continue.

"Dickerson told me the woman's murder had nothing to do with her brother and drugs. It was a crime of passion. I guess a woman's novel would call it 'unrequited love.' You loved Nhi, she rejected you, so you killed her, then shot her brother Van who happened to stumble in on the two of you. Is that the way it happened, Edgar?''

After a long moment Simpson nodded. ''Funny the way life works. When Tad was killed in Vietnam, I hated those people—Gooks, Slants. When some of them moved here, it made my blood boil. I watched them closely, even got involved personally in prosecuting some cases. Van, for example, and his dope dealing. I was in the Paddy questioning him one day last year, when I met his sister. Never saw anything so pretty, so delicate like a little doll. He offered her to me right then and there, like she was a cigarette. I felt like killing him.'' He stopped and smiled wryly. ''Two nights later I did go see her. She made my blood boil all night, but in a different way. I know what you're thinking—I'm some dirty old man who can't act his age. Wait'll you're as old as me, with nothing to look forward to except fishing and rattling around a big house with an old woman still mourning her dead son after almost twenty years. Do you understand what I'm saying?''

''You were planning to run away with Nhi? Just abandon your wife and disappear?''

''The house is paid for. I was going to leave Florence half the money. She'd of had plenty.''

''You went to Nhi's apartment that night with your suitcase and two plane tickets to Mexico, in the name of Mr. and Mrs. Simpson. Only the ticket wasn't for the real Mrs. Simpson. Those soiled tissues in the wastebasket were yours; they matched your blood type. I remember you had a cold.''

''Nhi said she couldn't leave her brother—he was her drug connection. I thought it was all set.

I gave her travel brochures. She said she must've been high to have agreed to go away with me.''

"So you killed Nhi and used the ticket you bought for her to take your wife on a surprise vacation. How could you kill her, Edgar?''

Simpson's face reddened. "She laughed at me. Said her brother would get a good laugh out of it too. I started thinking of Tad lying in the jungle with a bullet through his head. I just went crazy, took out the gun and . . .'' He shrugged.

"Why'd you bring a gun?''

"I thought Van might give me trouble. When I saw him walk in, his sister's laughter in my ears, I didn't wait for him to laugh. I'm not sorry about him.''

"Where'd you get the gun?''

"From the police property room. Who'd miss one weapon out of a hundred? After I shot Van, I wiped the handle and dumped it in the trash. Guess it must've been Basehart's gun, still had one of his prints from when the police first confiscated it. I didn't mean to frame him.''

Wilkes looked at the gun resting in Simpson's hands, then leaned forward and said, "No, you let Dickerson do that. You've been working with him all along, haven't you?''

"One hand washes the other—that's politics, Jimmy. Your daddy wasn't above doing a favor or getting one in return from the Senator.''

"My father was never involved in murder.''

"No,'' Simpson said quietly, "no, he wasn't.''

"Dickerson covered for you, got rid of Van, and in return you helped him frame Basehart, so that Pelham could take over the Guardians and bring them more tightly under Dickerson's control.''

"Help him frame Basehart . . . how?''

Wilkes shook his head. "You put me on the case."

"Jimmy . . ."

"You wanted to make sure Basehart would be convicted quickly and quietly. With the Senator's stooge Collinsby as defense counsel looking for a quick guilty plea, and me, inexperienced in this kind of case, seduced by the headlines and a chance for the job . . . Collinsby and I were even high school buddies. You really had everything going for you. Until Nate Rosen entered the case."

Simpson almost smiled. "You're the one who listened to him. Your daddy always said you were a smart kid."

Wilkes's intercom buzzed loudly. Martha said, "Sorry to disturb you, but Mr. Simpson's secretary wanted him to know that his nine o'clock appointment is here. Also, Lt. Canary called asking if he could wait to see you this afternoon."

Pushing the button Wilkes replied, "Have Mr. Simpson's appointments canceled for the day."

"All of them?"

"Jimmy . . ." Simpson began.

"Yes, all of them. And tell Lt. Canary to come here immediately."

Simpson's forehead broke into beads of sweat. "What are you going to do?"

Wilkes leaned over the desk, his folded hands only a few inches from the gun. He had gone over the words many times that morning, not once being able to finish them. "I'm going to have Lt. Canary take you downstairs, read you your rights, and charge you with the murders of Nguyen Thi Nhi and her brother Van."

"No, Jimmy, you can't. You can't do this to me.

I was your daddy's best friend. Christ, since his death I been like a daddy to you."

"Stop it."

"Remember who got you this job, who helped you get the down payment on your house. Why, your little girls call me uncle . . ."

"Stop it! Last night Dickerson said he was expecting me. There was only one person who knew I was going to his yacht. I left a message for you. You called Dickerson. You set me up to be killed. Now give me the gun."

Shaking his head Simpson stood and pointed the weapon at Wilkes. He was gasping for air like a drowning man. "Just a few hours. Just give me a few hours head start, that's all. In your daddy's memory."

Wilkes also stood. "What about justice?"

The gun shook in his hand. "Wh . . . What are you talking about? Two Slants—a whore and a drug-dealing pimp. All I'm asking for is a few hours."

There was a knock on the door.

Wilkes walked around the desk to face Simpson. "I won't let this office be used to subvert the law anymore."

Another knock, more insistent. "Wilkes, you in there!" Canary shouted.

Simpson glanced at the door then said, "I'm not going to jail. I couldn't face the . . . the . . ."

The face of another dead woman flashed before Wilkes. "The shame."

As the door opened Simpson sobbed loudly, pressed the gun barrel to his head and squeezed the trigger. It clicked loudly, the sound reverberating in the silence. Simpson brought the gun down and stared at it oddly, before Canary pulled it from his grasp.

Wilkes said, "I took the bullets out last night. I didn't want the gun to go off accidentally. I'm not used to guns."

"What's going on here?" Canary asked, lighting a cigarette.

"Take Mr. Simpson downstairs and charge him with the murders of Nguyen Thi Nhi and her brother Van."

Canary looked from one man to the other, the cigarette falling from his mouth. "You gotta be kidding."

"I said book him!"

Furrowing his brow the policeman shook his head. "Well, I'll be a son-of-a-bitch. Y'know, Jimmy, we had Basehart's bait and tackle shop staked out yesterday. Saw you and Rosen go in. When you left, I tailed you as far as Collinsby's apartment. A little while later, the dispatcher called in a report of a dead man in the apartment. Who was it called the police?"

"My secretary."

"Figures. When I went upstairs and found Burl's body, I sure wondered where you disappeared, what you was up to. I'll be a son-of-a-bitch." He put his hand on Simpson's shoulder. "Let's go."

Simpson let Canary lead him to the door then stopped. "Don't think this is gonna do you any good. You're not gonna become Commonwealth's Attorney by walking over my grave. I know a lot of people, no matter what. They know this is no way to treat a friend."

Wilkes checked his watch and knew he had to hurry. "A friend," he repeated. "Yes."

The bus had already pulled in front of the station, its door swung open and motor humming patiently. Parking his car around the corner, Wilkes walked back and saw that no one had boarded yet. Inside the terminal about a dozen people sat with suitcases or packages; a few were dozing quietly. One man looked up from a magazine. "Got about fifteen minutes before the bus leaves. Ticket counter's in back."

"I'm looking for someone who's returning to Washington this morning."

"Might try the coffee shop across the street. Just had breakfast there myself."

Rosen was alone in a corner booth, drinking hot tea and sneezing into a series of paper napkins.

"So you caught a cold too," Wilkes said, sitting across the table.

Rosen nodded and held up an envelope. "Birthday card for my daughter—her birthday's the day after tomorrow. Always have trouble writing it. When I get to D.C., think I'll turn in my report and fly to Chicago to help her celebrate. Easier to say things in person. At least, I hope it will be."

"That'll be nice. What about a present?"

Rosen looked away for a moment. "Trac helped me choose one last week."

Wilkes wanted to say some words of comfort but in the awkward silence thought it best to get on with the business between them. "I had Edgar Simpson arrested."

"That must've been tough."

"Yes, our families go back a long way." Shifting in his chair he said, "Guess I'm not much of a political animal. Both Simpson and Dickerson have a lot of friends. My daddy once told me politicians are like elephants—they never forget."

Rosen said, "I'm surprised at you, such an aficionado of Thomas Jefferson, giving up on the good sense of the common man. You're their champion, and they just may recognize it. After all, Jefferson was elected President.''

Wilkes said, "I don't think I'm presidential material."

"No, you're not." Rosen paused to take a long sip of tea. "You're something much more. I think you're a tzaddik, one of the thirty-six men of this world for whose goodness alone God spares the human race."

Wilkes laughed. "Aren't you laying it on a little thick. I was just doing my job."

Rosen shook his head. "Your job was to take the easy way out. Make a quick deal with Collinsby, get a conviction, run for Commonwealth's Attorney, Governor, etc. What you did was to surprise everyone, including me. You dealt justice."

"And what about you? Aren't you a just man, a . . . tzaddik?"

"No, I was just doing my job."

He stood and paid the check. Wilkes lifted Rosen's suitcase, and the two men walked into the street.

Rosen said, "One tends to become cynical seeing what I've seen the last few years. Lies and deception become truth, and truth becomes . . . a stranger. Like this case. From the day I arrived to last night on the yacht." Reaching the sidewalk he stopped. "I even tried to convince myself about Trac—that she was struggling with Junior for the gun and not the needle."

"She was."

They looked each other in the eye, Rosen staring hard for a hint of weakness, that Wilkes too was engaging in a lie. Finally he softened his gaze and whispered, '' ' . . . the mirror of your soul is clean of all the dust of the world.' ''

People brushed past them on their way to board the bus. Wilkes handed the suitcase to the driver who loaded it into the luggage compartment.

"Well," Rosen said, "guess it's time."

Hesitating momentarily like bashful schoolboys, the two men shook hands, each reluctant to let go. The bus's motor revved.

"Thanks for everything," Wilkes said.

"I told you, it's for me to give thanks."

Wilkes watched the bus disappear into the gray morning and continued staring for a long time after. Walking to his car he found himself smiling without quite knowing why, only that he would allow himself the luxury of taking a short drive before returning to work. The road that would take him along the coast, past the weathered bust of his old friend, Thomas Jefferson.